THE BIG NOTHING

ALSO BY BOB TRULUCK

Street Level (2000)
Saw Red (2003)
The Art of Redemption (2007)
Flat White (2014)

BOB TRULUCK

ISBN-10: 0-9908053-4-4
ISBN-13: 978-0-9908053-4-2

This is a work of fiction. Names, characters, places and incidents are products of the author's imagination or are used fictitiously and are not to be construed as real. Any resemblances to actual events, locales, organizations, or persons, living or dead, is entirely coincidental.

MurmurHousePress.com

This one is for those who will
never embrace repetitious
mediocrity as art. Thank you for
your steadfastness.
Namaste

The best things in life are free/But you can give them to the birds and bees/I need money (that's what I want)
Barry Gordy and Janie Bradford

Yet avarice is numbered among the sins, but stupidity omitted.
E.B. Farnum

There is a sufficiency in the world for man's need but not for his greed.
Mahatma Gandhi

Ambition is but avarice on stilts, and masked.
Walter Savage Landor

Greed is the inventor of injustice as well as the current enforcer.
Julian Casablancas

Grandma said, "Boy, go and follow your heart
And you'll be fine at the end of the line
All that's gold isn't meant to shine
Don't you and your one true love ever part"
Bob Dylan

The only two things you can truly depend on are gravity and greed.
Jack Palance

[1]

LATE SUMMER HERE after a rainy year, even a cemetery becomes an unlikely place to keep dead people. Plastic flowers and granite headstones be damned. Everything green as a Welsh poet's fuse and none of it acting embarrassed for the irreverence. Only the paranoid live oaks cringing away from the fickle Florida sky seemed aware of the somber situation.

The afternoon rains had all but moved on, now only big drops falling from the trees to thump on a funeral tent with no appreciative cadence. A tired pickup growled toward the tent and parked near an insensitive yellow backhoe.

Two gravediggers inside the truck stuck to the seat, finished cigarettes and watched a small group of mournful attendees in different stages of exit. The mourners moved between a man in an economical dark suit and a plastic wood-grained coffin—bottom of the line job—and on to waiting cars parked nearby.

The man with the cheap suit and a face full of nothing rose and began shaking hands, hugging people: generic consolation shit. A red-toned black man, tall and dressed well enough, remained seated in the back row of folding chairs. He wore the disinterested, patient face of a sin-eater, waiting, relaxed with a leg on a knee.

When everyone had drifted, the attending priest took the man in the suit by the shoulders and pressed some sincere words on him, hugged him and turned to go. A few feet, the priest turned back, tossed one last bit of sacramental hoodoo at the cheap coffin and moved away.

The gravediggers dropped from the truck. One of them grabbed a square shovel from the bed and both moved to stand just under the tent, out of the drip. The man at the rear acknowledged them. The gravediggers reciprocated.

The man at the front sat again. From the back he appeared to be looking off, looking at nothing.

The good suit of clothes swiveled in his chair, getting at a pocket. He came up with a money clip gripping some folded bills, peeled off a twenty. He straightened the bill, placed it between his index finger and its taller neighbor and leaned toward the closest gravedigger, the twenty fluttering out there.

"Looks like my man here needs a few minutes. Think maybe you and your partner might go grab a six of what makes y'all grin?"

The gravediggers traded looks and shrugs, the one closest grabbed the bill. "Yeah, we c'n work that. C'mon, Earl."

Earl and company loaded into the pickup, the truck splashed off as it had come. The two remaining men sat silently while the occasional sun looked quietly between the clouds.

A few minutes of that, the man by the coffin said, "Thanks, Dupree. How you been?"

"Been good, Marty. How you been?"

"Good, man."

It came too quick and Shad Dupree grinned a small one at Marty Pell's back.

"Sure you have, cuz. Sure you have."

Marty, still facing forward, shook his head and laughed through his nose. "Whatchu looking for, Dupree? Wanna see me break down, start crying?"

Dupree continued to stare at Marty's back but raised a hand in absolution. "Hey, ain't nobody here but me and you, bread. Just askin how you been is all."

"Nobody but me and you and some

asshole in a short-sleeved white shirt and Oakleys sitting across the way in a blue sedan."

"I saw im."

Marty's head bobbed up and down slightly. He stood, removing a carnation from his lapel. He doodled with it a bit, sniffed it and laid it on the coffin. He placed both hands palms down on the box. "The fuck you think I been, Dupree? I'm frigging burying my mom here. Last six months? I'm doing ant labor for fifty cents an hour over minimum wage. Hmmm. Before that? Let's see." Marty paused, thinking about it, maybe pretending to. "There was that three years Federal I did, but you know a little something about that, don't you?"

Dupree tossed up the absolving gesture again. "What'd you expect, Marty? Me own up, pay my debt cause they grabbed you? What good would that've been?"

Marty went on like Dupree maybe hadn't spoken up for himself: "Sum totaled? I'm an underemployed two-time loser. I got a six-hundred-dollar piece of Japanese shit with nearly three hundred thousand miles on it. Rent a two-room walk-up in an undesirable part of town. No money to speak of." Pause. "No nothing to speak of." More pause. "Yeah, I been just fine, cuz."

"Un-huh. Un-huh." Dupree swiped at

wispy chin whiskers, squinted at the recuperating sun. "But you know, bad as the last few years may've been, I do believe there's a bright, white future out in front. For both of us, Mr. Pell."

Marty turned to face Dupree, found a decent grin. He tossed on a pair of drugstore shades. "I believe you could be on to something, Mr. Dupree. What say we go knock back a couple of pops, discuss this improved future?"

"You ready?"

"Like you wouldn't fucking believe, cuz."

[2]

MARTY CHOSE IGGY'S for no other reason than it was the first bar on the way back from the cemetery. Marty's old beater had been parked in front and he'd led the way, Dupree's Caddy on his bumper. A quarter mile back, the dark sedan, cop-plain, had followed right along.

There was a sign out front that invited you to come inside Iggy's and enjoy an uncommon experience, but as close as Marty could tell, looking around, there was nothing uncommon about Iggy's. It was only what the fern bar had grown up to be—no more, no less. Wings and sizzling pretend-Mexican stuff from the kitchen, obscure college-radio emo from the speakers, perky college girls taking orders, walking away like their asses were in flames and they were trying to shake the fire out.

There was a small lake outside a long series of windows. Over the windows—and everywhere else—antiques and near antiques had replaced the ferns. The stuff was sad and dusty, like no one gave a shit, like the junk knew this was it, end of the line, and no one new was going to adopt it ever again.

Outside the windows the sun was back, showing off for the tourists, taking it out on the lake, ricocheting long shafts of light across Iggy's. The show was lost on Marty, probably Dupree too. They were natives—Floridians don't care shit what the sun does or doesn't do.

Dupree and Marty had found a tall table by the windows and were riding bar stools, backs to the bold August sun. Midafternoon, but no waitperson bothered them for a few minutes so Dupree hiked to the bar, returned with libations around.

"You broke down, told her and she made you promise, didn't she? Your mama, when she got the cancer on her?"

Marty played a finger in the condensation on the sides of a beer mug and studied the tabletop. "Yeah, pretty much."

"You had me worried, cuz."

Marty looked up, "What'd I tell you when I got out and you foolishly met me at the bus station?"

Dupree grinned at the memory. "Shook your ass up, huh?"

"It shoulda shook your ass up too.

Fucking Feds sitting across the street. What'd I tell you then?"

Ten months back:

Societally, bus stations represent. Concrete and asphalt and panhandlers and hustlers. All hard surfaces, nothing you couldn't hose down here. Cheap suitcases and duct-taped cardboard boxes filled with the sharp-edged shards of broken lives. Cops tilted to pissed at having to pull a bus-station shift. Everybody going somewhere, everybody getting nowhere.

A big Greyhound bus snorts, stamps, breaks wind and tethers up in a preappointed stall. A serious, gaunt Marty Pell steps down with a duct-taped cardboard box, hoists the box, freeing a hand to locate shades. He tosses the shades on and moves through the bus station to a front exit. He uses some big glass doors, adjusts the shades and moves down the sidewalk.

Shad Dupree leans across the top of a four-year-old Caddy watching Marty.

Marty sees him, tenses, repositions his possessions. Dupree finds a smile.

As Marty draws even, Dupree says: "S'up, cuz?"

Marty shakes his head, tosses up a hand, palm at Dupree. "Stay the fuck away from me, Dupree."

Dupree's face registers some changes. It sticks on perplexed for a beat, then settles for pissed off. He moves around the front of the car. "Un-un, Marty, that shit ain't gonna work. That shit ain't gonna work for a fuckin minute."

Marty stops, frees up an index finger, puts the finger on Dupree. "Listen, Dupree. Quit being stupid here."

Marty breathes deeply and moves his head around some. "It's gonna have to work for now." The finger's still up, working with the words. "My mom's got six weeks, six months, maybe a year. Who knows?"

Marty drops the finger. "She always liked you. You be your ass at her funeral. You hear me?"

Dupree doesn't like it. He takes his turn at deep breathing, his hands go to hips and he turns ninety degrees, looking off. "Yeah." Pauses. "I hear you."

Marty nods slowly, both hands under the box. "Ever hit you as funny how Feds sit across the street from you—dark sedans, short-sleeved dress shirts, ties and those ugly-assed Oakley sunglasses—and think you don't see them? And don't break your neck not looking around. I'm walking on, catch me a cab to the hospital, visit my mom. See you at the funeral, cuz."

Dupree nods at Marty's back, lips fretting

with the situation. His lips slack out and he blows some air at the disgust.

"Goddam, Marty, you're makin me nervous as hell, now."

Marty doesn't hear this—he's getting in a gypsy cab up the sidewalk.

Dupree drained his bottle. "What can I say, bread? You were makin me nervous."

Marty shrugged. Done was done. "It didn't kill you to wait."

"But, goddam, baby, it looks like you coulda called, told me *somethin*."

Marty shook his head. "Jesus, man, I'm funny just sitting here with you now knowing that Fed's outside. Shit, the chubby motherfucker's been part of my life for ten months now." Marty finished his beer, sat the mug down. "So how much is it worth? Now? Today?"

A waitress in black tux shorts and a tie-less tux shirt breezed up making sure everyone at the table noticed she had nice tits. Everyone seemed to notice.

"Two more of the same, boys?"

Dupree looked around, checking over both shoulders like he was looking for someone. "Where're you seein a boy at, girl?"

The girl put out a pretty smile; Marty winked at her.

"Sorry, sir. An inappropriate attempt at

familiarity and possibly interpreted as a racial slur. Gosh, I hope it doesn't interfere with that very large tip you were gonna leave."

"You got a boyfriend, sweetheart?"

The waitress backed up and posed in a sexy slouch. "Whadda you think?"

"He doin you any good?"

"See me smiling, don't you? I'll start you *gentlemen* a tab."

Marty said: "Thank you for the tab. Two more would be good."

Dupree said: "I'm dead serious, girl."

The waitress rolled her eyes and looked at Marty. "Does your friend ever stop?"

"No. And he's not my friend."

Dupree pushed his chin up. "Make sure you get my number before I get outta here."

Over a shoulder, the girl tossed: "Absolutely. I'll have it tattooed around my navel."

Dupree and Marty watched her ass retreat for the bar.

"So how are we gonna do this?" Marty off the girl, back on business.

Dupree looked peeved when he turned. "You wanna know how we're gonna do it, or you wanna know what's it worth? You're just sittin over there askin questions."

"What's it worth?"

Dupree grinned like a cat, not putting much into it. "The economy fucked up like it is, bullion prices've been goin ape-shit, in case you didn't notice."

"Yeah?" Marty'd noticed.

"Un-huh." Making Marty work for it.

"So how much?"

"Today? On the legal market? Oh, I'd say somewhere around twenty-seven, maybe a little better." Then turned it loose like he'd said nothing.

Marty says: "Million?"

"Hell yeah, *million.*" Dupree laughed, said, "Goddam startlin ain't it, cuz? Last I looked was at twelve hundred, forty-five smacks per Z—we're talkin thirty-one-point-one-gram Troy Z's now—and we've got twenty-one thousand, eight hundred seventy-five of those Troy Z's. Damn near fifteen hundred pounds of solid gold tomorrows, baby." Dupree smiled some phony bliss. "And the shit's just layin out there, callin to us, sayin, *come and get me.*"

Marty shot Dupree a grin, still stunned by the number Dupree'd tossed out. "We walk with half that, we're lucky motherfuckers."

"We're already lucky motherfuckers, my friend. At half prime, a share goes better'n six mil."

"You've put some thought into this, haven't you?"

"Damn right, baby. Almost five years,

thinkin how that shit's waitin there, all the joy it could bring." Dupree pushed his chin whiskers at Marty. "Like you didn't throw any gray cells at it."

The waitress breezed by with a tray, dropped a Miller Lite in a bottle and a Young's in a mug, all the while deftly dodging Dupree's dick again.

"Yeah, I thought about it some." Marty lifted his beer in salute.

Dupree lifted his beer in response, said, "Where're you at? Right now, where're you at on this thing, Marty?"

"I'm ready to go, cuz, which brings us to how do we get out from in front of the cop?"

"We ain't dull, we'll think of somethin. We need us a fresh ride. Next part—the gettin the shit—ain't nothin but semiskilled labor." More thought, then, "Maybe a truck since we've got haulin to do." Dupree nodded. "Okay, once we got our hands on it, what happens next?"

"You mean when it goes beyond just me and you?"

"Un-huh. You got ideas in that direction?"

"Maybe. I got a guy in mind."

Dupree dropped some beer and looked at Marty. "Tell me about it."

"A guy I met. Old as hell, but I think he can get it done."

Dupree sat the bottle down, said, "Here we go. I see this shit comin. You met this guy inside, right?"

"Right."

"And you say he's old?"

"Yeah, old enough."

"Reckon he got old inside?"

"Some, I guess."

"You see where I'm goin with this, don't you? You come around with some fossilized repeat offender and it makes me wonder . . . " Dupree let it dangle.

Marty shrugged. "You meet him, you'll be okay. Trust me."

"Been doin a lot of trustin, cuz."

Marty watched Dupree watch his beer bottle. "You got somebody else?"

Dupree must not have had anyone else—he said, "We get out there, you gonna be able to take us to that shit?"

"Like I had a map tattooed on my dick. How we losing the heat?"

"I'll call you tomorrow mornin. Travel light."

"Dupree, I can put all my worldly belongings in one bag—that light enough for you? We need a hand truck, lights, anything?"

"Nah. You just bring the dick, the one's got the map on it. Your daddy here'll arrange for the rest."

[3]

A LITTLE PHONE tag and a little decision making over what to lose, what to keep had Marty coming down his wooden steps with a small duffel slung over a shoulder. Bottom of the stairs, he tossed the duffel in the back door of Dupree's Caddy and slid in the front. He ducked his head to catch the car behind them in the side rear-view. "We ready, cuz?"

"Yeah." Dupree backed onto the street and pulled away. "He comin?"

"Oh yeah. Tried to fool us, act like he was asleep. This gonna work?"

Dupree wrinkled his face and wagged his head at Marty. "Please, Marty. The man ain't Dick fuckin Tracy. You've seen im—little fat boy with a crew cut."

"Maybe that's just a disguise."

"If it is, it's a good one."

Todd Milky was the shortest guy in his

training group at Quantico, only made the vertical minimum by fractions. But he felt like he made up for it horizontally—he was broad shouldered and barrel-chested and spent enough time on the machines to control it all. Usually.

FBI school had been tougher than Milky had suspected. The physical shit being pretty nominal but classwork out the ass. Milky pulled thirty-fourth in a class of thirty-five and had been on shit details for nearly two years now.

Like the present shit detail: following this guy Pell around for the last few months, off and on. Bor-ring.

Milky had found out the guy's mom had cancer of the insides and was in the hospital. And that's what the guy did—he went to the hospital.

It'd taken the parole office a couple of months to get Pell placed. Then, he went to work for eight hours, hospital, home. More bor-ring.

The sidekick, the black guy, was about as bad as Pell. Rolled bowling balls, hit softballs and chased pussy. Mostly chased pussy. Actually did okay—got laid way more than Milky did.

The guy Milky was doing the following for, Zellwood, must've had much ass. Milky wasn't even sure what the guy was, if he was armed services, Special Forces, DEA, Secret Service or a fucking spook. Milky'd been led to believe the latter, but found out if you called the CIA joint in Virginia they'd say they didn't know anyone by that name. But, in the guy's defense, he'd always call Milky back in a day or so.

Local seemed to be the whole continent to the man. Milky would call, small talk, ask where Zellwood was, Zellwood would pause like he was thinking, then say *local.* Meaning New York, the Beltway, LA. Or he'd say *outta town* in that slow semi-drawl. When he was *outta town*, Milky wasn't told where.

Milky became Zellwood's huckleberry when the branch supervisor stuck his head in Milky's cubicle, said, "Special assignment." The juiced up smile on the supe's face said it wasn't going to be too special.

The supe gave him Pell's name and address, told Milky a spook would be calling. Report directly to the spook. Hey, it sounded pretty dope when he heard it.

Zellwood called in a few days, gave Milky Dupree's description and an address to boot. Told Milky to stick on Pell though. Milky asked what these guys were that made them important. After an uncomfortable silence, Zellwood said, "A couple of blue collar opportunists." Then he told Milky don't ask anything else, just watch Pell. He watched, saw nada.

Milky had tried to report in a couple of times, and when Zellwood called back and found the status pretty much quo, he'd gotten miffed—both times. Second call, Zellwood gave Milky a phone number to a blind mailbox service. Told Milky don't call unless something changed, told Milky to stop wasting everybody's time, hung up.

In his abundant spare time, Milky ran Pell and Dupree, trying to find out what made a guy a blue-collar opportunist. Other than Pell recently pulling a thirty-eight-month hitch at one of Uncle's more sedate facilities, the guys were small change. Dupree had a couple of DWI's and one road rage incident—fines, no time. Pell had something from the way back: lifted a Vette, ran it like he stole it and celebrated his eighteenth birthday in the young men's prison in north Florida. Kid shit that cost him sixteen months of his life but clean since.

Whatever happened to Pell, the most recent scrape, went down at the now-defunct Naval Air Station here and the armed forces weren't sharing the details. Someone had put the seal on it and that was that.

So Milky followed the two nobodies doing nothing. So much fast food and junk food his ass and belly were fighting over space in his slacks.

Time moved like he was in hell. Months of it. Nada.

Now, after ten long months, Milky finally had what looked like something. The two guys were together till late evening yesterday and here they were together again this morning. Pell even had a bag packed. They were making a run. He really should call another car. Maybe in a few minutes.

All the stale juice kicked in and Milky was almost lightheaded. He locked in behind at a respectable distance, held that position.

The Cadillac turned toward downtown and pushed ahead.

Milky caught a light bad, ran it when the intersection was clear. The Caddy swung right into a parking garage; Milky grabbed an illegal spot and tethered the sedan at the curb.

A dark hand grabs a ticket. The yellow and black semaphore arm went up, the Caddy screeched inside.

Milky dismounted and walked to the garage entrance. The Caddy's taillights were going around the first corner, headed upstairs nice and easy. There was a traffic door with a picture of a stair on it. Milky pushed in on the excremental smell of every parking garage stairwell everywhere in the world.

Up a set of stairs. Milky pushed open door number two, spotted the Caddy's tail end going up. He jumped up another floor, number three. No Caddy. Number four, top floor: daylight and the same no Caddy.

Somewhere below, either second or third level, Milky could hear a car eating the concrete, rounding corners. Shit. Milky began jumping down half-flights of stairs—he could still hear the Caddy's tires screeching as he descended. He made street level and hit the traffic door in a line-backer move.

A bum in too many clothes was in front of the door. The force pushed him out into the street. Aggravated by a nasty stumble on the curb, the bum—coattails flying—head butted a big green SUV.

The woman driving the SUV slammed the brakes. Her fingers were pushing buttons on a cell phone and she was speaking before she was out of the car.

Early lunch traffic stacked up quickly, a few horns honking. Milky shook his head, looked at his hopelessly-blocked car and said, "Ah shit."

The bum stood, pointed at Milky. "He pushed me." The bony unkempt finger was indicting hell out of Milky. The bum went down in a heap, convulsed a little, went limp.

The woman from the SUV was going nuts into the phone, then she stared at Milky like he'd traded faces with Ted Bundy. She closed the phone and said, to Milky, "The police are on the way, buster."

Milky's hands came out, his head wagged. He pulled his buzzer wallet and flipped it open to show her the gold badge, his picture on the other fold. She studied it, finger on nine-one-one redial, phone out like she had Milky covered with it, keys hanging on a little finger.

"FBI?" The woman had doubts.

"Yes, ma'am."

"You sure?" She looked from the picture to Milky.

He'd added a few pounds since the picture was taken and he'd let the buzz cut go to a storm trooper flat top, white sides and all.

"Yes, ma'am. You need to move your car. I've got to get out."

The woman faltered.

"Now, lady. Goddammit, move."

She pushed redial and Milky grabbed for the keys. The woman yelped and popped Milky on the temple with the butt of the cell phone. She clenched her fist around the key ring and Milky held the keys in his fist.

Milky looked the woman in the face. "Lady, I'll break your fucking finger you don't let go of them keys."

The woman looked over Milky's shoulder and screamed *help* with conviction; a bicycle crashed to the sidewalk behind Milky; a sack of bricks hit him just above the hip. The sack of bricks turned out to be a bike cop. Milky and the cop went down with the woman and her finger on top on them.

While the woman screamed, the cop got his nightstick under Milky's chin and his knee in Milky's back. "Let go the keys, pal." The cop added a little emphasis with a jerk on the nightstick.

Milky made a noise that could have been anything but he let the keys go. The woman rolled away, holding the injured hand, the keys still in her possession.

Milky made some more gurgling noise.

"The hell you saying down there?"

Milky made noise again.

The woman was sitting on the street rubbing her hand. "He's trying to convince you he's with the FBI."

The cop repeated what the woman had said. Milky made a *yeah* sound and moved his head, as much as he could, up and down.

The cop said, "You gotta badge?" He eased up on the stick a tad.

Milky breathed like he'd been waiting all week. "Hell yeah, I gotta badge, asshole. Get off me."

The cop wasn't that easy. "Where's the buzzer?"

"Laying around here somewhere. I dropped it when you blindsided me."

The cop enlisted a guy in a post office uniform from the growing crowd to retrieve the badge wallet and had the man hold it up for him to read.

"You Milky?"

"Hell yes. See my picture there?"

"Don't look a lot like you."

"How can you tell looking at the back of my head?"

Another cop or two ran up, got clued to the situation by the cop on Milky's back, studied his badge wallet, then relieved him of his regular wallet. After some study and some radio traffic, Milky was cut loose. He stood, stroking his neck and putting some bad-ass on the cop who had knocked him down.

The woman was up, lots of cop help. Her finger got studied and she was pointing at Milky.

Didn't look to Milky like anyone was going to bail him out. He jumped in with: "Goddam, lady, I didn't intentionally knock the guy into you."

An older cop said, "What guy?"

"The bum, the one head-butted the lady's car."

Everyone looked around for the bum. There was no bum, so everyone looked at Milky. Milky looked at the lady since she was the only one who knew what the hell he was talking about.

He shook his head. "I've been fucking punked. Jesus Christ Almighty." Milky looked around at ignorant faces.

"How much you give the crack-head?"

"Crack-head? Shit, that's Fall Down Freddie, cuz. The man's an artist, lives in a two-hundred-fifty-thousand-dollar home."

"How much you give him?"

"Three hundred bucks."

"For five minutes of work? Jeez, I see how he affords the house."

"Good talent ain't cheap."

"I got twelve hundred bucks, man. That's my total net worth." Marty thought it sounded like an apology after it was out there.

Dupree wagged his head around some. "Chill, bread. I've been plannin on this shit four years and some. We're cool. You hang on to what you got. I get low, I'll let you know about it."

Marty looked at the side of Dupree's face. "You do that."

"Shit. You're gonna be good for it. I'll touch you back when you're a rich man. Dig?"

"Dig." Marty studied the windshield. "It's just me and you now, cuz."

"I hear you, baby."

"We play it out, no matter what."

Dupree nodded some. "Me and you, cuz, till the end of this thing. No matter, we play out."

"No matter."

Dupree said, "Here we go," and pulled in long-term parking near the airport.

A couple of rounds gave up a decent slot; Dupree slid into it.

Marty grabbed the duffel from the back seat. Dupree pushed a button, a lock clicked and the trunk lid rose.

Dupree sat out a mauve pigskin suitcase barely bigger than a boxcar. It had gold-resembling hinges, clasps and corner guards. He pulled its child—half the original's size—from the trunk.

Dupree pulled some handles and straps around until the smaller version was papoosed on the big job.

Marty: "That's packing light?"

"I've got a sartorial reputation to protect. That takes a few suits of clothes."

Marty walked on, grinning pretty good.

"Go ahead on. Say it, get it done."

Marty grinned, looked at Dupree. Dupree wasn't enjoying it like Marty was.

"Go ahead on."

"What color would you call that?"

Dupree walked, said nothing.

"Purple?"

"Shit ain't purple."

"Pink?"

"Ain't pink either."

"Purplish-pink?"

They stepped up as the short little shuttle bus knelt at the curb.

"Mauve."

Marty laughed at *mauve*, said, "Your granny die, leave you that shit?"

Dupree didn't dignify with a response.

The shuttle driver, an Asian guy with big rubber gloves, grabbed Dupree's bags. He looked at the luggage, smiled, said, "Very nice."

"His grandmother left it to him."

The driver was nodding, smiling like he got it.

"You got it outta your system yet?"

Marty said, "Yeah," used the steps. He stashed his duffel in the luggage rack and the driver carefully placed Dupree's beside it. Dupree passed the guy two bucks.

The guy looked grateful and said, "I take good care, sir."

Marty said, "Good man," sat next to Dupree. Dupree bent around to give Marty the peeved face again.

The driver used the outside lane and wound around to the airport. The bus hissed and knelt and people got off; the driver handed out the baggage.

Marty, Dupree and Dupree's loud

baggage walked into the airport, across to an elevator, down one floor, to a moving sidewalk that took them under the street above where the bus had just knelt. A sign said *Airport Parking.*

Spit out at a bank of elevators, up three floors, a walk past a few aisles then Dupree chose one.

Dupree freed a hand up and came out with a remote fob. He pushed it and a beep answered him.

"You're kidding me."

The parking lights on a big gray Ford pickup—an F-350, extra tall job—flashed a couple of times.

"What else we need?"

Duallies on the rear and the back window had a rebel flag stencil applied to it.

"What *will* this redneck mother say about your luggage?"

"I've heard enough about my suitcases."

The big truck moved off and merged into traffic after paying eighteen dollars' worth of short-term parking. Marty breathed deep, put his feet on the dash, grinned to himself.

Nothing unusual. Just a flashy brother and a two-time loser cruising down the boulevard in a jacked-up, glass-packed, redneck pickup truck. They could have been headed to Home Depot to pick up a bundle of furring strips or looking to dig up fifteen hundred pounds of gold that could arguably still belong to Uncle Sam. The Confederate flag tinting, Marty hoped you couldn't tell what they were up to.

[4]

TOMMY ZELLWOOD shifted a light bag on his shoulder as he moved across the terminal. A cell phone went to an ear as he shrugged a trench coat off his spare arm. He swapped the bag and phone to the other shoulder, shucked the trench coat, doubled it and stuffed it behind the strap of his bag.

Zellwood's suit was nice, but he might have slept in it. Open collar, boring tie loose at his neck. Late fifties, good shape. A professional package from head to toe. What he was hearing was making him happy.

The chirper went in a pocket and he moved to a phone bank, grabbed a free one. Fingers danced, paused, danced again. After a listen, one more key punch. When he spoke it was some uncharted version of Southernese, worn down from dropping anchor at many ports. "Milky? Tommy Zellwood." Pause. "Yeah, still local. Newark I think."

Zellwood looked around. "Yeah, looks like Newark. What you got, son?" Pause. "Yeah? Well God rest her soul. Lemme guess. Dupree showed at the funeral and they left together?" Pause to find a smile. "Well that don't exactly make me Nostradamus. Something was holding us up. Listen, Milky, I want this on the q.t. just like it's been. Just you and me for now, got it?"

Zellwood mimed some blah-blah-blah, looked tired.

His eyes came open. "Say what? *Lost em*?" Pause. "Goddam, Milky."

Zellwood rolled his eyes and shook his head. "Listen, get out to the place used to be the Naval air base. What's it called now?" Pause. "Yeah, Pringle Park. Pay particular attention around where the airstrip was. Hear me?" Pause. "Un-huh." Pause. "No. Don't do shit. Just try and keep up, hear me?"

Zellwood blah-blahed some more as he looked at his watch.

"Tell you what, pick me up commercial, four or five hours." Pause. "Yeah, I'll call soon as I hit the ground."

A look at the flight board. "Delta gate, quarter after twelve." Pause. "You can't miss me. I'll be wearing a blue suit and an ugly-assed brown trench coat." Pause. "Yeah, I'll call you when I'm on the tarmac. See you."

Zellwood cradled the phone like it was

crystal. He was far away, thinking. He turned in place and leaned back into the booth, smiling. His gaze slid out over the terminal and he tossed out a little headshake.

"Okay, boys. Here we go."

He leaned off the booth, found a ticket in a pocket and shrugged at it. He paused at a trash can and tossed the ticket.

The metal flap came down catching the ticket. It hung out there, flapping, and if anyone cared it would have taken them to Myanmar courtesy of the U.S. Government.

[5]

FUCK. THE FENCE is still up on this side." Marty had his window down, looking over a field. It was late afternoon and the sun had gone behind a row of trees across the road.

"I told you we could come in on the other side. No fences over where they're buildin houses."

"Love this country. They close a Navy base and two years later it's a housing development."

"Yeah, well, some rich folks that were friendly with city hall got themselves better'n a thousand acres of prime developmental real estate at a bargain price. Two, three thousand homes already, some stores, restaurants, apartment buildings sprouting up everywhere. Got their own fire house."

"Zero lot lines, no street system to get the traffic outta here, no sewer pipes to take the shit away. And it'll look like the projects in ten years. Pull over." Marty flicked a finger at the fence.

Dupree put the pickup on the wide grassy shoulder. Marty studied the landscape.

Beyond an eight-foot chain-link fence progress was still punching up houses a quarter mile to the east. Dozens of them. Slung together, priced to sell. Even in a collapsed market Pringle Park remained a desirable place to homestead—gridlock and urban sprawl had been a rude revelation to the masses who had rushed to the burbs a few years back. Now they were elbowing each other to get back in the city limits. Go figure.

"This is where we need to be tonight, Dupree. I don't wanna go in through the subdivision. We cut through that fence?"

"Like it was mostly air. This us?" Dupree's head was swiveling

Marty nodded, looked off. "By those pine trees."

"We humpin it to the truck?" Dupree gave Marty a face that weighed fifteen hundred pounds.

"Or we cut a big hole in the fence."

"Or we could drive around the other way, through the houses." Dupree looked over. "Why're you so jumpy?"

"I keep thinking if I was a smart guy watching me and you and I'd lost us, this'd be the first place I'd go to sit and wait on us."

"Shit. They don't even know it's out here. How could they know that, Marty?"

"They know neither of us left the base with shit that night—you stayed in the barracks, I left on a motorcycle. Next day, the shit hit the fan." Marty shrugged. "Where else they gonna look?"

Dupree nodded. "Seems a lot easier if we just drove out next to the shit, put it in the truck and went to the house."

"Humor me. Let's drop the luggage, grab some shovels."

"Got em."

"Wire cutters for the fence."

"Got em."

"Gloves."

"Check."

"Hand truck."

"I told you all you need's that dick with the map on it."

[6]

MILKY HAD SPENT the afternoon riding the housing project that Zellwood had suggested: the Navy's flight-training center a few years back. The gold buzzer shook up a project manager in a construction trailer but got Milky a good idea of where the runway had been. Then he checked out some model homes.

Not bad, two hundred grand—up to five or six you wanted down by the lake. But new bureau agents don't buy houses. Want to get transferred? Get a girlfriend or buy a house—you're out of here.

He had cruised on and off, pissed on the ground in some back lots a time or two. Zellwood finally called: it was nearly midnight.

Now it was almost one and Milky was leaning against his fender yawning. It was raining tiny droplets on the airport making his back moist even under the overhang.

Tommy Zellwood used some automatic doors to some concrete walk. He sat his bag on a bench and unzipped the trench coat's liner as he watched a young guy that had to be this Milky fella. He put the trench coat on loosely, left it unbuttoned, grabbed his bag and moved toward the presumed Milky. He stopped at a trashcan, stuffed the coat's now-redundant lining in it.

Milky looked over, saw the blue suit and brown coat, snapped to attention and moved toward Zellwood. "Sorry, sir. I didn't see you." Milky's hand was out either for a shake or to take the bag. Zellwood pointed a finger.

"Drive the car, son."

Milky trotted around and got in.

Zellwood said, "Watch yourself," and tossed his bag over the seat.

"Where to, sir?" Milky fired up the sedan and moved away from the curb.

"Let's go get us a decent rent-a-car. You might as well write FBI on the sides of this sled in white shoe polish."

"Yes, sir." Milky paused. "What do I call you, sir?"

"Let's keep it simple. Tommy works."

"Yes, sir. Uh, Tommy, there's Alamo and Hertz both up ahead. Which one?"

"Does it matter, son?"

"No, sir, I don't guess it does."

"Then just pull in one." Zellwood studied Milky's profile. "We on the q.t., right?"

Milky looked uncomfortable. "Yes, sir. So far, Tommy."

"Drop some of the sirs and talk to me. What does *so far* mean?" Zellwood ran his window down and lit a cigarette.

"I've got a supervisor. I'm not like you guys—on your own out here."

"Listen to me, son. You go tell your supe you need some days. This thing unrolls, I'll write a letter'll make you look like Melvin Purvis, get your leave back, probably get you a grade increase. How's that fit?"

Milky's head was wagging. "Some point, I gotta write a report, justify my time."

Zellwood turned, looked forward. "Good. We get done with all this, write your report. I'll staple my letter to it. Let's just stay low with this for now. Don't miss Alamo here, boy."

Milky turned in the drive and parked.

Zellwood grabbed his bag and pulled it over the seat's back. He placed it on his lap and folded his hands on the bag, cigarette smoldering between fingers.

"You were assigned to me, right?"

"Yessir."

"To use as I need, as I recall. I tell you how I want it done, you do it, son. Don't you fuck up my game here crossing T's and dotting I's after I tell you don't. There're worse field offices than the semi-sunny subtropics of Florida. You fuck me up, I'll fix you, son. Plain and simple. You get all that?"

"Yessir. I got it. Where do we leave my car?"

"Meet me at the Grand Bohemian downtown in a half hour. The lobby. We'll go look at this housing project."

"Okay, Tommy. See you."

Zellwood got out and puffed his butt until Milky's taillights blended into traffic.

"I do believe you're gonna fuck right around and become a liability, son." Zellwood shook his head, puffed. "And, unfortunately, I don't have time to dick with you."

He took one last hit, flipped the cigarette into the rainy mist, turned and went in the rental agency's doors.

[7]

MARTY POINTED TO a dark spot and looked over to make sure Dupree saw the indicating finger.

Dupree nodded, dropped the pickup into the wide shallow ditch, killed lights and engine as one.

The mist was heavy fog now, everything dripping wet since midnight. Marty looked at his watch. It was about two thirty and as quiet as civilization gets in this part of the world.

Dark clothes for dark deeds, he and Dupree climbed down from the tall truck. At the back, Dupree reached shovels, handed them out. Then he took a big pair of dikes to the fence and went to work by a post, clipping strands in the diamond weave.

When the slit ran about four feet high, Dupree pocketed the dikes and said, "Come on," and held the fence out.

Marty pushed the shovels through then squeezed himself through. He turned, held the fence open for Dupree.

Marty moved for the trees; Dupree said to his back, "Hold up, cuz."

Marty turned and watched. Dupree pulled some black wire from a coat pocket and clipped the slit shut in a couple of places. Satisfied, he turned to Marty and pointed with a chin.

Marty led Dupree across a grassy piece a hundred feet wide to a coppice of trees then to three skinny pines, the pines looking lonesome even as a trio.

Marty stood between the two bigger of the pines, lined himself up on center and took eighteen metered strides. Stopped. Turned left and strode off eight more. He poked a shovel into the sandy soil. Dupree was over his shoulder.

Dupree pointed a finger down and raised his eyebrows. Marty nodded and they put some muscle to the shovels.

The submissive sandy soil, a hole knee-deep and six foot wide wasn't tough work: a few minutes of tossing shovels of sand, a few drops of sweat.

Marty hit something solid, rapped it again, whispered, "Here you go, daddy."

Dupree turned and a set of headlights began to illuminate his face. The car came on. Marty and Dupree genuflected. The car slowed. They hit both knees like hard-shell Baptists. The car stopped and the two went in the hole, prone as a couple of Muslims.

Interior lights came on as doors were opened. A luxury sedan. Two guys coming around to check the truck out.

When the driver was in the headlights, Dupree asked, "That the fat-boy cop? Shit. Tell me that ain't him."

"It's him."

They watched a man in a trench coat open the tailgate of the pickup then walk around and pop a door. He climbed in like he owned it, went through the glove box, looked behind sun-visors. The fat-boy stood ready, flashlight hanging at arm's length.

The guy in the trench coat dropped out of the truck and the two of them went to their car. The car started up, sat idling for a bit then the fat-boy driver got out again, flashlight up.

He walked to the fence, maybe two feet from the spot where Dupree had cut it, and shone the beam across the field.

Marty and Dupree rolled onto their backs and watched the beam play in the mist overhead. Then the light went out, a grunt, a door slam.

The car disappeared into the void of the night with about as much noise as it takes for a memory to fade. The full silence came back; the shovels got busy and pushed it away again.

Marty dropped to his knees and threw aside some rotted boards and dragged a rusty cylinder head from the hole.

"Here we go, cuz. This is the shit I tossed on top."

Dupree dropped down beside Marty and pulled out another head. "Let's get on down to the part that counts."

Marty pulled sand away. There was nothing, only dirt. Marty looked up at Dupree—nobody was smiling.

Marty turned and located another rotted crate, threw the debris away. He pulled some engine parts off the top but same deal: nothing but dirt. Third crate, same deal: nada.

Dupree stood, stepped out of the hole. He abruptly walked away, palms of his hands on the sides of his head like it might explode. Marty watched, still on his knees in the hole.

Dupree turned, hands coming down, mumbling, then too loud: "Marty, some-goddam-body needs to be tellin me somethin. Four years is a long fuckin time to be waitin, cuz, waitin on nothin. That makes it a big goddam nothin." Dupree gave it a beat, slung his hands at the nothing. "I hope *to fuck* you ain't jammin me. You are, you know it's gonna get ugly."

Marty came up from his knees and was out of the hole, in Dupree's face, taking his turn at talking too loud in the timid quiet. "Hey, fuck you, cuz."

Dupree, hands to hips, turned his head off forty-five degrees. "Then where the fuck is it? It ain't in the fuckin hole, is it, Holmes? What? You already slipped out here, hauled the shit off so you could bring Dupree's big dumb niggah ass out here, say: *Look, Dupree, it's gone*."

Dupree turned back to Marty not a foot away. "We're gonna do better'n that." Pause to look mean. "Where's my shit at, Marty?"

Dupree's hands came up and out, pushing Marty pretty good. Marty stepped back with it, still on balance.

"I'd go easy, Dupree."

Dupree moved back in Marty's face. "That what you're countin on? Me goin easy?"

Dupree tossed a half-hearted punch at Marty's shoulder. Marty rolled out from under it.

"Go easy, Dupree."

"Nah. I ain't goin easy. Where's my shit, Marty." Dupree's hands came up again, pushing Marty harder.

Marty stumbled back by the hole, and caught himself on an upright shovel. Dupree squared off, crouched low, dukes up. He moved in on Marty.

"Last warning, Dupree."

Marty came with the shovel like he'd swung it from around the block. Dupree ducked off, letting a shoulder absorb the blow. Marty still clipped him a good one across the back. Dupree lost his wind and stumbled forward, down to knees then went over on all fours.

Marty drew the shovel back for another shot but the moment escaped him. He dropped the shovel to arm's length, then shook it at Dupree. "You fuck. You recall which one of us did three years over this shit? Fucking eighteen to life, Dupree. That's what's looking at me, I get caught fucking with this shit again. Get it? Eighteen to life. Federal time equals only fifteen fucking percent gain-time—I do eighty-five percent of the time." Marty shook his head. "And you think I'm playing you, playing the fuck around, hucking you."

Marty made a pooh sound through slack lips and threw the shovel down. He turned and walked for the fence. He turned back, still moving away but walking backwards, wiping grime off his face with a shirtsleeve, jabbing a finger. "Fuck you, cuz. You think I'm playing you, fuck you."

Dupree stood slowly, testing systems as

he came out of a crouch. Marty flapped a hand, gave Dupree another, *fuck you*, and turned away.

"Nah, man. I don't think you're playin me. I'm trippin or somethin. You'd be crazier'n a bag full of bats to come back out here. I know that. Let's get the fuck outta here."

Marty stopped, turned to see Dupree wobbling his shoulders, checking systems.

"Sorry about the shovel thing, dad."

Dupree wagged his head at Marty. "Shit, was me askin for it."

Marty walked back up, grabbed shovels.

Dupree said, "We do plan on pursuin all this, right?"

"Goddam, Dupree. My life is in fucking tatters here. I have no options. This is my one egg in my one basket. I-have-no-options."

"You gonna be able to figure this out?" Dupree worked at the pain in his back. "Cause it's you, cuz. I didn't even know where the shit was. It's all on you."

"Yeah. I got some ideas. Some good ones."

Dupree began walking off. "I'd be interested in hearin those ideas. Come on."

"We gonna put the dirt back in the hole?"

Dupree didn't look back. "Fuck the dirt. As it turns out, doesn't seem to be our hole."

[8]

TEN O'CLOCK in the morning:

The rain gone like it was never there. Tommy Zellwood, trench-coat over an arm, same rumpled suit as last night. Milky fresh, ready to go. A freshly dug hole.

Zellwood stepped in the hole, nudging pieces of discard around with a shoe, kicked at the earth inside each crate. "They didn't dig deep, did they, Milky?"

"No, sir."

Zellwood looked up and then around at the road then behind him where progress was at work, a hand over his brow to the morning sun.

"They never came home?"

"No, sir. I rode by both residences this morning. No one either place so I rode out here, saw the hole." Milky was proud as hell at finding the hole, but held back, wanting to make it look like something he did every day.

Zellwood looked back at the road beyond the fence, hand coming down as he faced west. "They could have."

"Sir?"

"They could have gone home." Zellwood sounding irritated at repeating it for Milky.

"Why's that sir?"

Zellwood turned to look at Milky, unreadable smile going. "It wasn't here."

"Sir?"

"What they were after. It wasn't here. If so, there'd a been more hole, more foot traffic." Zellwood climbed out of the shallow crater. "Somebody beat em to it." He walked over and studied the cut in the fence, walked back.

Zellwood stood there, looking off, deep in thought. "Milky, I want you to go to the office, do some research. I want everything you got on Pell's recent incarceration. Somewhere in New Mexico or Arizona or something. See who he slept with and talked to. Who he ate with and who he showered with."

"Yessir. Could I ask what it is they were looking for?"

"Something they stole, son. Stole it on my watch. You go on, do your research. You might figure it out, sooner or later."

Milky followed Zellwood to the dark Lincoln. Zellwood used the passenger door so Milky crawled under the wheel. He drove them out through a construction road and then out of Pringle Park—*NO DOWN PAYMENT-NO PAYMENTS FIRST YEAR.* A sign said so. Below that, in smaller script: *small signing fee.*

"Where to for you, sir?"

"Wherever your car is."

Milky caught a ramp and punched the accelerator.

A few minutes, he looked at Zellwood, asked, "Is this a problem? Whatever it is not being there?"

"Nah. These two boys are smart. They'll figure it out. We just need to find *them* before they figure out who it was jumped the game."

"You think we'll find them?"

Zellwood looked at Milky with a funny smile. "Of course, son. That's what we do for a livin, people like us. We find people, Milky." A nod and a wink, then, "We'll find em."

Dupree was herding some egg white up against a dam of grits. He lifted a forkful and hid it. Around the food, flecks of runny yolk at one corner of his mouth, he said: "And you think this lawyer may've had a key to this safe deposit box of your mama's?"

Marty nancied up his coffee, nodded. "Yeah. Pretty sure. Use your napkin."

Dupree took the advice. He put a face on Marty like his appendix was acting up. "And there's one envelope in there that's got my name on it?"

"Yeah."

"And what else did it say?"

"I told you what it said."

"Tell me again."

"To give it to you if something happened to me while I was in the pen."

"*Happen to you*? Goddam, Marty, you were in a fuckin country club."

"With big twelve-foot fences and concertina wire. Trust me, it wasn't that much fun."

"The fuck did you do somethin that stupid for? Leave a letter. Lookin back, doesn't it seem stupid?"

"Jesus, Dupree, I was going to prison. Maybe I was a little scared is all. And I goddam sure didn't know my Mom would get cancer."

Dupree dropped his face, moved his head around some. "That ain't what I'm sayin. What I'm sayin is why didn't you just tell me where it was before you left?"

Marty sat his coffee mug on the table, cradled his hands around it. He stared into the half-empty mug. Fuck it. There was no way to knock the sharp corners off the answer. "Dupree, I didn't know you for shit—

I mean, really know you. Yeah, we played some softball, bowled a few frames, had a few pops, ran some quiff. Besides that, it was work—you in your Navy cop outfit, me running a forklift." Marty paused, put his eyes on Dupree's. "Cuz, I was going off to pay for the right to that shit. I just didn't know you that good, not to put it all on the line."

Dupree pulled some soda through a straw, used his napkin again, balled it up like it was therapy and dropped it on his plate. "I hear what you're sayin, and I respect it."

A piece of silence was broken by a waitress with more coffee and soda.

"What'd it say? Inside the envelope? A map?"

"Nah. Words. Hints. You had to think about it some, use a calculator."

"And you believe this lawyer got into it?"

Marty nodded, sipped coffee. "It'd be him or my mom. Who you looking at?"

Dupree's jaw was clinched. "You sure on this? This lawyer?"

"I can't come up with anything else short of accident. And I don't wanna think about somebody just stumbling across it. That happened, we're done."

"Any way we can check out this man's finances?"

"Other than go ask him, no. But I think I know a simpler way to find out. Remember

I said you'd have to think about it? What was the score when we played Second Baptist for city champs and what year was it?"

"We beat em eight to three. Was drizzlin rain after the fifth, top of, I believe. Two thousand and ten."

"Pretty good. But it was two thousand eleven."

"You gotta know shit like that? Like a code?"

"Yeah. All right, bowling league inner-city, same year. You rolled a perfect game. What was my score?"

Dupree thought. "You were hot too, rolled two seventy, maybe better."

"You gotta have it exact."

Dupree wagged his head, flipped the check over and looked at it, winced. "Can't do it."

"Okay. You got your hands on the envelope, same question's looking at you, what do you do?"

Dupree dropped a couple of bills on the table. "I'd go my ass by the bowlin alley, ask Stanley Woo. He doesn't know, he'll check back on his computer. Come on."

"So where we going?"

"The bowling alley, then we gonna go see your lawyer buddy. This the motherfucker represented you at your trial?"

"Yeah."

"And your mama still used im?"

Marty shrugged. "He's a second cousin, maybe a third cousin, some shit." He stood.

"Umm. Seems like we're all cousins here, cuz. Let's go see Stanley. Then we'll go see our other cousin. What's his name?"

"Tony."

Dupree tried the name out a time or two. "Tony. Good ole cousin Tony. What's Tony's last name? Same as yours?"

"No. Wayne."

"Tony Wayne. That's right. Now I got im. Little wooly-headed fucker as I remember."

They stopped at a cash register and Dupree left some more money and pushed through a glass door.

Outside, on the sidewalk, Dupree said, "You know I may hurt this Tony Wayne motherfucker."

"I hope you get the opportunity, cuz, if that'll make you happy."

They used sidewalk until the big truck chirped at the dingus in Dupree's hand. Dupree said, "I believe it'll help some."

[9]

THE HOTEL PHONE sang out and Tommy Zellwood, undershirt and suit pants, cracked one reluctant eye. The room was dark, the heavy drapes holding out the daylight but for a few rebellious rays peeping around one edge. He got the other eye open and lay in the semi-dark for another ring or two, rolled over and found the phone.

"Yeah?" Pause, grin. "Bones. The fuck you at, right this minute?" Pause. "In the air, huh? How about you jump over to Djibouti, catch something up toward Frankfurt, slip into Virginia and go by the office?"

Longer pause, an arm that had been across eyes came away—a smile. Bones was already en route to Virginia. "You are the fucking man, Bones. Listen, you get clear, jump online, my files, go under personal, then financial, then retirement. Open municipals. There's a file called *Granddaddy's Stock* can only be opened at the office. Open it. All I got on this shit's right there." Pause. "You get every name on that file, run them. New found wealth, anything funny. Overseas accounts, trading. Run em all and run em hard, Bones. Somebody's gonna be leaking money. You find it, call me while you're getting on a plane this way. I need you." Pause, funny face. "The bureau boy? Nah. He's making me nervous. I don't know he's gonna make the cut." Pause. "Just stupid, Bones, is all I could tell you. See you when you get here, but call soon as you find the money." Pause. "Yeah, see you, partner."

Zellwood sat up and placed the phone on the cradle. He felt the lamp up until he found a switch. The sudden light in the darkened room slammed his eyes shut reflexively. He felt for the switch again, killed the light. A groan had him up on rusty knees and moving in the partial dark.

A wet towel to the face and neck, Zellwood was ready for quick one. It was nearly four o'clock according to the plastic radio alarm by the bed. He bought himself a neat scotch, watched CNN and wondered why anyone would think the free world was worth saving. Fuck the free world, you better save your goddam self.

He felt tired. No, he felt old. Fifty-nine. Big six-O coming at him warp speed. He walked over and looked at his face in the vanity mirror. To his face, he said, "You don't look a day over fifty-eight, son." He checked out his neck, his whisker status, decided he could use a shave.

Halfway through the shave, Milky called.

Zellwood patted down the shaved side with a towel while he listened to Milky. He smiled and licked a fleck of shave cream off his lip.

"Good boy. What's the guy's name?"

Milky: "Eduard—with a U—Margot. Eddie Margo. Fast Eddie Margot. Ed the Maggot. Eddie the Chute. It goes on. Then he's passing as Henry Clarendon the Fourth. He was Henry the Fourth for about five years before he got snagged."

"How'd they snag him?"

Milky related how Margot went entrepreneurial on a Canadian scheme, took off with the goodies *and* the money. "Turns out it was a sting. The Montreal crew was RCMP and the hot jewelry was bait. It pissed off the Mounties and they went after him even though he'd crossed the border and was out of their jurisdiction. Caught him in New York, turned him over to the Bureau. Margot rolled on everybody involved, still got forty-four months here for transporting."

"He hang out with Pell?"

"They worked together in the wood

shop. And, get this: they were cellmates Margot's last few months."

"What makes Margot hot, son?"

"His last fall? The one before the sting thing? He got caught in Tampa with a couple hundred pounds of gold bullion he was fencing off to one of the Trafficante crew. The goon goes down on a prostitution rap, rolls on Margot."

Zellwood smiled. Milky had found out what Pell and Dupree had stolen. "When did this Eddie Margot get out?"

"About four months before Pell."

"Un-huh. He wouldn't have ended up here by chance, would he?"

"Backed up to the fourteenth hole at the big country club."

"Shit, who says crime doesn't pay, huh? That's real good, Milky. You go check out Fast Eddie's house. You get drowsy, run by some of Pell and Dupree's old haunts. Locations may change, old habits don't. Check out some old favorites. They're bound to pop up."

Zellwood cradled the phone, went back to the cultured marble vanity. To his half-shaved mug looking at him from the mirror, he said: "Well, well, Mr. Pell, lookit you planning ahead and shit. I'm impressed. You are coming right along, right along indeed."

Zellwood turned on the water, put the razor back to his neck.

Milky put the cell phone on the seat. He'd used the country club's cart path to a bamboo hedge and backed into a notch the size of a compact car. Beat Zellwood to it: he'd already been at Margot's for a half-hour now.

He'd wanted to tell Zellwood about going to Budget and picking up a rental unit—a hundred-sixty-bucks worth at the economy rate but the girl had upgraded him to a compact since he got the weekly deal. It wasn't a Lincoln and it wasn't generous with legroom, but it beat the Bureau's Chevy Caprice all to hell. Fit nicely in the spot off the cart path.

From here, Milky could see Eddie Margot's house clearly, any comings and goings. He leaned his seat back and got out his pad, the one with the nice speckled cardboard covers and green paper, and opened it. He tossed a look at the house and began working on his report.

Fuck Zellwood—Todd Milky covered his own ass. A nice, well-documented report like they taught you at the academy. If Zellwood turned out okay, he could pitch it. If not, Todd Milky's ass was covered.

Milky got his book up to date and stashed it under the seat. He played with the radio, drank a lukewarm soda, peed in the bamboo bramble behind the car.

The house wasn't bad. A rambling ranch job with lots of porches and glass, the grounds as civilized as a trimmed poodle. The rear yard was large for Florida, nice oaks and St. Augustine stumbling onto the fourteenth hole beyond a crotch-high picket fence. Nice setup for an ex-con.

A car, an older Mercedes sedan, pulled in the drive. Milky found his company issue binoculars.

The car stopped. As one of the garage doors rose, a man got out of the passenger door. Hard to tell, but he looked to be seventy or better.

The only word Milky could come up with for dress was *exquisite.* Dark three-piece that hung like the silk worms had extruded it right onto the guy's lean body. Dark felt on his head, silver-headed cane over an arm. Dark shoes with some white explosions near the toe. Cranberry tie with a knot the size of New England and a diamond stick pin big enough Milky could actually see it, glittering like the stopper out of a cut-glass decanter.

The driver was a girl. Dark auburn or hennaed hair cut in a wedge shape, short in the back, long points under her chin in front. Pale skin, dark makeup on eyes and mouth. She could have been bored—her expression said so.

The car slid into the garage, the door

coming down to nearly pat it on the ass. The old guy used the front door and it was just Milky and the squirrels again. And the bugs.

The guy Stanley Woo saw come in the double doors with brother Dupree looked just like Marty Pell, but the closer he got the more he looked like someone else. That was it—the eyes.

And Stanley could tell Marty saw it, could see Stanley seeing it.

"Stan the man." Marty smiled the old one for Stanley, put out a hand.

Stanley slapped the hand. "*Que pasa*, bro?"

"Life, Stanley. Passing me by. How's the man with lots of balls?"

Stanley shrugged. "League season I make money, off season I spend it. Same old, same old." Stanley leaned, elbows on counter. "How long you been home Marty?"

"Ten months or so."

"And you just now come by?" Stanley tried to keep it friendly, but it had bothered him that Marty had gone to ground after getting out.

Dupree looked at Stanley, serious-faced, said, "The man's been busy tendin his Momma while she died with cancer. Maybe you weren't way up on the list, Stanley, of what the man had to do."

"Fuck you, Dupree." Stanley took it back to Marty. "Glad you're back, brother. Missed you."

"I'm glad I'm back too, Stanley."

"Go ahead on, Stanley, give im a kiss, let's move on with why we're here."

"You guys didn't come by to beat up my boards?" Stanley knew better.

"See what I told you, Marty? About how bright Stanley is? He knows we're lookin for somethin."

Stanley got an insincere smile from Dupree to go with the soft serve. "Twenty bucks." Stanley gave the smile back. Yep, knew where this was going. Maybe he'd find out something that had bugged him for months now.

"Damn, man, I just wanna ask you about a tournament a ways back."

"Okay. Double or nothing. I gotta think about it, free. I come off the head with it, forty bucks." No reason not to mix curiosity with profit.

"You gamblin bastard. Your people got a problem with that shit, you know it?"

Stanley used some eyebrows, looked at Marty. "Should I remind him about things people say about *his* people?"

"Hang on to it, Stanley. The man'll take the bet. He's bad as you."

"Hell yeah I'll take forty or nothin. Shit,

this thing I'm talkin about must be five years old. Ain't no way, Stanley. Gotcha cold." Dupree peeled a couple of twenties off his fold.

Stanley picked up the bills, smelled them like they smelled good, eyes closed. He opened his eyes, folded the bills and slid them in a shirt pocket that said *Stanley*. "Obliged, Dupree."

Dupree popped some eyebrow and Stanley said: "You rolled perfect, Marty did two seventy-eight; Tracy Gore blew up on his last two frames but still had a two sixty-nine. Terry Boggs tossed an ugly two sixty, but you guys took inner-city anyway. Was two thousand eleven, a crisp fall for Florida, as I recall, coming late after a beautiful Indian summer."

"Shut the fuck up." Dupree turned to Marty, shook his head.

"I answer your question?" Stanley knew he did.

Marty grinned. "Yeah, Stanley. What'd he look like? The guy asking after the scores?"

"Short guy. Loud suit. Frizzy hair."

Dupree said, "You seem to recall it well. How long ago?"

"Less than a year back. I remembered it because it ain't like everyday people come in off the street asking after tournament scores. And he was a weird little man."

Marty nodded some. Dupree said: "That sounds like your man."

Marty continued the nod. "Yeah. What'd he tell you? Why he wanted the scores?"

Stanley: "He said he was a reporter." Stanley gave them his best *yeah-right* face.

"You didn't buy it?" Marty wanting to know how Stanley knew.

"Nah. Too short."

Dupree cocked his head. "And that's how you could tell? Just from that? Him bein short?"

"Yeah. That and the fact that Cobbey Jergenson was behind the counter spraying down rental skids and said the guy was his brother's lawyer in a dope case."

Dupree nodded. "Cobbey's brother still in jail?"

"Yeah. The lawyer got him three years on a first offense."

Stanley watched Marty and Dupree trade looks. "I'll give the forty bucks back if you clue me to what's going on."

No one said anything for a beat or two and the moment went clumsy.

Stanley shrugged it. "Oh well. You need a hand, let me know. I'm just sitting around watching the varnish chip."

Dupree snorted. "What kinda help you gonna be? Whadda you go, Stanley? One thirty?"

"One forty-five."

"Ouch. One forty-five. What? You a karate man? You got nunchucks, some shit like that?"

"I gotta ten-millimeter Sig Sauer with an eight-hundred-dollar laser scope. I can shoot the eye out of a dog at a hundred and fifty feet."

Marty chuckled. "Goddam, Stanley." It turned into a laugh.

Stanley said, "What?"

Dupree looked disgusted. "*What?* You Chinese motherfucker out shootin the neighbor's dogs, like you're hungry, or something—that's *what*."

Stanley put his eyes to slits. "That some subtle racial slur, the dog eating comment?"

Marty pointed at the door. "We gotta go anyway." He put a hand out. Stanley slapped the hand with one of his own.

Marty said, "Thanks for the offer. We'll keep it in mind."

"Cool."

Marty and Dupree turned and used the ratty blue carpet to the doors.

To their backs, Stanley said: "I'm serious as a Mennonite, brother."

Over a shoulder, Marty tossed a wave. "I know you are, Stanley. That's why I love you, baby."

[10]

MILKY MUST HAVE dozed off. If not, the bug that woke him wouldn't have been on his face. It was big and flat and it was still in the car with him somewhere.

He hadn't seen it clearly but he suspected it was one of those big Florida cockroaches. Affectionately called palmetto bugs. You could call them cockatoos, they'd still be fucking cockroaches. Big greasy mothers.

Milky fought off a shudder, turned the move into an abbreviated stretch that the small car would allow.

More nothing going on at Margot's.

A glance at a dash clock told Milky it was nearly six, couple of hours until dark. Food and a piss would work nicely right now.

Milky fired the car up, put it in gear and bounced out of his hiding place.

Plan was: roll out of the ramble of streets, hit the highway, nab some fast food and piss, cruise a little. Maybe hit the bar down from Pell's where he walked to and drank cheap draft two-fers at happy hour on payday. That would be it on Pell's social life.

Dupree had a couple, three places he hung. A yuppie bar out by the airport, a rough place in the dark end of town, a cigar bar where the waitresses wore little black dresses you could ball up and hide in a fist. The softball field, the bowling alley.

Milky couldn't see Dupree dragging Pell to the dinge joint so he could X that one, check the others.

"Nah. That's not him. The house is a different color too."

"Maybe that's the yard man." Dupree tried to stay light. Wasn't easy. When they'd rounded the corner and saw the yuppie motherfucker in the yard, the adrenaline rush had made his eyes hurt.

"Right. Wearing Dockers and an Izod. Pull over, I'll ask."

Dupree pulled the truck in a driveway, Marty's last address on Tony Wayne. The yuppie dude was pushing leaves around with a rake like he could get dirty if he didn't watch his kiltied-moc step. Dupree didn't think the man took his yard work too seriously and had some Mexicans come by twice a month to do it for him.

Marty fell out, walked to the man. The man put on a bland noncommittal expression and smiled reluctantly. Marty tossed up a hand.

The man wagged his head, said something. Marty waved again, turned, showed Dupree a disappointed face on his way back.

Marty climbed in the truck; Dupree said, "He move?"

"Yeah."

Dupree played with that, said, "How long's he been gone?"

Marty grinned, put it on Dupree. "Three, four months. Guy says Tony's still in town. Just a better part."

"Mmm-mmm."

Marty shrugged. "He's still got an office downtown. This guy says so anyway. Let's ride."

They rode a bit, caught the interstate for no particular reason.

"I believe Mr. Wayne's spendin our money. What time lawyers go to work?"

Dupree was putting the truck in and out of slots in the thinning rush hour. No hurry anywhere, just hyped, burning juice.

Marty reached back and grabbed his seat belt and clicked it. Dupree looked over.

"I'd say nine thirty, ten o'clock."

Dupree jumped another tourist, jammed

away for a hundred feet to another tangle of autos. "And you don't know where he lives?"

"No. I did, we'd be there."

"You check the phone book?"

Marty rolled his eyes. "Same address and number as his office, same downtown zip. Chill out, cuz. We'll catch him in the morning."

Dupree absorbed it. "What's doin tonight? We're off, sounds like."

Marty shrugged, put a shoe on the dash and looked out the side window. "I wouldn't mind a couple of pops. And not at that racially conscious place on the other end of Church Street."

"The People's Bar."

"The Cut and Stab Saloon."

"And shootin. They got shootin too."

"Where we going?"

"They gotta bar at the motel. I go there on occasions, try and pick off a stewi if I can find one with a tolerable disposition. That's some hard damn women." Dupree meant it. Good, clean looking women, but could be downright ornery.

"Sky waitresses, daddy. Take shit all day from cheapskates." Marty had a shrug for it. "How much you go there?"

"Once in a while. Why?" Dupree knew why. Marty was into this watching his step so bad he was acting damn near paranoid. Not like the old Marty, the before-prison-Marty. Dupree hadn't noticed much except Marty had come back more serious. Even a little pushy. Not like the old Marty, the one didn't give a shit, the one wouldn't hit you with a shovel.

"We need to stay outta old places."

Dupree rolled his eyes, caught two lanes right. "The motherfucker's been followin you. He ain't been followin my ass."

Marty looked skeptical.

"Come on, man. I was military police. You don't follow my ass without I know about it. You hear what I'm sayin?"

"I see your lips moving, and I hear sounds, but it's just noise. You checked window decals and saluted cars, as I recall."

"Fuck you. I'm goin to get me some stewardess pussy."

"Sure you are. You wanna grab something to eat?"

"They gotta restaurant at the motel."

"Satisfying all your bodily functions at one facility sounds way too much like prison."

"You wanna try somethin else, I'm down with it." Dupree looked at the windshield. Yeah, Marty had changed. Maybe just the three years had grown him up some. But he did seem pushier.

Milky ordered two number threes, supersized both and told the kid he gave his money to that he'd be right back, he had to go to the restroom. She nodded greasy hair like she might give a fuck if he ever came back.

In the car he organized the burgers and fries, found a home for the huge sodas. Everything stored, ketchup in a drink cup lid, burger in hand, hand on wheel, Milky went cruising. He made a lopsided half-circle from Pell's residence to Dupree's, then by the cigar bar, since it was near Dupree's residence.

Less than an hour, the burgers were gone. And two bucketfuls of fries, six ketchups, one soda and half the other.

Milky cruised on, checked the ball-field, the bowling alley, Pell's local rail. No luck. But this was just fishing anyway. Killing time.

Now he had to piss again and needed to shit pretty bad, the greasy fast-food going right through him.

The freeway came up and Milky flipped a coin in his head. It was a jump to the airport bar Dupree frequented and about the same jump to Eddie Margot's.

If he went back to Margot's, the mosquitoes would be partying. He'd have to either run the car for A/C or sit there and sweat—rolling the windows down wasn't an option. He knew from training school that if he ran the car the catalytic converter might set the leaf litter on fire. He didn't like the sound of sitting in the hot car pulling pud. He'd go by the airport bar, maybe take that shit.

The light changed and he caught the freeway.

Dupree put the truck in a slot by the stair. He and Marty used the noisy metal steps to the second floor breezeway, used the breezeway to their rooms.

Marty's came up first; he pulled a plastic key. "How long till you're pretty enough to go get a drink?"

Dupree kept walking, stopped at the next door, tricked it. Before he went in he said, "I'll knock."

Milky caught his exit and wound around to the service road. He used the grainy road for a half-mile or so to the hotel entrance. A big ass stucco overhang jutted from the center of the facility. There was parking beyond, motel-side, and more across the asphalt drive.

Milky knew the lay, looked for a slot across from the motel and near the exit. He found a place to put his car, the little color-of-honey rental job.

A dome shaped canvas awning stuck out from the highway side of the building. Under the awning were a couple of doors. A sign above the awning said *Sky Room Lounge* in pencil-sized neon.

The bar doors were big pieces of wood fitted together, weathered and grainy, a couple of limbs for handles. Milky pulled one of the limbs and went in the bar.

It was so dark he first thought someone forgot to pay the light bill. He stood there until his eyes adjusted and saw the sign with silhouettes of a man and a woman over a hall to the right of the bar. No one behind the bar but a girl, no one anywhere but the girl.

Milky glanced at the bartender, a nice looking blond who must have worked out. He gave her a nod, almost embarrassed at coming in and going directly to the shitter. Oh well—you gotta go, you gotta go.

Dupree tapped on Marty's door in dark charcoal slacks, a collarless black shirt, open one button, and what could have been four hundred dollars' worth of shoe on each foot.

"You button your collar you'd look priestly."

"You get a cowboy hat and some boots you'd look Cowboy Bob."

The pale yellow western shirt with burgundy piping wouldn't make Marty look much like a cowboy even with the suggested hat and boots. Dupree was digging and it made Marty grin.

Dupree moved toward the stair. "Come on, cuz. Just don't stand by me should there be any ladies about."

"Yes, father. Shall we go and sin no more?"

"Shit, what fun's that gonna be?"

Milky finished up his business in the bathroom, washed up, checked himself in the mirror. The two super-sized number threes had his stomach pooched out. He pulled up on the stomach and smacked it with his hands. Too much sitting. He needed to hit the machines, tighten up the package.

Milky used the Men's door and avoided eye contact with the bartender, and now a couple of guys at the bar, as he came around. Not wanting to be viewed as some guy coming in off the street to take a shit, he headed for the light from the motel lobby where it was adjoined to the lounge by a wide, unencumbered opening.

The wide opening put Milky in the small lobby. One side of a double glass-door put him outside.

If he hadn't dropped his car keys, he'd have never seen it, he wouldn't have caught it. But when he turned and bent over in the parking lot it caught his eye: the rebel flag decal in a truck's rear window.

Milky walked down a few cars, checked the big gray truck out. Looked like the same one from last night. Too far away for coincidence. Pringle Park was way on the other side of town. Highly doubtful for construction guys up there to just happen to be drinking down here, miles away.

Milky duplicated the tag number on the palm of a hand and took it back to his car. A look at the notebook. Same tag. Too coincidental. Three possibilities: the truck was dumped here, the perps were staying here or they were in the bar. Un-uh.

Milky went back around to the side entrance, grabbed the handle of one of the wooden bar doors, eased it open. At the bar: a black guy and a white guy. Milky hadn't even looked coming out, being embarrassed about using the shitter and leaving like he did.

When one of the guys, the white guy, turned to see who was letting in sunlight Milky closed the door. He went around the building then back in through the hotel lobby. Behind the desk, a clerk he hadn't seen before smiled for him.

To the right was the lounge entrance Milky had used after coming around the bar. The barroom beyond was dark. A phone bank was outside the bar, by the doorway. Milky bent in the phone bank like a hunchback.

A few quick looks over his shoulder located the padded bar. His eyes adjusted more and he could see pretty good. The bartender was animated, serving up a couple for the guys. Shit, it *was*—his guys were sitting at the bar.

Milky went back to the humped over mode. He turned the other way and went for the front exit.

Holy shit. He walked right *by* them coming from the can. They were probably too busy checking out the barkeep's ass to notice him.

His finger got Zellwood's hotel number in after a couple of nervous tries. The phone began to purr, gave some options. Milky punched more numbers, then put the phone back to his ear.

"Tommy, it's Todd."

"Hey, Milky. You lonesome?"

"No, sir. I got em, sir."

"You don't say? Where? Margot's?"

"No. Like you said, *old habits*. I found them at one of Dupree's watering holes. Remember the truck? Out by the fence last night?"

"Yeah, Confederate flag, big gray job."

"That's them."

"Good work, Milky. Stay on em. Where you at?"

"Holiday Inn by the airport. Take the

turnpike to exit 98, go left on the access road. I'm on the right about a half mile down."

"Hang on to em, son. I'll be there directly."

"Yes, sir. I'm in a tan Mitsubishi." Hoping Zellwood appreciated the initiative.

He did: "You changed cars?"

"Yessir."

"Look at you. I'll see you in a few."

Tommy Zellwood re-cradled the phone. He took a long pull on his drink, held it up to enjoy the color of the single malt. "Too much luck," to no one.

He finished the drink, sat it down and said, to no one again: "Too much luck at the beginning and something'll pop bad in the end. Goddam it."

Zellwood shook his head. "Hurry up, Bones. I'm sitting here cursing my own good luck."

[11]

MILKY CRACKED AN eye. The beast was on the edge of his dash. It was cocked up on stiff legs, antennae reading Milky, a million years of instinct seeing what kind of mood the human was in.

Milky finessed with a snuffling turn, hand easing to a burger bag filled with other spent burger bags and spent burger accessories. Bag in hand with a good grip, then a sudden overhand flap.

The cockroach saw it coming from the locker room, did a dance, slid over the edge and Milky smashed the bag of trash, slinging debris all over his dash.

The commotion got the better of the cockroach—he jumped in the fray and spread his hard cloak, broke out his emergency wings and buzzed straight at Milky's face.

Milky panicked, began flapping the bag around, now empty and soggy-ended. The roach went by him like a special effects starfighter in a sci-fi flick.

Then, like a bad dream, the roach was gone again. Milky groaned, tossed the ragged bag and rubbed his face. Shit. Only six thirty. Barely daylight out. Still holding down the motel parking lot from the night before.

Zellwood had shown about ten—over an hour after Milky had called. They sit in separate cars side by side, Zellwood nipping the neck of a fifth bottle and burning cigarettes.

About midnight, Pell comes out of the bar, uses the stairs by the truck and goes in room 213. Milky knew because Zellwood had stepped over, gotten in Milky's car and told him to go get the room number off the door.

Milky does and a few minutes after that, Zellwood gets a call from someone he called *Bones*. Tells Bones to hold on. Tells Milky he'll see him in the morning—if anything pops, call.

Then Zellwood uses the asphalt between Milky's car and his own, still chatting as he pulls by Milky's car. Doesn't wave bye.

About two thirty, Dupree comes out with the bartender and a woman Milky hadn't seen: Hispanic and wearing a flight attendant's outfit. The three walk down the sidewalk to the stair.

In front of Pell's room there's some conversation, Dupree pulling at the bartender, the other arm around the stew. The bartender gives him a faux slap to the chest then knocks on Pell's door as Dupree and the sky-waitress walk on.

The door opens, the bartender goes coy, enters. Dupree and the other woman go in the room next door. Two forty-six a.m., last entry of the day.

Milky slept poorly, peed on the ground and on one of his socks about four thirty. Showed a rent-o-cop his buzzer about five, quarter after.

And here it was six thirty. Coffee. God, please let there be complimentary coffee.

[12]

THE ROOSTER HAD crowed about eight for Pell, and he does as Milky had done: coffee and pastry in the hotel lobby. Eight thirty, Dupree does likewise. Nine, the ladies fly.

About nine thirty Pell knocks on Dupree's door and Dupree lets him in. Pell had changed to decent slacks and a dark dress shirt, a darker sport coat on top.

Not long, they exit Dupree's room. Dupree's in lemon and lime silk and linen this morning, looking South Beach in his canvas espadrilles.

The boys leaving all dressed up like they were ready to go somewhere serious, Milky decides it's time to wake Zellwood. He did it with: "They're moving."

Zellwood makes some noise but nothing coherent.

"Yep. Here they come. Down the stairs."

Zellwood sucks his sinuses out and

croaks, "Stay on em, son," clears his throat. "I'll see you in an hour, tops." More throat clearing. "Don't call for twenty minutes. I'll be in the shower. Bye."

"Must be nice."

"Excuse me?"

"Must be nice, showering and stuff like that . . . " Milky tasted shoe in his mouth.

Heavy silence from Zellwood. Long silence.

Then: "Boy, I've lived in the fucking jungle for six, eight months at the time. No bathroom, no toilet paper. Not even a toothbrush. One night not washing your ass ain't gonna hurt you one goddam bit. You stay on em, son. See you in an hour."

Milky stayed on them all the way to the International House of Pancakes where they had a real breakfast. He dropped the Mitsubishi in parallel parking across a side street, watched Pell and Dupree through his binoculars and salivated.

An hour, Milky U-turned to follow the big truck and Zellwood called from his car, the number blocked. Milky told him where he was but never got if Zellwood was in front, behind, where. Milky held back, playing the traffic lights.

Momentarily, Zellwood drifted beside Milky. Barely acknowledging Milky, he slowed, then fell in behind.

Dupree found a parallel spot. It was short for the truck and gave him a hard go.

Milky and Zellwood both used some loading zone space on beyond the truck.

Dupree and Pell got out. Dupree fed the meter a few coins and the two men moved down the sidewalk, away from Milky and Zellwood.

Zellwood tapped his horn and jerked a thumb at Milky. Milky walked back, leaned in the passenger window.

Zellwood looked good this mid-morning: newer jeans, white button-down oxford-cloth shirt, tan corduroy jacket with suede elbow patches, well slept and shower fresh. Unlike Milky. Milky looked like he slept in the car, had coffee from a continental breakfast layout at the hotel. His neck was stiff, his head hurt and his asshole burned. The way Zellwood looked didn't help.

"I'm gonna follow them up the street here. You circle around, pick me up should I need."

"Yes, sir."

Milky went back to his car; Zellwood got out and went where the two guys went.

Hold back at the next cross street until Pell and Dupree cross. Then dodge light traffic and move on.

Halfway down the next block, the boys

turned into an alcove—the entrance to an office building. Milky showed at the curb. Zellwood pointed a thumb over a shoulder and Milky pulled on as advised.

Zellwood walked by, turned into the building. He hustled across a couple of miles of marble to a bank of elevators.

Pell and Dupree waited there, both looking at the unlit arrows over the elevator doors. Zellwood joined them.

A bell's ding lit up an arrow, doors withdrew. A few people disembarked.

Pell, Dupree, Zellwood and a young couple loaded up. Zellwood played elevator boy. "What number folks?" to the couple.

The girl smiled, said, "Six, please," while the boy pointed and mumbled something vague and tried to keep his large pants from falling down without appearing to be putting much effort into it.

"How about you gents? What'll it be?"

Pell stared at Zellwood; Dupree looked at Pell.

Pell came out of the stare, looked off, said, "Six'll do," like he didn't want to talk about it.

Dupree said, "I thought the tenant board said eight."

"Eight then."

Zellwood pushed *eight*, then *two* and leaned against the wall. He looked at nothing.

The bell dinged. Doors opened on two. Zellwood nodded cordially; his eye spending too much time on Pell's. When the doors closed behind him, he cursed himself for it. In the goddam jungle too long. He'd lost his edge at this local shit.

Pell had caught him off base somehow. Saw something, felt something, smelled something. Pell spooked.

Zellwood knew he'd have to step back now. Pell would know him when they met again. Good thing Bones was in transit.

The bell did its thing and dumped the young couple on six. Doors closed.

"The hell's wrong with you?"

"What?" Marty was clueless, gave Dupree some face to prove it.

"You know that motherfucker?"

"Who? The fuck are you talking about?"

"The man got on in the lobby? The man pushin buttons? You see his ass somewhere before?"

"Not that I know of."

"Then why the hell're you actin so funny?"

Marty shrugged, a bell dinged, the door opened. "Fuck, I don't know." Marty *didn't* know. The guy creeped him. For whatever reason.

They stepped out and the elevator took off without them.

"You think the motherfucker's a cop? Man that's got on a three-hundred-dollar pair of Johnston and Murphy ankle boots? Man that's got three-thousand-dollars' worth of Rolex on his goddam arm? Shit. Ain't no cop got that kinda scratch or taste. I wish you'd quit that paranoid shit. You're makin *me* nervous as hell."

"Sure. What's eighteen, twenty years in a Federal pen?" Marty followed with a face he hoped said he didn't want to talk about it.

Marty and Dupree used a hallway laid over with an expensive piece of carpet bordered by more marble. A hike down the carpet brought them to a sign that said *Burton, Wayne, Salibar and Associates.* A set of foiled doors took up most of the horizon.

Marty grabbed the knob, turned it. "You ready for this?"

"Shit, baby, I'm lookin forward to it."

People stepped aside while Zellwood and others got off the elevator. He looked across the lobby, saw a directory on a wall.

On a piece of paper, he copied the eighth floor occupants. Four law offices, a mortgage company and an ad agency. Zellwood wrote all the names down. He put the list in a coat pocket and went out the tall glass doors.

Zellwood slid in the passenger door of Milky's car. "Take me up to my car, son."

Milky put the car in gear and pulled away from the curb. "Could I ask what we're going to do, sir?"

Zellwood relaxed, tossed his left arm across the backs of the seats, hand resting on Milky's headrest.

"Sure. We're gonna follow em around until something means something. Right now, all I know is they might be seeking legal counsel or planning an advertising campaign. They could be planning on buying themselves a starter home. That's what's on their floor: lawyers, mortgage brokers and ad men. Whatchu think, Milky?" Zellwood didn't look over. He didn't really give a fuck what Milky thought.

"I'd say the lawyers."

"Un-huh. Me too. You think maybe their conscience got to em? They wanna turn themselves in, pay their debts to society?"

"I doubt it, sir."

Milky stopped parallel to Zellwood's car. Zellwood popped the door.

"Me too. Circle on around, son. Park before the building. They come out, let em come on. I'll follow them, you just follow me. And stay close."

"Yes, sir." Pause. "Tommy, I don't have your cell phone number—in case I lose you."

"I got yours. I look back and don't see you, I'll call."

Zellwood stepped out, stepped over and was in his car.

The waiting room of Burton, Wayne, Salibar and Associates was spacious, lots of wood and what some designer might consider power colors. A bold place.

A woman sat in a transaction window behind a desk. She was answering the phone like she probably did it a couple hundred times a day.

The woman said: "Burton, Wayne, Salibar. How may I direct your call?" Pause. "Hold please."

She pushed some numbers on a phone console and swiveled to the transaction window. A smile found her face. "Well, hello there, Marty Pell. How are you?"

"No complaints, Ava."

Ava was better than fifty but could have passed for ten years younger, no problem. Nice trim lady in a nice trim black-and-white polka-dot suit today.

"Marty, I'm so sorry about your mom."

"Thanks, Ava. Me too. Listen, after Mom died, you or someone called and said there were some personal items here."

The phone complained; Ava held up a finger and nabbed it. "Burton, Wayne, Salibar. How may I direct your call?" Pause. "Hold please." Buttons got punched.

"Sorry, Marty. Yes. I think so. Let me go look." Ava rose, the phone rang. "Burton, Wayne, Salibar. How may I direct your call?" Pause. "Hold please."

Ava pushed several buttons, lifted the receiver, pushed another and lowered it. "I'll be right back."

Ava disappeared and the phone began ringing. A machine whirred and Ava's voice came out of it: "Burton, Wayne, Salibar. Hold please." The phone clicked a couple of times and went silent.

Ava came back with an accordion file. "Come on around, Marty. I'll buzz you in."

Marty moved to a door at his right, Dupree crowding behind. Marty tossed a glance over his shoulder. "This ain't a toll plaza, cuz. You'll get in, no charge."

"Move along, bread. We got business."

The file sat on a foot wide counter separating Ava's workspace from a hallway. Marty shook the contents onto the counter.

Some keys and a couple of envelopes slid out. One envelope had *Shad Dupree* written on it. Marty grabbed that one and said, "I believe this is yours, Mr. Dupree." He handed it to Dupree, then looked at the other envelope, tossed it aside.

Marty looked at tags on keys. Her house keys—sold. Her car keys—sold. An iron key to an antique roll-top his mom had been handed down—sold. Everything the woman owned sold to pay the hospital while her baby boy was doing his Federal time. He scooped up the keys, segregated one and said: "This is a funny little key. Wonder what that's for?" Marty tossed Dupree some deadpan.

Ava came back from a stock phone conversation, looked over cat-eyed cheaters, said, "Oh, I'd say your mom's safe deposit box. When she first got sick and you were still . . . " Ava searched for words.

Marty helped her. "In prison."

"Yes. She lost consciousness and when she came around she asked Mr. Wayne to go through her stuff, see what was solvent enough to sell. She had a safe deposit box at the downtown bank. Mr. Wayne brought the contents here to review and appraise them."

Dupree and Marty traded looks. Dupree looked at the envelope in his hand, squeezed it by its edges. The envelope gapped where it had been cut open.

Under his breath Dupree said: "Motherfucker."

Ava looked at Dupree through the cats'-eyes then over them like she'd just now seen him.

"I beg your pardon?"

Marty grinned, said, "He says my mother was lucky."

Dupree smiled good for Ava. "A quality

lawyer like Mr. Wayne lookin out for her interests and all."

Marty watched Ava almost laugh, almost smile. Her eyebrows went up alone against the statement.

After a suitable pause, Ava looked at Marty and said, "He doesn't know Mr. Wayne, does he?"

"No, Ava, my friend's never had the pleasure of Tony's legal expertise. I thought I might break his streak of good luck. Tony in?"

Marty leaned on the counter, close to Ava. Ava made a face meant to be noncommittal maybe, said, "Mr. Wayne doesn't come in much these days, Marty." The face was dying to say more.

"His prospective clients should appreciate that. What's he doing *these days*?"

Ava looked around, making sure the copy machine wasn't eavesdropping. "Nobody says officially, but the rumor mill has it that Mr. Wayne's into development now, not much law anymore. Has some hush-hush overseas partnerships putting up gobs of cash."

Dupree said, "Oh yeah? What's he developin?"

Ava shrugged. "He's bought and sold several pieces of commercial property, a few big residential pieces. I know because I typed up the contracts. Other than that . . . " another shrug, "Who knows?"

Under his breath again, Dupree said, "Shit, I bet I do."

Ava looked up at him again.

"Just talkin to myself. Don't mind me."

"I don't mind you a bit, sugar." Ava was looking at Dupree like she really didn't mind him, like he was chocolate ice-cream.

Marty asked, "Tony doesn't live in the house downtown anymore, huh?"

Ava looked at Marty, mock shock going. "Oh heavens no, Marty. Mr. Wayne bought a house up at Alaqua Lakes."

"You have the address? Tony's got something else of mine I need to get from him."

"Sorry, Marty. Absolutely *verboten*." Ava's face wasn't convincing.

Marty made a hmmm sound.

Ava said, to a fingernail. "It's hard to believe they'd let someone paint a house *that* yellow in such an exclusive neighborhood, right on the lake and all."

"Yeah? Tony's house downtown, it was pretty yellow at one time."

"Same color." Ava leaned on her elbows while she smiled.

"He must like it. On the lake, huh?"

Ava shrugged. "That's what they say. I wouldn't go there on a dare. Bye, Marty and Marty's friend."

The phone rang and Ava said: "Burton, Wayne, Salibar."

Marty and Dupree used the door to the waiting room.

"How may I direct your call?"

Marty turned and tossed a wink.

"Hold please."

Then to Marty, through the transaction window: "Marty, whatever Mr. Wayne has of yours? I hope you get it."

"Thanks, Ava. Me too."

[13]

TOMMY ZELLWOOD USED the car's cigarette lighter to spark a butt, tossed the lighter and plugged in a laptop. The screen came up.

Maneuvered online, headed to Virginia. Security held him up at the front door. He fed them a password. De-nied.

Seemed someone was currently on that site using that password. A rude little box wanted to know was this a security breach? Should this action be reported? A click on *no* let him make a note explaining the collision to the cyber-security guys and he backed out.

Zellwood found his cell and fed it some numbers. A few purrs later: "Bones. You're at the office, huh?" Pause. "Yeah, I went online and stumbled into you riding my password. You still in there?" Pause. "Go ahead, get it back up." Pause longer. "Okay. Who was my boy Marty's lawyer? Got that?" Pause with a smile and a look at the eighth floor list. "Anthony Wayne, Esquire. Un-huh." Pause. "Yeah. He's up there now." Pause. "That's good. I'll see you then."

The phone came away from the ear then back. "Yeah, I'm still here. What you got?" Pause. "Hmmm. Wayne handled mom's affairs too." Pause. "I don't know. It could mean something. We'll see. Get your ass down here."

The tall glass doors put Marty and Dupree on the sidewalk. Eleven o'clock sun looking over the canyon lip of downtown.

"Tell you what, bread, I got some fuckin developments for Mr. Tony Wayne. My goddam fist's gonna develop upside his head."

"That how we do it? We beat it out of him?" Marty could see a problem coming.

"Goddam, cuz, I hope so."

The truck chirped and winked its lights at them.

Marty said, before climbing in, "How about you don't knock him out until we hear about the shit."

Zellwood watched the nose of the truck push into downtown traffic. He turned the A/C down and watched the rearview mirror.

And, goddam, there was Milky, right behind them.

Zellwood shucked his jacket and put a hand up to his face as Dupree and Pell rolled past. He punched his window down and put out a hand for Milky. Milky stopped next to him, put down a window.

"Son, you hear what I said about I follow them, you follow me?"

"Yes, sir."

"Then pay attention. We wanna follow them—we don't wanna steal their damn shoes."

"Yes, sir."

Milky gave Zellwood a face that was probably supposed to say he was properly reprimanded.

"Well, come on."

Zellwood pulled out, Milky in tow. He dragged Milky out of the tall buildings, around some lakes where houses began to pop up. Onto an interstate for ten or fifteen miles. Off at a bucolic exit, an eye catching arrangement of feral ground and red brick shopping opportunities, the concrete fresh and new. Burbs pastoral.

The parade followed a piece of young concrete around to a strip mall. The truck signaled a right at the second entrance. Zellwood jumped in the first entrance and the dumb kid almost rear-ended his car. Zellwood shook his head and mumbled about the FBI.

The truck drew a slot close to the storefronts and dumped its occupants. Pell and Dupree crossed between cars and went in a sporting goods store.

Zellwood had his choice of slots on the distant end of the parking lot. He grabbed one with a view of the sporting goods outfit.

Milky pulled alongside, dropped a window.

Milky looked at the side of Zellwood's face through the Lincoln's window, the window still up. In a bit it began to descend.

"Morning, son."

"Good morning."

Zellwood looked over at Milky. "Damn, boy, you look like hell. Come on over here, ride with me."

Milky locked his car and walked around. "You want me to drive, sir?"

"Nah. Come on around, take it easy. I believe we're close to wherever it is we're going. We weren't, we wouldn't have gotten off the interstate."

Milky got in, enjoying the room and luxury of the big American car. He leaned his head back, closed his eyes.

He'd nearly floated off when Zellwood said, "Here we go."

Milky sat up. He watched Pell and Dupree come out of the store. Dupree brought something out of a small plastic bag. They stopped by the trashcan, Dupree tossed the bag, used his teeth on tags then tossed the tags, spitting plastic.

"The hell's he got, Milky?"

"Don't know, sir. I got field glasses in the car. We need them?"

"Yeah. Grab em right quick."

Milky jumped out, jogged around, unlocked, nabbed glasses, locked, jogged around, jumped back in the car.

He passed the glasses to Zellwood.

Zellwood put up a hand. "You look—my eyes are old."

Milky looked. Under the glasses, his mouth said: "Gloves. Like workout gloves. Full finger jobs."

Zellwood turned his ignition key looking at Pell and Dupree, eyes focused on beyond them, grinning good. Then a funny little, *un-un-un*, then, "This may get interesting, Milky, you stay awake to see it."

Dupree pulled on the leather gloves. The fit was tight and he was animated with the struggle, doing O.J. on the walk to the pickup. Once the gloves were on, he stretched and wiggled his fingers then smacked each fist in the other palm.

Marty watched, amused. "You get what you need?"

"Yeah." Dupree struggled out of the gloves. He unbuttoned a back pocket and stuffed the gloves in there.

"You do this before?"

"Some." Dupree unlocked the truck.

"When?" Marty wasn't sure he believed it.

"Here and there. Do it for Grady once in a while."

"Grady? Shady Grady the limo man? What? Somebody doesn't pay the meter, you beat it out of em?" Marty saying it over the hood of the truck.

Doors opened; Dupree and Marty climb in.

"Grady doesn't necessarily make all his money runnin limos. There's some body-guardin work and then there's also some phones in the back room don't stop ringin, you get my drift."

Marty let it sink in. "And sometimes, somebody makes a bad bet and doesn't have the ends, you go see him?"

"Hey, they always got the ends. What you do is try and help the man realize the overlooked resources is all."

Dupree fired up and pulled straight ahead through the empty space in front of them. Marty watched the pickup's big side mirror miss an SUV by fractions.

"So you enjoy that shit? Helping people realize overlooked resources?"

"You judgin?"

"Nah. I'm asking."

Dupree sat on his response while he pulled back on the concrete road, caught it the same direction they were going before the stop. Then: "I guess—compared to limoin anyway. That shit ain't nothin but sittin around waitin on the Man."

"You never chauffeured women?"

"You know that ain't what I mean, but yeah. They go out, a bunch of women? One of em always vomits. If they're all good and drunk, maybe another one or two might vomit lookin at the first girl vomit." Dupree made a disgusted face. "Then you're drivin along with all these sick, silly white bitches and the car smells like a Roman vomitorium."

"So you're saying it might not be you necessarily enjoy collecting so much as you don't seem to care much for limoing."

"Collectin pays better too. Mileage plus a percentage on the collect."

"Plus you've learned a new trade."

"True. True. What'd you learn? While you were on the chill?"

"Toy making. Wood toys. Made them in the wood shop for orphans and homeless kids, I guess. I mostly made wheels outta closet rod, used a bandsaw to cut it into little slices."

Marty looked over to see Dupree nodding, knowing they were gaming but doing it serious like Marty was.

"Sounds like an interestin and fun trade, but ain't much call for that nowdays."

"True. True." Beat for drama—they were playing anyway. "But you never know. I mean look at you. Something as discreet as leg breaking, and here you go getting your entrepreneurial game on with it already. Wooden wheels could go viral at a moment's notice."

"True. Never know. This our turn?" Dupree pointed to an elegant entrance into a lush and docile community.

"Yeah."

"There's a gate?"

"Yeah. Pull up and stop. We'll get the guard to call Tony, buzz us in."

"Un-huh. You think the man wants to see us?"

"No, but if he doesn't buzz us in, it might look like he doesn't wanna see us."

"We don't want that, do we?"

"No. Me and you could misread the situation, do something foolish."

"We wouldn't want something like that to happen, would we?" Dupree dropped the side glass.

"No. We wouldn't want that."

The truck stopped at a white and black

bar next to a guard shack, the shack a half-glass deal. It was finished with the same smooth stucco job applied to the wall that ran like the Wall of China around the enclave and a two-hundred-acre lake, the lake chaining off to several lesser versions. Ten-foot-high walls and armed guards—the things you have to do these days to keep the riffraff out.

The shack hatched a rent-a-cop, blue-gray uniform, a vinyl-billed cover, fat ass and a big blue-steel revolver from a cowboy movie up on the hip. He had a face that could make a basset look optimistic. He put it on Marty and Dupree. Maybe he didn't like the truck.

It seemed to be a lot of trouble for him to walk out to the truck but he managed with a good bit of sloth.

"What's up, gents?" He was getting a good look at faces.

Marty leaned out so he could talk around Dupree. "Tony Wayne. We're friends dropping by. Tell him it's his cousin Marty and a friend."

The guard let it soak in for a bit. "Mr. Wayne? Two seventeen Alaqua?"

Dupree was looking congenial as hell. "Sounds right. Ugly yellow motherfucker sits on the lake?"

The guard lost composure and grinned. "Yeah, that'd be it alright. Hang on."

The guard retreated, still conserving energy. In a moment, he appeared inside the glass cubby, sat and only his head and upper body were visible.

A phone came up, his eyes went down.

After a brief hibernation, knuckles propping his face up, he came to life. His lips moved. He shrugged, the spare hand came up in animation. He looked out at Marty and Dupree. It didn't look good.

Dupree said as much.

Marty shrugged, relaxed back. "Chill. He's gonna let us in."

The guard nodded and the receiver disappeared. He rose, smiled and waved a hand, motioning them on. The semaphore arm jumped to attention, saluting the truck's passing.

"You called it, cuz."

Marty grinned. "I was bluffing."

"Good work still. Which way do we go gives me the chance to put my foot up Mr. Wayne's ass?"

Uh-oh. Here we go. Marty rolled his head to see Dupree. Dupree's jaw muscles were flexing all the way to his temple. "How about we see if we can find us a more discreet way to go home?"

"Why?"

"I don't wanna meet some cops at the one and only gate, in case we have to whip somebody's ass inside this fence."

"Oh somebody's definitely gonna get their ass kicked."

"And people like lawyers tend to call nine-one-one when somebody kicks their asses, so let's go find us a new way outta here."

"Sounds good. Like I said: which way?"

"The road less traveled, daddy."

[14]

HOUSES WITH TWO commas in the selling price. Even the shabby, off-lake trash would get you a solid six zeros. A place where you could find guys who chased different balls; transient theme-park execs whose longevity was determined by park sales stats; the children of hundred-acre, hard-scrabble, white-trash chicken farmers and orange pickers yanked into prosperity by the surge of wealth oozing from the edges of a tourist town. Probably a thug-done-well or two trying to insulate themselves from the violent streets they'd created, keep their own kids out of the frenzy.

Sum totaled, money so new the ink was still damp on the most of it around here. It could have been shameful if new-money didn't kick no-money's ass. No one here cared what people thought about it. They were too busy spending their large lucky streaks.

The high hedges gave way to the back lot. Construction had grabbed ground in all directions, pregnant with houses in varied forms of gestation. Block walls with wood skeletons on second and third floors came up first. Then nothing but some concrete slabs with pipes sticking up. Progress and asphalt finally petered out like the economy had, yielding to sand roads and sewer stubs. No signs of life or recent growth.

A few bad choices broke good and brought the large truck to a dead-end by a dusty vacant construction trailer. A padlocked gate of tall diamond-weave fence on an aluminum frame filled a twelve-foot void in more diamond weave that seemed to continue to infinity either way.

"Hang on, my brother." Marty jumped out and waded through the dust to the gate. A quick look showed him what he expected. He flexed his knees and gripped the mesh gate low.

The gate lifted off the hinges and swung free.

It took Marty half a dozen tries to get the dual eyehooks of the gate back on the dual L brackets in the support post. He brushed his hands on his pants, went back to the truck.

He closed the door, said, "Construction guys always have a way to get in and out.

These guys used an old one: they reversed the top pin, turned it up, so they wouldn't have to wait on the super in the morning."

"You learn that inside?"

Marty laughed but it wasn't funny. "No. I learned that in the day-labor pool after I got out."

Dupree looked contrite for a bit, said, "Which way to Tony the motherfucker's?"

Dupree was bright eyed, keyed to the cap. Marty watched the side of his face. The muscles of Dupree's jaw were still undulating in ripples.

"Maybe we should come back later to see Tony."

"Why?"

"Right now the guard knows we're here. Tony calls the cops—and he will—we're fucked. We leave, come in this back way later on, nobody'll know we were here."

"Tony will. He's the only one I care about."

"How about you humor me—we go out, come back around dark, do this deed. I don't believe it's a daytime duty anyway."

Dupree thought about it. "I bought new gloves."

"They aren't perishable, they'll hold."

Dupree fired the truck up, put it in reverse. He did a three point on a 180.

"We're goin to see the man. Right now."

"No, we're not." Marty put it out there with a little more juice in it than he intended, but it was out there now.

Dupree looked over. Marty knew Dupree had something to say but he sat on it. Marty went again. "Listen, Dupree, while you've been running the numbers, figuring gold prices, I've been figuring this part. I know how it needs to go, and rushing in and throwing blows ain't how it's done. This is slow, steady work. Let's get outta here."

Dupree sat long enough Marty didn't know which way it was going to go, wondered it if was going to go to blows. It didn't and Marty was relieved—Dupree wouldn't be fun to spar with.

"You okay if we ride by, see where it is, the man's house? See what he got for our money?" Not friendly. Formal.

They rode by. Nothing fancy for this hood, maybe a million and a half, a nice place. But the color should have come with a warning label. It was catsup and mustard—a blend of. More orange than the yellow Ava had promised. Marty thought about it, thought he could have done better with his money, even with his stunted sense of style.

Dupree motored back around and he and Marty waved at their buddy, the hired gun in the guard shack. The guard disregarded them other than raising the traffic arm.

At the road, a right turn had them going as they had come. Dupree had a death grip on the steering wheel, veins rigid as cables under his skin, pushing the truck hard. "We shoulda got him, Marty. Right then."

"You need to chill out, cuz." Marty could feel himself getting agitated. "I bug you being so paranoid; you scare me being Mr. Sluggo." Good pause, then, "I'll chill if you'll chill."

Dupree looked over from his tailgating. Marty turned to watch the car in front for him.

Marty said, "One of us needs to watch the road. Seems like it should be you."

Dupree looked forward, eased off the bumper in front of them. "That why you didn't wanna go see Tony? You afraid I'll be *Mr. Sluggo*?"

Marty shrugged. "Like I say, I know how it needs to go. And, no, I don't want you to kill the fuck—nor beat him unconscious. You're topped out. We need the bad-ass stuff, but we need to control it." Some pause. Then, "We gotta control it, cuz. Let's chill, put it at arm's length, make it business, talk it through some."

"How're you suggestin we do that?"

"We go by Stanley's, have some beers and a low quality alley burger, side order Mel Fries."

"Thanks, but if I gotta eat there, I pass. I

get the urge to gamble, I'll go to 7-Eleven Saturday night and play my lucky numbers. Beer sounds good though."

"Whatever your pleasure. I'll buy. That twelve hundred bucks is burning a hole in my pocket."

"My pleasure to let you buy." Dupree went off in thought, absently caught the left to the interstate ramp and zipped to speed, driving almost courteously, blending into traffic.

"Marty, what if this motherfucker's cashed all the chips in and got it in paper and shit?"

Marty flicked his eyebrows, said, "I should be spending more time thinking about that but I keep avoiding it." It wasn't a good answer but it was all Marty had.

[15]

DUPREE WAS RIGHT, of course: you want to gamble on food, eat at a bowling alley bar. Stanley's joint, the Majestic Bar, was no different. And it was no more majestic than his Majestic Lanes.

Before his jump, Marty had spent enough time here to know it would never change. Him, Dupree, Stanley Woo and two, three other guys who swung at softballs and played tenpins hung out at the Majestic, downed pitchers of beer.

A look around—same as it ever was.

The bar enclosure had no front wall or door or other designation from the rest of the bowling alley. Only the ratty worn carpet growing ever darker as it ventured into the food and beverage zone demarked it. A few sad vinyl booths nestled to a wall wrapped in cheap dark paneling. A tired wooden bar came from the back wall, zipped around ninety degrees to quickly collide with the wall opposite the booths.

On the bar top, a bagel carousel inside a clear plastic case jerked nervously. The plastic was streaked with something that resembled ambered varnish but was probably once pretend-butter. The glass sides of a popcorn machine that was new about the Carter administration was similarly streaked, maybe more streaked.

The percussive sounds of bowling balls bullying the pins and the sharp-cornered electronic sounds of video games from the adjoining room competed with George Jones and Englebert tossing out near hits and tired old favorites for fifty cents a pop. The place smelled of grease and sweat and stale bits of clabbered beer.

Marty and Dupree were in one of the booths, both looking at a rinsed-out middle-aged blonde behind the bar named Charlotte. Charlotte could have passed for someone who tends bar and overcooks burgers at the bowling alley.

Across from Charlotte was a guy with sideburns, frantically retreating hairline and a comb he didn't mind pulling from a hip pocket and using. His hair went back from a Mohawkish spear point, flared across his head then blossomed down in back to ducktail nicely over his collar. Profile, Marty thought the guy looked like an iguana in a plaid cowboy shirt. Mostly he looked like someone who wouldn't mind spending a few bucks on a piece like Charlotte.

Charlotte half-turned from her conversation and flipped a couple of thin hamburger patties on a blackened grill. She was speaking to the man, turned back and laughed obscenely. Smokers' hack bent her out of sight, taking her breath down there behind the bar. She got her breath past the laugh and came back up.

Dupree said, "Hey, Charlotte, you get done tellin dirty jokes, you think you could pull us a couple?"

Charlotte squinted until she recognized Dupree. "Hey, Shad, honey. I'll be with you in a minute. Lemme flip these burgers. You want draft?"

"Yeah. May as well make it a pitcher."

"Okay, hon." Another squint, then, "Marty Pell? Is that you?"

"I think so Charlotte. How you doing?"

"I'm good, honey. Where in the hell have you been? You move or sump'n?"

Marty glanced at Dupree, Dupree waiting to see what Marty would say. He said, "Sorta."

"You move back?"

"For a while." Marty looked at Dupree, Dupree now grinning a little.

"Well good, sweetheart. I missed you."

Charlotte went back to propping on the bar and her conversation with the alley wag.

"Shit. We may never get any beer with Charlotte makin goo-goo at the handsome stranger at the bar." Pause. "Tell me about this old man. The one from inside."

"Whatcha wanna know?"

"What he can do. What he's gonna do for us."

"He's moved some gems and metals." Marty used a shrug so he wouldn't have to ask Dupree again if he had anybody else.

"How much's he gonna want?"

Marty put out some dunno. "We'll ask him when we get to that part."

"Keep in mind, cousin Tony looks like he's cashin out some. We need to go a percentage on what we recover, not a flat rate."

Marty thought he'd heard himself say they'd talk about that when they got to it. He changed directions. "How much you think Tony's pissed away?"

"Lookin at the house, where it is, lifestyle goes with it? A cool two, three mil by now. Maybe more. Course all that shit's about to end sometime this evenin."

Stanley Woo sauntered in, took in the scene, the few customers. Took in Marty and Dupree then Charlotte and her frog prince.

"*Que pasa?*"

"No beer to slow beer. How about you pull us a pitcher, put it on your tab, innkeeper?" Dupree had one of his big insincere smiles for Stanley.

Stanley looked at his watch. "Twelve thirty. I buy the beer, you buy your own food."

Dupree extended the insincere smile. "I'd have to leave the damn premises to find something could legally qualify for food. I do that, then the beer goes even warmer while I'm gone."

Stanley put up an innocent hand. "What's wrong with my food?"

"Same thing that's wrong with fugu, Stanley. And I mean that in the best way."

Stanley blew a kiss at Dupree and went to a place in the bar that hinged up to become a pass. He raised the section until it locked in place.

Charlotte turned and said something to him, he waved her back to her burgers and grabbed a couple of glass pitchers. He sat the pitchers on a mat under taps and pulled the taps open a tad.

Stanley found a tray and pulled three iced mugs from a cooler below the bar. He turned to the taps, pulled them full open for a bit then killed one, then the other. Pitchers went on the tray. The tray went on Stanley's upraised hand.

Through the bar break, across the carpet. At the booth, Stanley spun the tray down like he was trying out for the Service Industry Olympics. He slid mugs into place and sat the pitchers—one golden, one deep brown—on the Formica top.

Marty moved condiment caddies to make some elbow room. "Go, Stanley. What's the occasion?"

Stanley put the tray in an empty booth. "Hey, I haven't seen you in what? Three, four years till the other day. You mind? I'm having a generous and sentimental moment here."

"We won't have to hug or anything, right?"

"Nah. Not unless you want."

"Sit on Dupree's side anyway."

Dupree slid over, sliding the pitcher of pale beer with him then pouring himself one in a single continuous move. Marty held the pitcher of brown beer up, Stanley nodded and Marty poured Stanley then himself.

A few sips and a little silence that had some sharp corners, Stanley said, "So. How'd you find jail?"

Marty laughed; Dupree looked at Stanley, showed Marty the bewildered face, put it back on Stanley.

"The fuck's wrong with you, Stanley? You mean how he found where it was at? He didn't have to. They sent a van to the courthouse for his ass, took him all the way up there. Oh. You mean how did he *like* it? He liked it fine. He liked it so much, he's savin his money so he can go back there this year on vacation." Dupree nailed some free beer. "You don't ask a man shit like that."

"So kill me cause I'm not up on jailing protocol. I've never had any ex-con friends, you don't mind me calling you that."

Marty was getting good entertainment value and didn't mind being called an ex-con a bit and said so.

"So I shouldn't ask any questions about possible nefarious homosexual encounters a man has on the inside, right?"

Dupree looked at Marty. "You see why he serves us free beer, right? So we'll sit here while he fucks with us with his superior eastern mind and ten-dollar words. What'd you do, Stanley, buy a new thesaurus?"

Marty said, "You two don't knock it off, I'm gonna go sit somewhere else."

The silence came back. Stanley broke it with: "So. How's your post-incarceration rehab going?"

"You're a funny motherfucker, Stanley. Nothin but a wonder somebody ain't built you a stage out there at the counter where you stay with all those stinky shoes. Why don't you put up a spotlight, get stoned-ass

Cobbey over there on a snare drum, do a roll when you hit the zingers."

"Jeez, Dupree, ease up. I'm just curious." Stanley sipped. "I was in jail one time, you know."

Dupree lifted a pitcher, shook himself another one. "Yeah. For what? The health man find domestic animal pelts in your dumpster?"

"Public urination."

Marty passed; Dupree played. "They lock you up for that shit?"

"Depends on where you are."

Marty jumped in: "And how many times you shake it."

Dupree: "Un-huh. And where were you?"

Stanley: "City hall. But that's a long story."

Dupree: "Un-huh. I bet. How much time did you get?"

"Two."

"Two years for public pissin? Stanley Woo, you ain't ever been in jail for any two fuckin years."

"Two days."

"Shit. Two days." Dupree dismissed Stanley's short-time with a pooh.

"Changed my life though."

"How's two days in jail gonna change somebody's fuckin life?" Dupree, just like old times, was buying into Stanley's bullshit.

Stanley sipped his beer. "Going to jail naked changes your life, brother. Take my word for it."

"Wait now." Dupree's forehead accordioned. "You were naked? At city hall? Pissin? They oughta got your ass on indecent exposure."

"There was that too."

Dupree wanted to know: "How'd you come to be naked, Stanley?"

"It's a long story."

"This already is a long story. Tell it."

"Okay, there's a long boring part about being pissed off that the city pissed on me when they condemned my storage building, and my deciding to piss on the city—more accurately the mayor's car."

"Good concrete target." Marty held his beer up in salute, drank.

"And a seemingly foolproof plan." Stanley put a positive nod on it. "Well thought out."

Dupree. "Uh-huh. Sounds like it. You have drawins, diagrams and shit?"

Stanley ignored Dupree. "With a fatal flaw."

"You gonna tell the story, or you gonna wax around like Carl Sandburg?" Dupree tossing around poets like he knew what he was talking about.

"The fuck's Carl Sandburg?" Stanley played totally sidetracked.

Marty said, "Doesn't matter. And the plan was . . . ?"

"Okay. I'd go downtown, piss on the mayor's car. In it, if it happens to be unlocked."

Dupree looked over at Marty. Marty was already smiling.

"But, I'm thinking . . . "

"Bad mistake."

"Fuck you, Dupree. So I think: *How do I get away clean?* And, *eureka*, it hits me."

Dupree said, "*Eureka*? You say shit like *eureka* to yourself?"

"Fuck you, Dupree. I say: *that's it.* If I soap myself up and the cops show, I slip away, pun intended."

Marty nodded. "So then you over analyzed and tossed in a few safety clauses, right?"

Nodding Stanley said, "Yeah. The soap got supercharged to grease."

"God knows you got plenty of that." Dupree put up a phony smile.

"Fuck you, Dupree. Then I was thinking: *wetsuit.*"

"And a wetsuit ain't but a hop, skip and a jump from bein greased-up buck-ass naked downtown?" Dupree was asking like he didn't know.

"Fuck you, Dupree. It was artistic civil protest. Something you and Carl Sandburg would never get. This was more a Thoreau thing."

Dupree smiled the phony one. "Nor is it somethin you could do in your country of origin and not get your ass executed in the town square."

Marty shook his head, said, "So what went wrong? I mean besides the part where you fucked up and inserted getting naked downtown into your scheme?"

"Slipped, dude. All that oil. My foot slid out of my sneaker and I busted ass. Falling on concrete naked hurts like hell—stunned me severely."

Marty: "But, luckily, you still had one shoe on?"

Stanley: "Yeah."

Dupree: "You went to jail naked but for one shoe?"

Stanley: "No. Somebody got my other shoe for me."

Marty poured another brown one for himself and topped Stanley's off. "So. How'd you find incarceration, Stanley?"

Stanley pushed long bangs from his face with delicate Asian fingers. "Mostly bad."

Dupree: "Oh. There were good parts?"

Stanley shrugged, slow like he was sitting on Zen. "The part where the jailer tells everybody to shuck duds and spread em? For the delousing? You're already naked, you're first up. First to get your orange jump suit and paper shoes."

A laugh crawled out of Dupree. "Fuckin Stanley goes to jail, turns it into a contest. See who could be first gettin deloused."

Marty sipped, asked, "So, Stanley, you have any nefarious homosexual encounters during your unfortunate incarceration for government protest and civil disobedience?"

"Sorta. When I was tossed in the tank, there was this rough, biker-looking dude. He didn't say anything, but he kept looking and grinning. Nasty guy. Ragged beard with part of his last few meals stuck to it. Greasy hair. The works."

Marty said the guy sounded untidy. Stanley agreed.

Dupree asked, "Didn't anybody ask you why you were in jail naked?

"Nah, man. Contrary to what you may have heard, people tend to avoid you in jail if you're booked in naked."

"I guess so." Dupree finished his beer, poured another. "That your homosexual experience?"

"Oh no. That was later. After delousing. We're in this holding cell waiting to go upstairs, sitting on these benches around the wall, and this biker's sitting directly across from me. Watching me again."

"In a bit, he leaned forward and held up

a grubby index finger and said, *They put me in with you, I'm gonna stick this finger right here in your asshole tonight.*" Stanley did a good imitation of a redneck biker.

Dupree leaned against the paneled wall. "Say what? What'd you do?"

"I asked him why."

Marty laughed; Dupree rolled eyes.

Marty: "And he said . . . "

"He didn't like to go all the way on the first date."

Marty: "Lose respect for you?"

Stanley shrugged. "I let it go."

Marty nodded. "I can see why. So, you had to put the moral of all this on a fortune cookie slip, what would it say?"

Stanley sat for a while thinking about it, looking into his beer like the answer might rise with the bubbles. Then he said: "Civil disobedience often leads to fines and probation."

Marty raised his mug. "Well said, baby."

Dupree added, "Take it to the bank," mug in the air.

Stanley raised his glass and said, "Outside the trains don't run on time."

[16]

IT HAD BEEN a scramble back in the suburbs and Milky was glad Zellwood was behind the wheel. Still dopey from little to no sleep, Milky had been trying to hang on to his half-drowse without looking stupid to Zellwood.

When the perps pulled in the gated subdivision, Zellwood had pulled by, gone up the road. He'd three-pointed in the opposite direction and parked on the shoulder. Then, no perps for a bit so Zellwood gets itchy, pulls in the drive.

Zellwood was trying to finesse the fat security guard without having to show him a buzzer when their guys come by on the other side of the guard house. Dupree waves through several layers of glass and the security guard turns, looks, pushes a button on a console. The black guy, Dupree, doesn't appear to make them, doesn't even make eye contact. The truck rolls out of Milkey's line of vision.

A car was behind them, so Zellwood pushes through the semaphore, breaking it, and U-turns around the guard house, breaks the exit gate. The guard yells and runs maybe two steps after them. His hand is on the big dinosaur on his hip but he doesn't draw. Zellwood pulls off, waves at the guy.

Zellwood slows just enough for Milky to get out across the road from the strip mall where he'd parked the little car. Dodges SUV's and vans to the car, zips out and catches the interstate highway.

He runs ninety or better back to civilization but he never glimpses the other two vehicles. He catches an exit and parks on a side street and waits.

A half-hour, Zellwood calls: the bowling alley.

Milky drives over and pulls between two buildings with a bowling alley view. Zellwood's there, using Milky's binoculars to watch the bowling alley across the street.

Milky backs in like Zellwood, next slot. He puts his window down. He watches Zellwood talk on the cell phone and look through Milky's glasses. He watches through Zellwood's raised window. Milky tosses on his Oakleys, loosens his tie and ignores Zellwood.

Zellwood doesn't seem to mind.

Thirty minutes of that, Zellwood puts

down his passenger window and says: "Well, Milky, I'm leaving you with it. Call me at the ho-tel."

That's what Zellwood had said. He was leaving Milky with it. Call him at the *ho-tel.* That was maybe one o'clock.

Now it was four and Milky needed a bath as bad as he could ever remember. The backs of the knees of his suit pants were accordions. His hair was stiff. His underarms smelled.

Milky was out of the car stretching and there were his people, coming through the bowling alley door. Into the truck. Moving.

A call to Zellwood's hotel message box: "They're traveling."

Milky pulled onto the street. The truck was at the next light. The light was red; Milky dawdled. His phone chirped. The light changed.

"This is Milky."

"We moving?"

"Yes, sir."

"Let me know when y'all light down, I'll come spell you so you can shower and eat. I bet you didn't get lunch, did you, son?"

Zellwood knew goddam well he hadn't had lunch. "Thanks. I'll call."

The trek was straight to the Holiday Inn by the airport. Milky called Zellwood back.

"All right, hoss. I'll be there shortly."

And he was. Milky had never been so glad to be off duty in his fucking life.

Tommy Zellwood, sitting in the lot at Holiday Inn, was on the property appraiser's website. He had a map up but he was hitting zip.

Everything was new at the upscale neighborhood with its big stucco wall and its rent-cop guard. Too damn new. Streets not on the map. Transactions too fresh to be registered. Contradictions. Shit, he wasn't even sure he was in the right township section.

Zellwood sat back, hand to mouth. The laptop jingled telling him he had mail. Bones. It said: *Been busy at this. Had luck. Commercial 8:45 P.M.,* then the two colons separated by a hyphen that was Bones' casual signature.

"Good," to no one.

Eight thirty, his boys were on the stair. Pell looking like the yard help as usual but Mr. Dupree actually going out dressed like that? That ghetto? Got his Lakers warm-up suit on. Sneakers. Terry headband and wristbands.

Pell was jabbing words at Dupree. Seemed the words were affecting Dupree. He went more animated, adjusted the headband, checked himself out in the truck's big side-view, lost the headband.

The boys loaded up, fired up and drifted. Zellwood kept a respectable distance as the truck glided onto the Beachline and attached itself to the stream of lights in the late dusk.

Zellwood felt for his phone, unplugged the computer jack and punched Milky up.

"Milky, wake up boy. Put your shoes on and get vertical." Pause. "Yeah, we're moving. I got a good idea where we're going this evening." Pause to think. Then: "You're close to downtown ain't you?" Pause to listen. "Just hang tight in your driveway. We peel off the toll road and catch the interstate like I think, we'll be coming right by you." Pause to think again. "Matter of fact, I'm so good on this, why don't you head on up to where we were this morning." Pause. "Yeah. The ritzy burb out there. Cruise around back, see what it looks like. I'll call you."

Zellwood was on the money. Beachline to the interstate, to upgrade country road. Around the curves to the gatehouse.

Wait a minute. Are we turning? Maybe? Look. Now we're turning. Well before the guarded gate.

The truck turned again on an even lesser road, one the previous progress had overlooked. It was lonesome and Zellwood didn't risk it; he drove on by.

Cell phone up. "Milky. Where you at, boy?"

Smile.

"You'll see them coming right now, then. Sit tight. I'm turning around. Flash your lights when you see me."

Zellwood turned at a private road with a chain across it, backed out and went as he had come. At the next road, he went as the truck had gone, letting the car idle forward, giving the boys some time.

A half mile, headlights flashed in an orange grove. Zellwood slowed and swung across the broad shoulder.

Milky pulled out, around and then beside Zellwood.

"They lifted the gate off the hinges then put it back."

Zellwood nodded. "All right, son. You leave your car back in the grove and run across the road and lift the gate off for us."

"Yessir."

Milky backed into the orange trees, got out of his car and locked it before crossing the shoulder and the road to the chalky drive at the gate. Zellwood shook his head as he watched Milky walk away. To the inside of the windshield, he said, "Whadda we got keeping America safe and secure? Dumb little fat fucks. Lord have mercy." More headshake, some *mmm-mmm-mmm*.

A look and a lift, Milky pulled the gate back. Zellwood slid through in his black car. Milky wrestled with the gate getting it back on the pins, then went to the car and opened the passenger door. Zellwood sat in the passenger seat.

"How about you drive, son? Lemme work my little computer here."

Milky closed the door and went around.

The truck was hard to find in this hood like a rat turd in a rice bowl. Parked on the brick drive of a house so yellow it glowed. Pell and Dupree were still in the truck, doors open, interior light on. They appeared to be having some serious dialogue.

"Get the house number, Milky."

Milky's head swiveled. "Forty-three seventy-two."

Zellwood pushed numbers on his keyboard as Milky did a three-point and parked.

The glow from the little screen lighted Zellwood's face. He looked puzzled. His gaze drifted to Milky then to Pell and Dupree walking to the door of the blithe house.

"His lawyer again. The boy needs to see his lawyer something awful, son."

[17]

UP CLOSE, MARTY could see what Tony had himself was a faux mansion. Call it a mansionette, a mansion*ito*. Stucco and glass. Established tile roof but patinaed so perfectly it raised suspicions. Pinkish paver walks went off a main circular area. Some Aztec crap patterned into the center in a darker paver led to the entrance of the house.

The plant life was new and vigorous. Plenty of it. The moon, nearly full, competed with peanut-colored lights accenting the house. Marty thought the moon was getting its pale, oval ass kicked by the peanut-colored lights.

He pushed a button beside a door that had an egret etched into its glass. A chime sounded inside.

Maybe half a minute, Marty pushed the button again. The chimes tolled like baby bells.

More nada from no one.

Marty leaned over and held the buzzer. The bells went for it nonstop.

Tony Wayne stepped out of a doorway down a hallway off the foyer and could be seen coming to the door. Marty let the buzzer go and the chimes ran away to hide behind wide, high cornices.

Tony, late forties, was pudgy-soft. A halo of reddish brown curls frizzed out a perfect inch and a half in all directions—the neo-fro something new since Marty had seen him. He wore a poncey Japanese robe open over a caftan that might have been dyed using coffee grounds. Tony had always thought he was pretty hip, even when they were kids. He wasn't then either. Marty wondered if Tony ever once looked in the mirror and saw a short fat fuck with frizzy hair in poncey outfits.

Tony made his way down the hall; he was poking ice cream in his face from a fancy cut glass bowl with a cute little silver baby spoon looking hip as ever.

At the foyer, never looking directly at Marty and Dupree, Tony unlocked the door, spun delicately, robes aflutter and walked off. He motioned with the spoon over a shoulder, a *come hither* thing.

Marty turned to watch Dupree watching Tony. Dupree looked at Marty, eyebrows up.

Marty popped the glass-heavy door and swung it in as Tony retreated down the hall.

Dupree struggled with a nasty grin. "Seems Mr. Wayne goes a little sissy on his day off."

Marty smiled blandly. He shrugged out a nod. "I guess. Watch your cherry."

Dupree put on a pained look. "Please."

Dupree followed Marty down the long hall, both admiring what Tony had done with their money. Marty looked over a shoulder, said, "That doesn't give you pause, does it?"

"What? Him bein sissy? Oh no. I'm equal opportunity when it comes to kickin a motherfucker's ass that stole from me."

Marty nodded, had a comeback ready but he turned right and was in a room with Tony Wayne—the living room. Big windows were accenting the lake, hence the living room in the rear of the house.

The room was bright and shiny, very busy with glass and chrome and knick-knacky shit. Tony stood in the curve of a leather couch that bent around a low table and ran a couple of miles each way. Marty and Dupree entered, checking out the decor in Tony's crib.

Tony had turned, facing them now. It looked to Marty he maybe remembered Dupree but let it go.

"Hey, Marty. You get lost?"

Marty grinned like it hurt. "You mean this afternoon? Yeah. Change of plans." Marty's gaze wandered over the overly decorated room. "Nice place, Tony. You must be doing alright."

"I get by. I wish you'd called first—I'm jammed schedule-wise. What you need?"

Dupree stood near the door; Marty moved into the room, again appraising what his money'd gone for.

Marty could sense Tony watching, keeping Marty in his field of vision, if only indirectly.

Marty began fumbling and fingering things in a tall glass case. He moved on, doodled with lamps and other accoutrements along the wall. Tony turned more, staying face-on to Marty as Marty wound around the room's perimeter.

"I got lots of needs, Tony." Move a little, doodle a little.

Tony turned, being cool with it, eating his French vanilla. Dupree remained at the door, silent, watching.

Nerves insisted Tony say: "Hey, sorry about your mom."

Marty laughed a little, he opened a glass box and picked up a clay figure of a duck. It looked like it was made by first graders leading Marty to believe it must have been expensive. Marty pitched it up a couple of times like he was trying to guess its weight, but really doing it to fuck with Tony.

Tony was stock-still, baby spoon suspended between bowl and mouth.

Marty moved closer to Tony, tossed the doodad up. “You missed the funeral.” There was a table abutting the back of the couch and Marty sat the figure between a potbellied vase and a wireless phone that looked like it was made of glass.

The shovelful of ice cream went to the mouth. Tony made a face around the mouthful that said he was sorry about it. He swallowed, said, “Yeah. When was it? Last week?”

Marty strolled around the couch. “Your mom was there.”

“Well there you go: represented by family. And I really meant to go.” Tony shrugged as Marty stepped closer.

Marty was two feet from Tony, nothing in his face, talking to Dupree, but looking at Tony. “You believe this motherfucker, Dupree? Standing here throwing out small talk like everything’s hunky fucking dory. Everything hunky dory with you, Tony?”

Tony found a hard look. “Marty . . . ” the spoon hand came palm up in apology, “ . . . you’re upset about the funeral. I understand that. Again, I’m sorry. I’m busy—it slipped my mind is all.” Tony licked the spoon, dug in. “Look, I’d love to sit here all evening and chat with you and your friend here . . . ”

Tony put the ice cream in his mouth and pointed at Dupree with the spoon.

Marty held the deposit box key up in his right hand.

Tony reacted some but rolled out from under it with a what’s-that face. His mouth opened to speak around the ice cream currently sharing real estate with his tongue.

Marty punched the right side of Tony’s neck.

The chunk of ice cream went across the room like a meteor, the bowl flew up, Tony went down. He hit the couch at a bad angle, bounced into the coffee table then to the rug. He made some funny sounds from down there between couch and table.

Dupree stepped over to get a better look at Tony. He showed Marty a hurt face. “I thought me and you talked about this and agreed I was the one got to tune Tony.”

“Sorry, cuz, just slipped out. In defense, I did punch him with my wimpy left. He’s all yours. Tune away.” Marty moved off, leaned against the wall to give Dupree a chance to work with Tony on some misplaced resources, see how that trick got done.

Dupree put the gloves on and asked Marty to pass him a straight back chair sitting nearby. Marty passed the chair over the couch and Dupree sat it in a vacant spot, grabbed Tony by a handful of silk lapel. He stood Tony upright.

Tony looked confused, like he'd been yanked out of bed in the middle of the night. The afro was a little askance, high spots and low spots here and there now. He cleared his throat loudly like Marty's fist had stuck in there.

Tony's knees sagged and Dupree jerked him up. "Got a frog in there, Tony? Stand your sissy ass up here."

Dupree freed a hand and slapped Tony lightly, forehand and back. Tony cleared his throat again, coming around a little. His legs were still squirrelly and he looked at Dupree like he couldn't focus on him.

"Hey, Tony, remember me? Yeah, we talked a couple of times. When Marty had his little problem. Remember? Uncle Sam had me confined to base and you called and took a deposition from me on the phone? Came by another time, got my signature? Remember, Tony, I said I didn't know nothin about nothin?"

Tony was losing the baffles and seemed to be focusing on Dupree. A light went on somewhere in Tony's head. He copped a dopey smile but he didn't look happy. Tony wagged his head and croaked, "No. Don't recall."

Dupree looked disappointed, then smiled. "See, Marty, Tony remembers. He says he doesn't, but he does. See his face?" Dupree turned Tony so Marty could get a look at Tony's face.

"You know what he's thinkin now, don't you?"

"*My expensive new hairdo's all a mess*?"

"Nah. Right now, he's thinkin: *Why's this motherfucker used to be a Navy cop holdin me up by my Geisha robe?*" Dupree gave Tony a jerk. "You think he's comin around on it yet, Marty?"

"Yeah. He's smarter than he looks. He's just still trying to adjust to his sudden change of luck."

"Maybe so." Dupree pulled Tony up to him. "You are indeed fresh outta luck, Tony," and smacked him a good one, open handed, on the side of his head.

Tony put a hand on the offended ear.

Dupree traded hands and offended the other ear. Tony had a hand on every ear.

Tony yelled, "Stop it. Make him stop, Marty. He's crazy."

Marty moved laterally and sat on the wing of the sofa away from the slapping. A thumbnail bothered him more than Tony's dilemma so he fretted at it with his teeth some. He rubbed his other palm over the couch's leather surface, admiring. Nice skin but the aqua was a bit much.

Dupree spun Tony around and slammed him in the chair. He grabbed a wad of Tony's hair and walked around to stand behind Tony.

Dupree jerked the hair back; Tony yelped at the ceiling a time or two.

Dupree looked down on Tony's face without kindness or anything. "Tony, ain't a soul gonna help your ass here. You're gonna hafta help yourself. Hear me?"

Dupree pulled a little harder on the hair as he leaned over Tony's upturned face. "And we *ain't* goin away, cracker. Not without what you took."

Maybe Tony wasn't convinced of Dupree's sincerity, thought a word play would work. He said, "What'd I take? Am I supposed to know what you're talking about?" Tony took his appeal to Marty again. "Hey, Marty, am I supposed to know what he's talking about?" Tony's face was pointed up, but his eyes were walking around, searching for Marty in his peripheral vision.

Marty gave Tony a distant grin that Tony never saw. "Save yourself, Tony."

Tony rolled his eyes back to see Dupree. "Hey, listen, pal. You're gonna get tired of hitting me eventually. What say we try talking about this thing? Whatever it is."

Dupree yanked the hair up and the head followed. Tony may have caught a brief glimpse of Marty sitting on the couch, relaxed, leg on a knee, hands draped across the back of the couch. He'd have to have been quick.

Dupree smacked Tony on the side of the head again. Tony writhed off the chair. He spun to his knees, one hand on his ear, one on Dupree's hand in his hair.

Dupree pulled Tony upright by the hair, grabbed the lapels again, got Tony in close. "We're done with the bitch slappin, Tony. You listenin?"

Tony nodded, not looking at Dupree.

Dupree yanked the lapels. "Stand your ass up. Look at me, Tony."

Tony looked, his hair mussed like it had fallen victim to Don King's barber.

"I'm gonna ask you one more time about that shit buried out there. Then you're gonna see can't you find somethin to keep me from hittin you in the face with my fist. You want me to hit you for real, Tony?"

Marty liked how Dupree said it: slow, enunciating each word like he was dealing with a naughty child.

Tony said: "No."

Dupree looked relieved. "Then talk to me, Tony. Tell me somethin, baby. Marty, he's on the fence. Help him out. Tell him what he needs to do."

Marty sighed, tried to make it sincere. "You need to talk to him, Tony."

Tony fucked up and put a used-car-salesman's face out there. Nobody was buying, so he said, "Guys, come on. I swear I don't have a clue here." He laughed a little, glanced at Dupree, then back to Marty. "What shit? Buried where?"

Dupree pushed Tony out to arm's length. "Here we go, Tony. One the hard way comin up." And he punched Tony in the forehead.

Tony's head went back, his body went limp and he slipped out of Dupree's grip and went down again.

Dupree pulled limp Tony up and put him back in the chair, held Tony's head up by the hair.

Dupree said: "Tony, I'm gonna hit you whether you got your eyes opened or closed. Doesn't matter to me."

Tony's eyes fluttered a little.

Marty reached back for a pot-bellied vase behind him, tossed some fresh yellow roses on the poly-carb coffee table and said, "Here."

Dupree let the hair go, grabbed the vase and poured the cup or so of water over Tony's head. Tony blew out when the water reached his lips.

"Say somethin, Tony. You don't, I'm gonna knock you the fuck out for real." Dupree was close in on Tony now, fist poised to deliver on the promise.

Tony surprised Marty, miraculously came back to life.

"Jesus Christ, people. This is crazy. You're both nuts. What shit?"

Marty smiled at Tony.

Tony said, "You realize I'm gonna send your asses to jail over this."

Marty held the smile, said, "I don't think you will, Tony."

"You willing to try me, Marty?"

Marty nodded, "Yeah, Tony."

Tony watched Marty a few beats. "How about I call the cops, let you tell them about this *shit* buried *out there*? How's that sound?"

Marty reached behind him, grabbed the glass phone, tossed it to Dupree.

Dupree looked at the phone, put jacked-up eyebrows on Marty.

Marty said, "Give it to him."

Dupree hesitated but dropped the phone in Tony's lap. Tony looky but no touchy.

Tony thought on it, said, "Look, Marty, I don't know what you and your friend think I did, but I've got nearly eighty thousand dollars in a safe upstairs. I'll give it to you right now."

Marty smiled at Dupree, asked Tony why he'd do that since he had no idea what was what.

Tony said, "Call it go-away money. Call

it what you want. Just don't think you can come by any old time for more."

Marty found a coffee table book and flipped through it. "He's pretty good, Dupree."

"Un-huh. So far. He's just now seein how serious things are. Hear that desperation in his voice? He's comin around. Hey, Tony, check this out."

Marty looked up to see Dupree drop a nice left hook on Tony's neck. Hit him in the same spot Marty'd hit him earlier.

Tony's head went the other way pretty fast. Dupree snagged Tony's collar as he went by and dragged him upright again, fist coming back. "Look here, Tony. Got another one just like it. Here it comes."

"Let him go, mister."

The beat dropped and the scene froze.

A young boy, late teens somewhere, with long lashes and numb dark eyes was being led into the room by a big chrome revolver using a two-handed grip he'd probably seen on TV.

The boy was well made up and pretty in an androgynous sort of way. He wore an identical robe to Tony's, open, nothing else. He put the gun on Dupree.

Dupree half-stepped, put Tony between himself and the kid, holding Tony up there like a shield.

The kid dropped a cap high, well over the heads of Dupree and Tony. They reflexively ducked as the sound took its time dying.

Marty was sitting off to the kid's right. He found a pistol under his shirt as he stood. He stepped toward the kid, the pistol out in front of him, the serious end sighting on the kid's temple.

Marty said in a low calm voice: "Kid, you drop another cap, I'll pop you. Grits ain't groceries if I won't pop your young fucking ass."

The kid didn't act like he heard Marty. He said, "I'm gonna shoot the nigger."

Marty took another step toward the kid. "No. You're not shooting anyone. Nobody is. What we got here is a stand-down. Right, Tony? Tell him we're gonna stand down."

Tony tried to see the kid over a shoulder but Dupree had Tony crunched down. "Back off, Toy. It's just jailbird Marty and his big psycho friend. Put the gun away."

Toy didn't seem to hear Tony either; his face said he was circling out around Alpha Centauri somewhere. Marty watched his mouth twitching from a near smile to a nasty frown.

Marty said, "What's his name? Toy?"

Tony said it was.

"Hey, Toy." Marty eased in a half-step on Toy. "Partner, you relax, put it down, we'll go out the door, find some other way to deal with this business we got. How about it?"

Toy clued in a tad and the big gun went down slowly. But Toy still had a finger on the trigger, thumb on the hammer. Marty backed himself down a little too in a show of faith.

Dupree let go of Tony and Tony straightened, touching himself here and there on the head and neck.

Tony turned to face Toy and Marty, said, "Jesus, people."

The kid's gun came back up. Marty's came back up.

Dupree rushed Tony, grabbing him around the neck, from behind now, making Tony a shield again.

Marty tightened up. "Goddam, Toy, you had it made. Come on, kid, lose the piece."

Toy stepped once toward Tony and Dupree. "Un-uh. I'm gonna shoot the nigger."

Tony rolled his eyes. "Toy, knock it off. You're high as hell, acting stupid. *Put-it-down.*"

Toy stepped again, sighting down the barrel at Dupree's head over Tony's shoulders. Marty stepped in on Toy.

Toy turned, put the gat on Marty. Four beats—maybe half a beat before Marty shot the kid—he swung back to Dupree. His thumb brought the hammer back and it made a clicking noise that everyone in the room heard.

"Don't move, Tony—I'm gonna shoot the nigger." Toy moved around to the right, toward Marty, looking for his shot on Dupree.

Dupree swung Tony around, let go of Tony's neck and took him by the shoulders, disappearing behind Tony. From back there, he said, "Some-goddam-body needs to do somethin here."

Marty half stepped.

Tony said, "Put it down, Toy. You're gonna shoot somebody."

Marty took a big stride, snatched Toy back by the collar and laid the barrel of his piece across Toy's pretty nose. It sounded nasty, a melon thump noise.

Toy went horizontal, dropping a cap on his way down. A mirror by Tony and Dupree shattered. Tony grabbed his head, screamed. His legs went queer on him and he went down.

Dupree looked at his hand, showed Marty some blood. "Aw shit." He reached over and wiped his hand on the couch.

Marty shook his head. He was weary. "He shoot the fuck? Say he didn't shoot the fuck."

Dupree bent down and turned Tony's head. Marty leaned over, looked at Tony. There was a little blood at his hairline.

Dupree parted the frizzy mat and said, "Shit. He ain't hurt. Piece of glass or something cut him, made his pansy ass faint." Dupree stood, wiped his hand on the couch some more. "Motherfucker's luck's holdin steady as hell."

Marty reviewed the scene, the limp biscuits on the floor. "I'm thinking it's starting to show." Marty did a slow wag with his head, looked over at Dupree.

"What's that, cuz?"

"How green we are at this shit." Marty floated an exasperated hand across the room. "This is a fucking mess."

"I hear you. You ready to get cousin Tony up and goin again?"

"We're done here, Dupree. For now."

"I ain't fuckin done. Neither is Tony." Dupree nudged Tony's foot with his foot. "Get up, Tony. You ain't hurt."

Tony stood mute.

"Come on, Dupree. We're getting nowhere. You keep knocking him silly and pouring water on his head, and you're getting nada. Let's go, try to regroup."

"Please clue me as to how regroupin's gonna help?" Dupree didn't like it.

"I don't know, Dupree. Maybe start with a fucking plan instead of work-out gloves next time."

"I gotta plan—kick Tony's ass till his nose bleeds and he tells us somethin."

"Yeah, and it's not working too well either. What's next, Dupree? Buy a bigger pair of gloves? Come on, man, before we kill the fuck."

"Marty . . ." Dupree was hands out at his sides.

"What if someone else is here? We didn't know the kid was. What if we got someone else upstairs calling the cops right now. Let's fucking get outta here, cuz."

Dupree breathed deeply and noisily, shook his head, shook it off. Shook his head more, said, "Cousin Tony, I'll be back motherfucker." Then to Marty: "You ready?"

Marty nodded and stepped across Toy, moved to the door.

"Hey, cuz, the hell you come up with that grits ain't groceries shit?"

When Marty and his thug were history and nothing was left standing in the room but quiet, Tony Wayne rolled over, groaned at the quiet and sat.

He looked around at the mess, at Toy lying on his back, passing for asleep but for a tiny trickle of blood from each nostril and a nasty bump on the bridge of his nose. Tony groaned again, touched his ears, then his head. He winced and grabbed the phone from the low table.

Tony punched in zero-one-one, then four-nine, then some local digits.

He waited a bit, looking at the blood on his fingers, touched the cut on his head again, looked at the fingers again. He reached over and grabbed a soft pillow from the couch and made a compress out of it, pressing it to his head.

"Yeah, is this Haas Mueller's answering service?" Pause. "Good. I need him to call me ASAP." Pause, incredulous hand rising palm up. "No. Right fucking now. I don't give a rat's ass what time it is there." Pause in irritation. "Yeah, yeah, bet your sweet patoot I want to leave my name and number."

[18]

IF ANGEL'S DINER was a car, it would be a '57 Chevy, the radio blasting an oldies station. Rolled and pleated, chromed and glass-packed.

The food's pretty pre-prep, from freezer to microwave to your table. Don't even think about ordering a Reuben—you wouldn't recognize it. But the draw is a dessert tray a few feet shorter than the QM2. A complete soda fountain eruption as well as cakes and pies of varied colors and textures. Marty wouldn't even toss a guess at how many heart failures per square inch were on that tray.

He and Dupree were in a big rounded corner booth. Dupree lounged in the center, chin cupped in hand. Marty was to his right nancying up coffee with cream and sugar.

An older gentleman was to Dupree's left and Dupree was studying him intently. The way the man was dressed, he could have been a retired banker or broker or something.

Snow white hair, well behaved in a swept back style. Trim build. Nimble blue eyes that absorbed. He was Eddie Margot. Marty knew him, knew he was neither banker nor broker nor Indian chief. He was a career criminal Marty had jailed with at a federal correctional institution.

There was a question on Eddie's face, fork and knife poised on ends in fists. Several dessert selections were in front of him. There was a crumb of chocolate on his chin. Marty didn't mention it.

"I could turn up the volume on my hearing aids, but all I'm getting so far is what a couple of dumb-asses you two are." Eddie dug into a scoop of ice cream, dug on down to excavate a respectable chunk of sinfully dark chocolate cake that was holding the ice cream up. "Let's try it in a straight line. Once upon a time, you two work together at what was then the Naval Air Station here, know each other pretty good, right?"

Marty shrugged out a nod, looked at Dupree. Dupree put on a maybe face, shrugged.

Eddie put a little impatience on his mug. "Okay, could we agree on worked some shifts together, maybe had a pop or two after work once in a while?"

Eddie got dual nods. He pointed his fork at Dupree. "You're a Navy cop at the time."

Dupree nodded unenthusiastically. "Un-huh."

"And Marty's livin out the American dream: a civil-service, forklift-jockey gig." Marty got the knife pointed at him.

Marty did: "Un-huh."

Eddie took a dainty bite of ice cream and let it dissolve in his mouth. He swallowed, said, "So this plane comes in one night. The crew goes for what? Grub? Showers? The rain's comin down. Marty here's got some merchandise to load on this transport plane. The plane's goin where?"

Marty said, "A place called Ho."

Eddie paused to be sure he heard right. "Ho? The hell's Ho?"

"Ghana."

"And that's in what? Africa?"

"Un-huh." Marty looked at the non-participating Dupree. Dupree gave him back some bored eyebrows.

Eddie speared a piece of pecan pie and studied it. "Doesn't matter. So Dupree's got officers' club duty, but this plane drops outta the sky. He gets called out, in this dead weather to watch Marty's ass, make sure he don't steal no bullets or nothin." Eddie took pie into his mouth. He chewed a couple of times then said, around the mouthful, "How am I doin so far, kids?"

Dupree looked bored; Marty, trying to

look a little less, shrugged and nodded. Marty said, "So far, so good."

Eddie used the knife to scrape a portion of Boston cream pie onto the pecan pie. He carved off a bite of the blend, bit it until cream and goo oozed from the corners of his mouth. Some head bobbing and neck stretching got the bite down the tube. Eddie slurped some strawberry shake to clear his pallet, smacked a time or two and leaned forward.

The quick blue eyes danced between Marty and Dupree. "So, the part about Marty ridin a forklift in the rain while Dupree tugs his pud and watches? Start me off there, and take me all the way to this mess about the mom's safe deposit box and the lawyer you went to see last night." Eddie wagged his head slowly, wrinkled his brow. "I gotta be missin somethin, some slight glimmer that might tell me you two got a clue what you're doin."

Dupree sat up. "You hear the whole thing, you're still gonna be listenin for that. See, that's how we come to be sittin here with you today. You're the expert, ain't you?"

Marty got a foot free and kicked Dupree's foot; Dupree looked at him. Marty warned with his eyes.Dupree let it go, rolled his own eyes and slumped back down in the booth's seat. He mumbled out something that sounded like *shit* then he said, "You wanna hear it all, from the git-go, that's a-whole-nother chapter."

Eddie placed a couple of fingers on his wrist, concentrated like he was taking his own pulse. "Strong vitals—I got time. Read me the chapter."

Dupree slumped down even farther, a drape on the tuck-and-pleat bench. "Tell im, Marty. You're the only one knows it all anyhow."

Marty killed his java, slid back in time a bit.

[19]

FOUR YEARS EARLIER:

Serious weather has the night down kicking its dark ass. Rain heaves in torrents, ripples across the tarmac. Chain lightning bitches and moans overhead, putting out a decent but unreliable show.

A pot-bellied pig of a plane drops through the low ceiling and onto the runway. The landing isn't pretty but it does the job.

The cargo plane taxis around and squats near a couple of hangars and ignores the weather. The engines whine down; the back bay door drops. Light emanates.

Not too many minutes, a blue Humvee with a Navy insignia on its doors hisses across the tarmac. It stops, sheltered under the plane's body. Someone in dress blues with a rifle disembarks from the passenger door.

Several men in jungle wear come down

the ramp. The dress uniform salutes crisply. The jungle suits reciprocate so unenthusiastically it looks like they're shooing flies. The jungle suits load into the Hummer and it goes as it came. Dress blues goes up the ramp into the plane.

Lightning smokes something close by as a forklift slides through the big door of a hangar. The forklift pushes through the rain making for the plane.

The forklift uses the ramp, leaving the dark wet behind as it disappears into the plane. The operator is Marty Pell when Marty Pell was the guy with the good grin and the game eyes. Tonight he's the guy needing the yellow rain suit he wears.

Inside the plane's belly, crates and equipment are stacked and lashed here and there. A jeep is bucked with chains to one side.

Dupree sits in the jeep reading a jack mag. He's laid back in his dress uniform tonight, feet up, expanding his literary horizons.

Marty wheels the lift around to rest—steel to steel—against the jeep, tagging it harder than Uncle Sam would appreciate, making it rock, fucking with Dupree. Dupree doesn't care enough to look away from his magazine. He puts up a fist for adoption; Marty bumps the fist with one of his own.

"Jesus, Dupree, you make admiral or something?" Marty brushes the rain suit's hood back, pulls a ball cap off and flaps it against the lift with a spray of water.

Dupree puts a little distracted agitation on his face and wipes errant drops from his reading material. "Officers' Club duty. At least till I got called out in this shit. The hell're you doin workin this time of day?"

Marty re-blocks the ball cap and reapplies it. "Same as you, daddy: somebody with much ass needed something; I was accessible."

"Un-huh. That and the fact you're about one more shenanigan away from the unemployment line and can't say no."

Marty shrugs the shot off, putting a grin on it. "Yeah, that'd be a tragedy too, lose this cushy opportunity."

"Ain't you got somethin to do that involves getting wet?" Dupree turns the mag sideways and folds down the bonus flap.

Marty makes a dismal face. "Yeah, I do. You gonna make the game Friday?"

"Who else you got can hit and play third base too?"

"We counting me or besides me?"

"Shit. You go ahead on and include anybody you like, Mr. Team Manager."

Marty laughs some. "How long you stuck here?"

Dupree shrugs, refolds the bonus flap. "Fuck if I know. I guess till these serious actin motherfuckers get em a hole in the clouds. You see em?"

"Yeah. The fuck they supposed to be? Marines? Specials? What?"

Dupree has moved on in his book. He shrugs like he doesn't really give a shit. "Jungle Jim outfits, no insignia, no nothin? I'd say the spooky motherfuckers are at least special forces of some kind. You don't think anybody told me anything, do you?"

Marty ignores the question if it was one. He finds a clipboard, reads a bit. "I believe you're right. Next stop Ho, Ghana. The fuck's going on in Ghana?"

"Who knows, bread? Secret wars. We got us some."

"I bet. Well, keep your eye on me."

Dupree hums an unenthusiastic: mmm-hmm.

Marty punches the forklift accelerator and moves away too fast. The lift hits a wet spot and shifts directions erratically. The forks rip into one of the tarp-draped crates strapped to the wall.

The end of something that looks like the end of a gold ingot slides from under the tarp. Marty backs away. When the forks move, two ingots and a pile of sawdust hit the diamond-plate steel floor. The noise seems loud inside the aluminum tube of the airplane.

Marty says, "Holy fucking shit, Batman, I believe I just solved the mystery of why you and your rifle're here. Check this out, dad."

Dupree looks over slowly, reluctantly, an almost inadvertent gesture. He loses the magazine and steps out of the jeep in a flow of movement. "Goddam, blood, the fuck did you find?"

Marty kills the lift, gets off, throws the wet hat on the seat. He and Dupree move to the crate. Dupree nudges an ingot with a patent leather toe. It doesn't move. They squat on either side of the two bars.

Dupree touches one, lifts a corner. "Bread, that shit's the McCoy. Look at the markings—straight outta Fort Knox."

Marty huffs out some breath. He stands, does a hand-through-the-hair move, then tosses the tarp back. Two more crates just like the one he cracked. He gives one of them a knock with knuckles—sawdust sprinkles from the tapped crate.

Dupree stands. His face says he's bewildered. "Candy bar like that'd take a man's sweet tooth a long way, cuz."

Marty, hand at the back of his neck, looks back at the hangar. When he speaks, he's distracted. "How'd I get lucky enough to be your cousin, Dupree?" Looks at the hangar again.

"When that shit fell outta that crate. You dig?" Dupree's holding back, not wanting to sound like he'd entertain the notion of stealing some of Uncle's gold.

Marty looks around again, looks at the two gold ingots, looks at Dupree. "You suggesting we grab a couple?" Marty's eyes stay on Dupree's.

Dupree finds an innocent face. "I ain't suggestin a fuckin thing. All I'm sayin is a man could go a long way on that kinda ends."

Dupree and Marty trade looks for a few. Marty turns, hand to mouth. He does three-sixty, the hand moves and he's smiling. "You think they won't miss it? We just do two?"

"Hell yeah, they'll miss it. Just seems like they might have trouble figurin where it fell off."

"Shit, I wouldn't count on that. What it'll come down to is holding your face straight. You think you could do it, dad? They came right at you, think you'd be able to hold your face?"

Dupree does incredulous with eyebrows. "You're kiddin, right? That kinda cheese? Goddam right I could hold my fuckin face. How about you?"

Marty nods slowly, not even in response to Dupree's question. He's reading Dupree, thinking in the deep grass. He tosses another quick glance at the hangar over his shoulder. "We know they're gonna miss it, why only two chunks? Looks like three crates, all just alike. We're gonna do it, let's fucking do it—cuz."

Dupree looks around, raps on the other crates, blows sawdust sprinkles off gloved fingers. "You got somewhere to drop this shit till things go chilly?"

"You bet your dark ass I do. We're burying scrap over by the west fence, got holes dug everywhere over there. Where you at, cuz?" Marty smiles.

The smile infects Dupree. He smiles, says, "Marty, my man, you are fucking beautiful."

[20]

EDDIE MARGOT WAS down to bits and pieces of his desserts. He used the back of his fork to scrape a plate, studied the fork then put it back to work. "So I'm guessin you guys put junk in the crates, put the good stuff in some other crates. Marty takes off, finds a convenient hole, drops the stuff in it.

"The plane takes off, no problems. Later, the government boys miss the stuff. Some guys in suits come talk to you two, being the most obvious pigeons. They get Marty's prints off the shill you put in their crates. Now Dupree—he got called off officers' club duty, has on his nice special-occasion outfit, white gloves, the whole bit—he don't leave prints.

"The Feds check the gate log. Nobody left with anything contraband. They check the whole Navy base out good, I'm sure—gets em nertz. I'd say they figured you clever lads slid it out a backdoor somehow." Eddie gave his mouth a break but no one put anything in the void. He looked from Marty to Dupree, said, "You boys awake?"

Marty looked over. Dupree might have been. His eyes were nearly open.

Marty shifted around some, trying to seem awake. "Yeah. We've heard the story before, Eddie."

"Well I haven't and I'm old. I'm almost dead. Humor me while I get the details straightened out, how about it?"

A waitress showed and re-upped coffees around.

She drifted and Eddie took it up again. "So the Feds ain't got shit they can make stick. But this fifteen hundred pounds of goods are gone for damn sure." Eddie hid the last bite of dessert. "They take a pound or two of it outta Marty here's ass. Pin his ears back for tamperin with government property—all they could get to stick to the boy since nobody was sharin what sorta goods got lifted."

Eddie scraped a dessert plate with his fork's edge again. He licked it, studied the fork, licked it again. His gaze went to Marty. "And they put you on ice for three years and change, the max they got on such chicken shit as that."

Marty nodded, said, "Yes they did, Eddie."

Eddie took a break and added a few

pounds of sugar to his coffee. Added cream. Tasted. His mouth sampled then said, "Not a bad piece of bein in the right place at the right time at all. But you boys realize where you went wrong, don't you?"

Eddie again left a spot for someone to jump in. Again, no one did.

"You guys say the Feds knew you didn't leave with nothin. Explain please."

"They had the gate log." Marty shrugged. "That'd be my guess."

Eddie: "They search every vehicle leavin the place?"

Marty: "Pretty much."

Eddie: "They search yours?"

Marty stirred around. "No. I was on my bobber."

Eddie asked: "The hell's a bobber?"

Marty told him it was a motorbike.

It left Eddie baffled, but he let it go. He said, "Here's where you fucked up: you shoulda kept your product movin till you got it somewhere you could control it. You never let the product stop movin. You just don't operate like that."

Dupree rustled around some, partially sat, his eyes on Eddie. "The fuck you think we do? Go to work some-fuckin-where ain't even got toilet paper fit to steal, wait around four, five years, see maybe doesn't somethin fall off a truck? You think that's how we *operate*, Eddie?" Dupree shook his head. "Shit. Seems pretty fuckin evident we ain't done much of this before. You dig?"

Marty was tired of being referee. They wanted to go at it, fuck them.

Eddie's clear blue eyes were hanging on to Dupree. "I dig. I was just gettin it straight, all right? For me. An idle comment, not meant to insult."

Dupree folded, waved a hand at Eddie. "What else you need?"

Eddie thought. Said: "So, while Marty's payin societal debts, the government closes the base. You guys thought you had it cold, huh? Don't even have to trespass on government property now."

Dupree said, "Yeah," looking to seem a little more civil.

"You guys go out there, dig. It equals nada. You think it out, go see the lawyer, kick his ass. Gets you some more nada."

Eddie added a couple more spoons of sugar to his joe, stirred it languidly. He looked at Dupree then Marty, gaze settling on Marty. "Now for the undeniably stupid shit. Tell me about the envelope in the safe deposit box again with some detail if it ain't too painful."

Marty grinned, wagged his head. "I thought we'd pretty much agreed on me and Dupree being amateurs, right?"

"Not no more, son." Eddie winked. "Start actin like you ain't."

Dupree looked over at Marty, smiled a sly one.

What the smile got for Dupree was: "You think it's funny, tough guy? That's who you were last night, right? Tough guy." Eddie dissed Dupree with bushy white brows. "A fuckin fairy hustler's got you runnin around the room, your asshole buddy here's the only one remembered to bring a gun to a twenty-somethin-million-dollar ass kickin."

Eddie heard his raised voice, dropped it. "With all due respect, boys, you people are gonna have to pick it up here. Tell me about the letter and the lawyer."

Marty sipped coffee through a grin. "I'm going up, I figured I croak or something, some-*fucking*-body should enjoy it. I left a kinda coded thing for Dupree here." Marty motioned with his head, "In hopes of changing his luck."

Dupree said, "My luck changed all right. It went from poor to worse."

Eddie studied his coffee. "You pretty sure the lawyer went in the box?"

Marty shrugged out: "Gotta be, Eddie. No one else went in there but my mom. No way she's looking in an envelope with Dupree's name on it. Considering where I was at the time, she wouldn't want to know. Then the guy, the lawyer, goes by the bowling alley, asks about the coded hints." Marty sipped, nodded, met Eddie's eyes. "He's it."

Eddie nodded slowly until the waitress showed, settled on one last slice of red velvet. The waitress took off to get it for him while he thought about the situation.

Dupree sat, put his hands on the Formica top. He watched Eddie think. He said, "Why don't you eat anything but sweet shit, Eddie?"

Eddie looked at Dupree like he wondered if Dupree was fucking with him. He must have decided not: he shrugged thin shoulders, said, "I don't know. I don't get out much? I don't get this kinda shit at home? Take your choice. Mostly, it's just I ain't got that many meals left in me anyway. Why piss it away on healthy shit ain't really doin your heart or prostate any good anyway. So fuck it." Eddie showed them an ancient set of dentures.

The waitress brought Eddie's cake; he dove in. After a few bites and a sip of coffee to clear his pallet, he said, "So we gonna talk my eatin habits or you two wanna hear what I think?"

Dupree looked peeved again. "What I wanna hear is how big a piece of this you're lookin for. That is, we get around to somethin I didn't know before I got here."

Eddie smiled at Dupree. "The man gets right to it. Good. You get the whole pie, I get a twenty-cent piece on what we roll out from under this lawyer. What you're talkin about, sounds like we should be able to get ten to twelve minimum, fifteen or so max. That puts my part at a couple of mil or so, give or take. Less than the whole pie or he's scattered it and we gotta find it, then we negotiate again. The scale could slide either way."

Marty knew that wouldn't make Dupree happy.

"Enlighten me on that slidin scale, please."

"Less than jackpot, I work less, I'll reduce my points. He's scattered it, I'll have to work my ass off to get at it. That'll cost you."

Not good enough, Eddie. Marty turned to Dupree, knowing he'd ask.

"What's: *That'll cost you*?"

"Could go high as fifty points."

"Ouch." Marty didn't care, but it was time to move on. "Go ahead, Eddie, tell him what he gets for his two to four mil. He's gonna ask anyway."

Eddie was skinning the icing from the cake, then he was eating it. He nodded slowly like he understood all things. "Bright ideas mostly. Info you'll need; the means to get it. Put you in front of some good contract labor should you need it, and you will. You need some right now, you just don't know it."

Eddie thought about it a few seconds,

then: "Should we recover product, I'm the man to roll it. I'd like to, since I get an extra bump from the other end on puttin the deal together. But that ain't no skin off you two birds." A little more thought, Eddie shrugged out a uncommitted frown. "That's pretty much it. Bright ideas. You boys'll have to do the heavy liftin, but I can get you to it."

A little nagging silence edged out the golden oldie blasting from overhead speakers—Sam the Sham doing his take on a Grimm's Brothers' job, howling like a motherfucker once in a while. Marty waited knowing Dupree would do a little howling of his own.

Dupree made the wait short. "Sounds like a lotta money for bright ideas and introductions."

Eddie interrupted the red velvet destruction, fork poised halfway to his mouth. He looked across his eyes at Dupree. "Your shit's gone. You couldn't beat it outta the guy that took it." Pause. "And your sittin here tells me you got no bright ideas. You did, you'd be out pursuin em." Another effective pause. "I got bright ideas. I got contacts. I done this before; I know how it goes; you don't."

Marty rolled a hand out that said, *there you go,* hoping Dupree was done.

Dupree had some more grumbling so

Marty went lateral, see could he move this thing along. "We got a shot, Eddie?"

Eddie put down his silver, found a napkin on his lap and wiped his lips. He raised his cup stylishly, ringed pinky showing off, and sipped delicately. "Maybe." The cup went back to the saucer. "Maybe."

Eddie went off in thought again. His face adjusted. His mouth said, "It's a lot easier to get somethin tangible outta somebody's ass than somethin intangible. For our purposes, intangible would cover bank accounts, money markets, stocks, bonds, paper shit like that. I ain't sayin we can't get to it; I'm sayin it's harder is all. You two keepin up here?"

Marty nodded, said, "Yeah. You're saying it'd still be easier to lay hands on the . . . ."

Eddie's hand came up, warning Marty.

Marty looked around, didn't see anyone who looked like a cop. "The shit, whatever. If he's still got it, it'd be easier to locate and move than chasing down bank books, raiding his accounts."

Eddie was happy. "Lookit Marty actin smarter'n he looks. So tell me, Einstein, what's next?"

Marty looked stupid for Eddie, so Eddie looked over at Dupree. Dupree was doing the same.

"Come on, boys. You got anything you want at your disposal. Whatchu gonna do?"

Dupree said, "I believe I'd look into the man's business, see how much sudden wealth he's come into the last few months that's recorded somewhere."

Marty tossed: "And hope like hell you don't find more than what's obvious: the house, new cars—the flashy shit a guy like Tony is apt to gravitate to."

Eddie beamed. "Goddam if you boys might not squeak by, pull this thing off. You got me feelin better'n better. What's next? Come on, think about it. Cover your bases."

A pause brought nothing. "Come on. You paid the lawyer a visit, shook his tree. He knows you know."

Marty got it. "What he hasn't rolled, he will soon. Or move what's left physically." Marty thought about it. "Yeah. He'll be moving it real soon, he's got anything left to move."

Eddie was nodding. "He's got some left. Just for laughs, say he got in the bank box a year and a half back . . . "

Marty: "He didn't. He hit it maybe nine, ten months ago, but I'm guessing. Right before I got back would be close."

"Even better. Say it took him a month or two to get the balls to go get it. He sits on it for another two or three, lookin for a chute. Okay, even when he finds somebody can take it off his hands, you don't move that kinda weight one shot, one place. The stuff's still red hot. You take somethin from Uncle Sam, it stays that way a long time." Pause to figure. "Tops, he's moved four, maybe five hundred pounds. Considerin he's not able to move more'n a couple hundred pounds at the jump."

Dupree had some numbers. "So you sayin he's moved five mil, maybe five and a half?"

"Nah. He wouldn't have got that sorta nut. Say three mil, maybe four—outside."

Dupree looked at Marty. "Looks like we get to stick to Tony like stink on shit next few days."

Marty nodded. "Yep. So, Eddie, how do we get inside Tony's new empire, see what's left?"

Eddie was smiling like it was graduation. His hands fell open priestly. "Bless you, my children. You two come by tomorrow, I'll show you how to put the game in play. Now let's get the hell outta here. Who's gettin the check?"

[21]

TOMMY ZELLWOOD'S CELL chirped. He looked at the caller ID and smiled.

Zellwood looked at Milky apologetically. "Excuse me a minute, son."

Milky sat for a moment before he got it. "Oh, okay."

They were in Zellwood's car and it was sitting in the breakdown lane of the interstate highway. Below the berm of the interstate was a shiny chrome diner. A neon sign, red, said *Angel's Diner*; white bulbs marched around the sign's perimeter.

Milky opened his door and nearly lost it to an eighteen wheeler. He stepped out, closed the door and heard Zellwood say: *Bones.*

Milky walked back and leaned on the car's trunk and let the traffic zephyrs pummel him.

"Yeah? Found some goodies?"

Zellwood paused to listen.

"Don't have to guess. I got it: the lawyer."

Zellwood grinned at what Bones was saying.

"They kept chasing around after him. Caught up with him last evening and came away disappointed. You find a guy in there name of Eddie Margot?"

Pause.

"Well, they're with him right now. My Bureau boy found that for me."

Pause; smile.

"He *is* dumb as a stump. It wasn't actually his idea where to look but he does take direction pretty good, long as you keep it simple. So what you got I don't know already?"

A longer pause to put on an interested face.

"Yeah? This Kimmel Diversity Group, they legit?"

Pause.

"Shit. Haas Mueller? Why does that sound familiar?"

Pause to listen.

"You're kidding? Well that's all the pieces. The fucking lawyer's out past the breakers and drifting fast, the company he's keeping nowdays."

Pause.

"Yeah, it's getting crowded. My boys and

their fakir, the South African now. This shit's about to go snatch-n-grab right quick, Bones. You in town?"

Pause.

"Good. Good."

Pause.

"Nah. I'll be in shortly. They hooked up with Margot so I know where they'll be. Margot's too old to run too fast or hide too deep."

Pause.

"Hell, I don't know. Late seventies, early eighties I guess. Why?"

Pause to smile.

"No shit? Sixty-eight ain't old." Zellwood thinking how he'd be sixty next year, but saying: "That's in'tresting. That's real in'tresting."

Pause.

"Yeah, I'll see you in a bit. Stay low, alright? I still don't know about this boy I got schlepping for me. We may have to figure something out about him before this is over. We do, it'd go easier if he doesn't know you."

Pause.

"I love it when you agree, Bones. See you."

Zellwood closed the phone and looked through his window at the diner below. As he watched, Pell and Dupree exited with Eddie Margot.

The three of them chatted on the sidewalk until a newer Cadillac the color of pearls dropped anchor. Eddie Margot used the front passenger door. The door shut and the Cadillac moved away as only a Cadillac can. Pell and Dupree stood there and watched the taillights round a corner then they moved toward the truck parked across some asphalt.

Zellwood smiled, said, "Boys, y'all are in so far over your heads you'd have to stand on tippy toes to even get a glimpse." He reached over and tapped the horn.

Milky got in a little pouty at being dismissed. Zellwood didn't seem to give much of a shit one way or the other.

"Let's go, son. Drop yourself at your car."

Milky started the car and pulled into traffic. "What then?"

Zellwood thought about it. "They'll end up at Margot's. He's the linchpin now, calling the plays." Zellwood tossed it some more. "You don't have to camp out anywhere but keep an eye on everybody. I got other business this evening."

Milky looked around for something to add that wouldn't make him sound like a dumb-ass. He asked: "When will things start happening, sir?"

Zellwood watched the city's adolescent skyline slide by outside.

"Things are already happening, Milky. Like you would not believe. You hang on. We're about to get busy as a new pair of jumper cables at a Mexican wedding next day or so."

"Good."

"You bored, son?" Almost sarcastic.

"I just thought it'd be a little more exciting than sitting in cars. Hell, that's all I've done since I've been at the Bureau."

Zellwood grinned. "Shit, son, that's what it is, this whole goddamned business. Pissing in Co-Cola bottles, eating junk, heartburn, BO, cramps. Waiting, son. That's the whole game. It's what you do to catch the big fish. Waiting. And watching."

Zellwood leaned over and broke wind but not too loudly. "That's all I've done my whole life, Milky—wait and watch."

Milky let the back windows down an inch or two and stared at the windshield wishing he had a clue what was building up around him right now. Maybe if he did, he could lose the uneasy feeling about Tommy Zellwood—the one that had Milky gobbling Tums like they were fucking M&M's.

[22]

TONY WAYNE—Speedo, flip-flops and a two-toned cocktail—was sporting some nice bruises at several locations. Sitting in the lanai, the patio part that was under roof. The screened pool skipped undulating shafts of secondhand sunlight across the poured-rock floor then bounced them off the glitter-hint stucco wall beyond. Tony could see his reflection in the French door to his right and the odd light accentuated the discolored marks on his skin.

The lanai was a knock-off of Tony's former digs. The new place, he'd furnished brand new throughout, but hadn't done the exterior crap yet. He'd just transplanted whole cloth from the lanai at his house downtown when he moved.

Present was the expected wrought-iron patio set of round glass-topped table and four chairs. The ironwork didn't necessarily stop short of unnecessarily ornate but Tony had liked it when it was new. A ceiling fan rotated indefinitely overhead, the paddles moving slowly, about eye speed. A cheap, heavy Tiffany knock-off was sconced off a wall over a Naugahyde wet bar. Floats and other pool toys were scattered around the pebbly floor. The walls were sparsely decorated with the usual accoutrements for a Florida lanai: a piece of varnished driftwood; a nautical-theme clock—not working; a Michelob sign—unlit. A gas grill was tethered in a corner, dusty because it didn't get out much.

The Speedo wasn't doing anything for Tony. His reflection had a lot of ass and belly going unprotected. Oh, well, so everyone had been right: age and decadence were running him down. Nothing lots of money wouldn't cure.

He was wearing wrap around shades, laid back in his iron chair, feet protruding into the sunlight where it slipped under the eaves. He put the glass to his lips and sipped. Its sweetness made him smack.

Another set of French doors stood open on a playroom full of a snooker table, several tall commercial-sized video games and a big-ass TV. Toy drifted through the doors and onto the patio. He danced casually to music coming from a boom box sitting on a low table. The box was playing softly. Toy was naked.

He danced to the table, bending over to turn up the music in a move meant for Tony. The music raged and Toy got into the sound, moving with it in earnest, hands raised over his head, hips telling stories. Tony didn't know the song—the radio was on Toy's station and it was some pop shit with a jingling sound. Didn't matter, Toy was the show.

A fancy twirling move on one foot got Toy facing Tony. Tony tried to hide the wince that took him every time he saw Toy's nose. There was a big bandage across it and Toy still had a bad case of raccoon eyes. Tony overlooked it, watching Toy, the sweat shining clean and strong on his young body.

Toy's moves were bringing him to Tony at a teasing pace. Tony was smiling, arms out to Toy.

The phone on the table's glass top chimed. Tony ignored it so it rang some more.

Tony gave the phone an agitated glance. It rang again.

Tony looked back at dancing Toy, inadvertently lifting the phone. He punched it on with a thumb without looking at it, put it to a bruised ear gently.

"Yes?"

Tony sat up, losing the shades, losing interest in Toy and the dance. "Yes, yes. This is Mr. Wayne. What?" Tony put a hand on the other bruised ear, gently. "Yes. Put him on." Pause, squinting like that might help him hear over the music. "What? Hold on."

Tony put the phone to his chest and looked at Toy. Toy was standing, hands limp at sides, unhappy. Head cocked, hip cocked.

"Toy, turn that shit off."

The music didn't go off.

"Goddam it, Toy. *Turn-it-off.*"

Toy walked over, yanked the cord out and heaved the boom box across the lanai and into the pool. He folded his arms, glared at Tony.

Tony smiled demurely. "Thank you, sweetie. Sorry, but this is Haas."

Toy didn't care a shit who it was; he spun and stamped into the house. The French doors slammed one after the other, neither staying shut.

Tony shook his head and put the phone to the ear again.

"Haas?" Pause. "Oh, it's not Haas." Pause. "I don't speak whatever it is you're speaking, dear." Pause. "Yes, I'll hold."

Tony held. Then: "Haas. Jesus Christ, man, I've been going nuts here. We got big problems. *Big* problems. The guy knows. He's outta jail and he knows." Impatient pause. "The guy that took it. He came here, knocked us around some, him and this black guy." Pause. "The Navy cop. The guy that was in with the first guy when he took it." Pause. "By all means think for a minute. I'm fresh out of ideas."

Tony gave Haas Mueller a few moments to think.

"No, Haas, I didn't tell them shit." Pause. "Nothing. I acted dumb." Pause. "What?" Pause. "Yeah. Twelve hundred pounds. That's about five hundred kilos, I guess. What does it matter? We've got to move it all anyway. These guys'll be back, no doubt. I wanna be gone." Pause. "Yes. It's at my horse farm. I can get to it anytime—day or night." Pause. "Yeah, I guess you could land a small airplane there. When're you coming?" Pause. "Good. Should I send Toy to pick you up?" Pauses, smiles. "Yeah, he got his license the end of last year." Pause. "Well, let me know, I'll send him." Pause. "I won't, Haas." Pause. "I won't do anything stupid. I won't do anything at all if you'll hurry up. See you." Pause. "Yeah, see you." Then, "Hey, Haas, you still there?" Pause. "Good. Listen, how about you grab me fifty, a hundred grams of white from your friend?" Pause. "No. I don't want that much. Toy'll kill himself." Pause to laugh wickedly. "*Have him stuffed*—that's ugly. Bye. Hurry."

Tony dropped the connect and put the phone down. He sat a few, thinking.

Decided he felt better now that Haas was on his way.

He felt so good, he opened a Chinese box that sat on the table and took out Toy's glass pipe and lighter. He found a pearlescent rock in the box, examined it and sat it in a depression in the pipe. He heated up the barrel, rocking it slowly in his fingers as he slid the flame up and down its length. Tony went pipe-to-lips and fired the rock. He held the fumes and watched the bubbling subside in the shallow bowl. Exhaled. Another quick bump and the pipe went away.

Tony pushed off the table and sat back as he was before the call, feet in the sunlight.

He steepled his fingers, looked at the ceiling fan and called: "Toy. Oh, To-eey."

It got him nothing.

Louder: "To-eey. Sweetie pie. Come out, come out."

Nothing.

"Come on, Toy. I'm sorry, baby doll."

A four-foot ceramic cheetah crashed through one of the French doors and completed its destruction on the poured-rock floor. Tony shook his head, smiling.

He leaned his head back to rest on the chair and closed his eyes. He said, "To-eey. I'll suck your dick if you come out here." Beat. "To-eey."

Broken glass tinkled and Tony rolled his

head around, peeped through shuttered eyes. Watched Toy step through the battered doors. He was still naked but he had the big silver revolver, holding it up in two hands. He leveled it at Tony.

Tony closed his eyes. He could hear Toy moving in on him, pretending—Tony now the imaginary perp, Toy taking no chances.

Tony brought his head up and opened his eyes. He took a sip of his drink, wagged his head.

"Don't cut your feet."

Toy didn't care—he was into the game. "Shut up, mister. Get on your knees." He moved in on Tony, still in his action-ready stance.

"Baby, watch where you're walking. Jesus."

Toy lay the barrel on the center of Tony's forehead. "I said on your knees, mister."

Tony rolled his eyes. "I'd love to blow you but, please, tell me you didn't find the bullets and load that thing again."

[23]

HAAS MUELLER STARED at the telephone sitting on his ebony desk for probably five minutes after the call. Thinking.

The American was a mouse. A femme. He would disintegrate under the lightest pressure.

The man who went to jail for taking the gold would be motivated. Now the man had a partner.

They weren't afraid of Wayne; they would be back. Soon.

Wayne would crumble.

The thoughts came around to yield two necessities. First, Mueller needed to go to the States. No matter what, the two thieves needed to be eliminated immediately.

And Tony Wayne may as well be dealt with at the same time.

Toy. What to do about Toy? Maybe he'd keep Toy for a while.

Mueller smiled, picked up the phone again.

He pushed some keys and swiveled to look out the window to see the statue of Bismarck, his back to Mueller.

He was in his Hamburg apartment, late afternoon, dressed in a charcoal suit cut in an Italian fashion. Oyster shirt, gray tie with tiny raspberry dots. The weathered face, the cropped brush of silver hair, Mueller prided himself in being just as comfortable on the decks of a motor yacht in the Aegean as he was lurking in the shadows of Munich's money machine.

Tonight he was to dine with an Austrian duke, a pretender actually. Mueller was touting the faux-duke to recover some inheritance lying about unclaimed since the war. The prize was several pieces of excellent art, legally registered. A nice take but the faux-duke was a pretty dunce, an idiot and possibly a waste of time. Maybe there was a sign in Bismarck's backside. Mueller needed a sign—the market had beaten him senseless in one swift short-trade leaving him worse than broke.

Course change: his fingers detoured on the phone pad, killing the call he'd placed then pressing familiar digits.

The machine gun purr of the phone trying the number came out loud through the speakerphone. Second purr, clicking came on. Mueller felt better already.

A woman's voice, a nice voice with the slightest bit of Teutonic in it, said, "Yes?"

"Gretchen, my love."

"Haas, darling. How are you?"

Mueller read the message. She was with someone—probably the American industrialist she allowed to keep her when she wanted to be bored—so she would speak English.

"Where are you, dear?"

"A place called Hilton Head, in South Carolina. Do you know it?"

"I'm familiar. Can you get free?"

"Haas, dear, I am always free. Where am I going?"

"Florida."

A pause. Then the nice voice said, "The government bullion?"

"Yes. Things are developing quickly in a troublesome manner. When you get there, see if you can locate a small aircraft. Something that would take you and me and five-hundred kilos of luggage to Freeport."

"Rented or borrowed?"

"Borrowed."

"From someone I know or someone I do not know?"

"Someone you don't know."

"Anything else?"

"Bring toys. Mine are in Johannesburg."

"Anything in particular?"

"No. These people are amateurs and not very smart amateurs it seems. It should be a frolic. Bring what you will."

"Splendid. I await you with bated breath." It was openly sarcastic.

"Ah, Gretchen, if you weren't such a heartless bitch, I wouldn't care for you so deeply."

"That seems to be one of my more lucrative qualities. *Ciao*, darling."

More clicking then dial tone.

Mueller pushed a button. The sound died. He turned to a laptop opened on the black desk, typed in *travel* and hit *enter*.

[24]

GRETCHEN GERTZ pressed a finger against the cell phone in the palm of a pale slender hand. The rest of her was draped over a long, low couch. She wore bra and panties, beige, almost skin tone. A glass of wine was near.

Hair the color of moonlight framed a heart-shaped face wars could be fought over.

Below the face was a body to make men forget war.

She gulped the wine, stood, looking defiantly at the man on the bed. "What is it, Howard?"

Howard was seventy-one, vigorous enough for his age, good hair. He was under a sheet of Egyptian cotton as white as nothing itself.

"Don't tell me."

Gretchen did what could have been a pout. "Yes. Work calls, Howard."

"Work?" Howard put a smile on his

tanned successful face. "What is it you do, now?"

A smile parted full lips. Temptation to tell him. "You would not believe it."

"How much will you make? I'll double it."

"But you are boring, Howard. I only love you for your money."

"I don't care."

Gretchen smiled warmly, walked to the bed and tousled the good hair. "I know, darling. That is why I always come back. But how can I return if I do not leave. Goodbye, Howard."

"You're not leaving *now*?" Howard grew a can't-believe-it face.

"Yes, dear. Right now."

"What about . . . " Howard motioned at the part of his body under the sheet. "I just took a Cialis."

Gretchen's hand came down to caress Howard's cheek, down his chest, down to his medicated member. The hand fell away as she turned to a closet.

"Oh, poor Howard. You have my permission to think of me as you masturbate, darling."

Gretchen found a small carry-on suitcase and took it into the dressing room off the bedroom. She closed the door on Howard shaking his head.

The carry-on was placed on a bench, loaded quickly and closed. Gretchen chose a pale loose silk blouse over clingy jeans, suede mules, Gucci sunglasses, linen jacket over an arm.

She and the suitcase came out of the dressing room. Howard looked pathetic.

"I can't believe you're doing this."

"Doing what, Howard?" Gretchen sat the suitcase down and walked to the dresser.

"Leaving."

"Oh? Leaving? I thought it was leaving you with a hard on that was bothering you." Gretchen picked up a wallet, rifled bills out of it and tossed it back on the dresser. "I need US dollars so I am taking your money, Howard." She paused, took Howard's keys as well. "And your car."

"Come on, Gretch. Give me five minutes. Tops, five minutes."

Gretchen picked up the suitcase, sat the Gucci's on her nose and walked away. Over her shoulder, she said, "Goodbye, Howard. Have fun."

[25]

MILKY WASN'T CLEAR on whether he was supposed to spend the night or not.

Zellwood hadn't answered at the *ho-tel*, so Milky cashed in about midnight, left the boys in the bar at the Holiday Inn on Jetport Road. Six hours in the rack, a shower, an electric shave in the car on the way, knowing the pigeons would be sleeping in.

The truck was gone when Milky pulled in, only minutes before eight.

He bumped the steering wheel with his palms. Goddam. Zellwood was going to have a shit fit.

Milky's cell phone had made its way into his hand. He said, "Fuck it," and tossed the phone in the seat.

He'd wait for them at Margot's. They didn't show there, he'd check back here, come up with some way to find out if they'd moved on.

That's how Milky spent half the morning: in the big bamboo at Eddie Margot's. Maybe ten, he rambled back to the motel.

Still no truck, but the maid's cart was only two doors down from Dupree's room. Shit. Maybe she was working this way.

Fifteen, twenty minutes a room? What the hell could you do in a motel room to clean up that took that long?

Short change on an hour, Milky was using the stairs, praying the big truck didn't show, catch him in the open.

A short piece of breezeway, he was looking in Dupree's room. The TV and vacuum were competing. A Hispanic woman, thirty to fifty, in a maid's outfit was glued on Springer dubbed to Spanish. She looked at Milky and pushed a button on the vacuum. That made the TV louder yet. The woman punched the power button; the TV crackled to dead.

"Yessir?" She looked like she hoped Milky didn't want towels or something.

"Just wondering when you were getting to my room."

"Whish room?"

"Down the way."

The woman looked cautious. "You stay here?" *Here* had a couple of syllables.

"Yeah."

Milky stepped in, saw a pigskin suitcase

he would have called feminine. He had to back up to check, see if he had the right room. He did.

"Ah, never mind. I'll just go ahead and go to my appointment. Thanks."

The lady put a little confusion on a wary face. "Thans for what?"

Milky drifted to his car, drove back over and hid in the bushes at Eddie Margot's and hoped Zellwood didn't call.

About three, maybe a quarter after, the proud pickup popped over a rise and into Eddie Margot's driveway. Milky's nuts fell out of his stomach. It was all Milky could do to keep from shouting with glee. Goddam, he was a happy man.

The truck claimed a piece of concrete and got quiet. Doors opened and the dynamic duo was using the front door like regular people.

Milky got the specs out, watched as Margot answered the chime. He was shirt sleeves, but that's all the fun he was allowing himself—tie and vest still in place.

Small greeting, the pigeons go in the door.

Milky was feeling for his cell phone, looking through the binoculars. He located the phone Stevie Wonder style, dropped the glasses in his lap, punched up Zellwood.

He fed the hotel's electronic receptionist

three numbers to Zellwood's room. He won four rings to an electronic hotel secretary saying Mr. Three-Digits wasn't available.

Milky got a few options, chose one, said, "We're all at Eddie's. Bye."

The phone went in the passenger seat, the glasses back up. The passenger door popped and Milky almost screamed it caught him so cold.

"Jesus fucking Christ."

"I scare you, boy?" Zellwood slid in and sat on Milky's phone.

Milky didn't mention the phone. He said, "I wish you'd give me some warning."

Zellwood smiled. "Warning, huh?" He got comfortable, let the seat back to its limit. "You finally get you some sleep, son?" It didn't sound to Milky like Zellwood really cared whether he did or not.

"Yes, sir." Milky looked straight ahead. Thinking.

After a bit, feeling like Zellwood was lounged out over there waiting on him, Milky said: "Sorry about this morning, sir. I'm glad you were on them."

"You didn't miss a thing. Had us some pancakes at the Pancake House, we drank coffee and read newspapers until about nine thirty, ten o'clock. Then we took a spin down to the hood, made a few stops, and, if I'm not mistaken, Mr. Dupree bought himself a handgun *and* something longer. Actually, two long guns. And ammo."

Milky took it as a warning to watch his ass and nodded like he was smarter than yesterday. "Why do you think he felt like he needed a gun? The lawyer?"

Zellwood did a dodge with his head over a shrug. "I don't know. I can't see the lawyer being that kinda tough." Some thought. "But something happened the other night. They eased off with their tails between their legs, empty handed. Next day they run straight to Margot. One of two things: they didn't get shit but they know who's got it, or they know where it is. Either way, they're ready to move on it."

"Which way are you leaning?"

Zellwood waged his head, frowned. "They didn't find it. They did? They'd a gone to it."

[26]

EDDIE'S HOUSE WAS a fucking museum. Old shit. Classy shit.

A rug of Far Eastern descent so old it looked like it had maybe been thrown on the street and cars had driven over it. A three-hundred-year-old Chippendale upright something, ancient and withered and cracked, a few off-color necessity repairs visible. A small dark painting of a child with a pricked finger holding it aloft in exquisite Dutch lighting. A Kutani vase and pitcher set on a noble buffet in the dining area.

The furniture didn't look fit to sit on. Maybe one of the Vanderbilts would have been able to.

Marty decided fragile was another good word for Eddie's crib. He chose a pretty sturdy looking leather ottoman and parked ass. Dupree hit the couch. It creaked but held. Eddie was in a velvet throne, a wing-back chair so deep he might have to be airlifted out.

"So whatcha think?" Eddie's hands were out and he was showing off the top of his dentures.

Marty nodded frank approval. "Nice, Eddie. Very nice place." Pause. "Eddie, what're we doing here?"

Eddie's mouth began in one direction, stopped, then said, "Anybody want something to drink?"

Shrugs around.

Dupree said, "Don't go to any trouble." Marty flapped a hand.

"Ain't no trouble." Eddie sat up, twisted around, yelled, "Annie Mae. Annie."

Nothing happened.

Eddie mumbled: "Goddammit." Then louder: "Annie. Goddammit, Annie Mae."

Marty said, "Don't worry about it."

Eddie yelled for Annie Mae anyway.

A woman with a sienna face of amused dismay appeared behind Eddie. She had eyes the color and shape of walnuts and happy round cheeks. She was downhill end of fifty somewhere. What she wore could have been a domestic outfit or not: a plain black shift but belted, onyx earrings and necklace.

The woman crept up behind Eddie. As he drew breath to shout, she put a hand on his shoulder. "Settle down, Margot. You still fumin from all that sugar you inhale yesterday." Very island.

Eddie looked over his shoulder. "Hey, sweetheart. These are the boys I was telling you about. They're the ones made me eat all the sweet shit."

"I see. I been wantin to ask, he have caffeine also?"

Marty and Dupree tossed out stereo nods.

"Un-huh. As I thought. You old liar. No wonder you stay in the bat-room all mornin." Annie Mae shook her head. "Hello, fellas." A hand to her breast, then, "Annie Mae."

Nods.

"And who do I have?"

"Marty."

"Shad."

A wise nod, a twinkle from the walnut eyes. "Martin and Shadrack. Good strong names."

Eddie said, "Jesus, Annie, leave em the hell alone. They'll run off screamin." He motioned with his head at Annie Mae. "She reads a mean entrail, you need her to."

Annie Mae rolled her eyes. "Get away, you old liar. What can I get for you two?"

Eddie said, "Brandy for me."

Annie Mae said, "Red wine for you."

Marty shrugged out, "Beer?"

Annie Mae looked at Dupree. He dittoed with a nod.

Orders taken, Annie Mae went out.

Eddie, coming back to the game, laid it down matter of fact with: "You need computer work."

Marty tossed out a pregnant, *okay*.

"I can hook you up."

Another expectant, *okay*.

Eddie's mouth looked like it was ready to say something and then Annie Mae was back with a tray.

Beer, beer, and red wine.

Eddie looked at Annie Mae, disappointment furrowed his brow.

"Don't you give me that evil eye, mister."

Eddie flapped a dismissive hand and Annie Mae withdrew with thanks for the beers. A coo-coo jumped through double doors up on a wall, yodeled once at the half-hour and went doggo again.

"And you're in luck—I got somebody in-house. I don't know you recall, Marty, reason I moved here, my only grandbaby was going to school out at the university. Only person I got left. I'm all she's got. Top it all, the kid dances around in computerland like Gene Kelly dances in the rain."

Dupree cleared his throat. "She here?"

"Yeah. You wanna meet her?"

Dupree's hands came out, palms up, brow wrinkled, looking at Marty, then looking at Eddie. "Why, hell yeah we wanna meet her."

He looked back at Marty—Marty deadpanned.

Eddie said, "Well, come on. You might enjoy this. I'm still deciding."

They rose as a covey. Dupree said, "Deciding what, Eddie?"

Eddie said, "You'll see. Come on, gents. Bring your beers."

Eddie led the way down a hall, swooshing through carpet the color and height of a wheat field. He stopped at a closed door. The door couldn't hold back the music spilling out around its edges. White Stripes were beating hell out of *Dead Leaves and the Dirty Ground*, making much noise for a two-piece.

Eddie knocked. Whoever was inside couldn't hear anyone coming down the hall, couldn't have heard a piano fall.

A harder knock followed. "Edy," followed the knock.

Nada.

Eddie wagged his head. His face registered mild irritation. "Goddam kids." He tried the door. It gave way.

Eddie stuck his head in. "Edy?" He pushed the door open, wincing at the audio assault. "Jesus. Come on." The last to Marty and Dupree twiddling thumb in the hallway.

The room made Marty think all it lacked was some twisted up track and a stoned Amtrak operator.

There was an unmade bed, a dresser with drawers opened at various depths. There was a long chaise, a mirrored vanity and the other furniture that shows up in bedrooms. There were clothes on every horizontal surface in the room.

The only exception was a path that led from the bedroom door to branch off into two smaller paths. One branch led to the cluttered bed. The other led to a long counter taking up one entire wall. There was more electronic gadgetry than at a Best Buy on the counter. Considering the rest of the room, the counter area was immaculate.

From four corners, speakers as big as tubas blared so loudly the dimmed ceiling light vibrated as did the rest of the room.

In a chair at the long counter was a girl Marty would have put mid-twenties somewhere. The headphones on her head begged the obvious question about the excessive speaker noise. Her head bobbled almost imperceptibly; she was oblivious to visitors.

Hair hennaed that popular color that's as subtle as a red-violet Crayola. Pale, pale skin, stranger to the sun. Eye shadow the color of a two-day-old bruise. Lipstick to match eye shadow and hair. Thin to a fault in black skinny jeans, form fitting on narrow hips and bird legs. Small breasts subdued even more by a thin fleece hoodie zipped to a spot a few inches above the breasts. Experienced black high-top All-Stars, sock-free. No visible tattoos or piercing but not out of the question.

Marty liked her, liked her laid back relaxed style. Liked how, when she looked over to see her grandfather and two strangers, she didn't react beyond doing something with a mouse that dropped the volume to not much more than a memory.

She lost the headphones and exited the program running on the only lit monitor of four on the counter. She swiveled in the chair to face the men but she didn't smile. Marty wasn't sure she wasn't a little pissed or something. Maybe disappointed.

He still liked her, liked her eyes. The palest gray eyes he'd ever seen.

"Edy, these are the boys I was telling you about. This one's Marty and that one's Shad but everyone calls him Dupree."

Edy did a quick and bold appraisal. It didn't look promising.

Eddie made eye contact with everyone in the room, said, "Somebody needs to say something like, *let's talk business.* Who's first?"

Dupree wasn't shy. "How much's this gonna run us?"

"What do you want?" The voice was not what Marty expected.

He didn't know what he expected and not getting it wasn't bad. The voice was low, but not mannish. Sultry wouldn't work and neither little-girl nor come-and-get-it were involved in its strains. Pleasant. Relaxed. A sound that would never chafe against the male ear.

Eddie brought Marty back to ground with: "And one of you guys say something like: *we need you to run a guy for us*."

Marty volunteered, repeated the need.

Edy gave it a beat. A perfect beat. She said, "How deep?"

Marty and Dupree traded looks, question marks floating over their heads.

They looked back at Edy. Something less than kindness was curling the corners of her mouth. She leaned back, eyes sad like a little girl's, the points of her unlikely-colored hair falling back from her chin. "Gramps?"

"Yeah, sweetheart?" Eddie's hand went to caress her face but she brushed it away.

"I don't believe your friends have a fucking clue what they're doing."

"No, sweetheart, they don't. What's the guy's name, one of you."

Marty: "Tony Wayne. Anthony J. Wayne. No idea what the J is. He's a local lawyer."

"You know where he lives?"

Marty said, *yeah*, asked was she ready.

The girl, Edy, said, "Shoot."

Marty rolled Tony's address off his memory.

"Got a pen, Gramps?"

Eddie felt himself up, found a pen, said, "And don't forget where you got it."

Edy wrote something in the palm of her hand. Marty assumed it was Tony's christening name and address. She sat back studying the palm, pen in her teeth.

Eddie snapped his fingers, said, "The pen, girlie."

Edy wiped the pen on her pants and handed it up to Eddie.

She said, "Everything there is on the guy? Ten grand."

Dupree did the one where he looked like he'd been slapped. "Goddam, girl, why don't you get a mask and a gun?"

"Okay. Five grand—up front."

Marty watched her work Dupree. Not bad for a skinny little girl.

"Up front? Ain't gonna be any up front. You get yours when we get ours. Five thousand dollars?" Dupree put a head jerk on it. "You think we got money like that? Right now?"

Edy decided, carney eyes studying Dupree then Marty. Back to Dupree. "I'd say a guy like you, it would take six maybe seven grand to make you feel large. You're close. You got it, but the hit would put you lean. Leaner than you'd like."

Marty could see Dupree admired her read but tried to sit on it. He just shrugged and poked his chin whiskers at her.

Edy put the gray eyes on Marty. "And Mr. Pell here, considering his recent past . . . " She ran the eyes up and down Marty, being playful with it, " . . . I'd say he's got maybe a grand in his pocket. Depending on how his tastes have run since he's been back in general pop." Near smile. "How have your tastes been running, Mr. Pell?"

"Haven't had much time to redevelop any tastes." Marty was sticking with it, having fun. "Considering my recent past." He moved the conversation over to Eddie, eyes on the girl. "Is that the going rate? Ten?" Eddie paused so Marty looked at him.

Eddie lifted thin shoulders inside the starched white shirt. "Going rate's more like twenty, considering the take. You're getting family rates. Say thank you."

Marty did; Dupree didn't.

Dupree wanted to know: "How long does this kinda thing take?"

Edy dittoed Eddie's high shouldered shrug. "A few hours harvesting. A couple more printing it all out. Some sorting. Organizing'll take some time." Another shrug, some pursed lips. "I'll have it tomorrow, the next day."

Dupree didn't take it well but he gripped

it. Very subdued: "And what exactly're we gettin for our money, now?"

"Personal and financial data. All of it. Bank justifications. Stock holdings, trades. Tangibles. I hear bullion is involved. I'll track any trading with gold investors and brokers. Any sudden improvements in status." Edy turned to the monitor, moused up a screen. "Besides that, you'll get it all organized, consolidated, collated and interpreted. You'll know what brand underwear the guy wears, where he bought them and what he paid. But what you're really paying for is discretion. You guys did want discretion, right?"

Marty did and said so.

Then Edy said, "So get outta here and let me do my thing. I'll call you tomorrow." She looked from the monitor to non-retreating faces. She made flipping motions with a hand. "Begone."

They became begone. The door closed; the Whites slammed against it, oozing out around the hinges again and taking their sweet little time about it.

[27]

ZELLWOOD WENT Japanese. A Lexus. A nice pewter color.

Told Milky the Lincoln was getting too well known. Milky took the advice to heart, traded rental units himself. Now he had a white Mitsubishi, otherwise same as the other, same tan interior even. Milky hoped like hell the bold-ass cockroach hadn't somehow slipped into the new ride.

It was parked in the dark, one street over from Tony Wayne's place with a clear view between a couple of versions similar to Wayne's digs. Zellwood's Lexus was tethered in the orange grove outside the sneak gate that all players but Wayne were using—he and Zellwood were rotating cars for stealth.

Zellwood grunted, said, "Pull up where we can see my boys, make sure they're still there."

Milky moved the car forward slowly. The truck sat in a sandy lot outside a half finished house. Dupree and Pell had gone in the house and were at the rear, drinking a twelve-pack and watching Wayne's house through vacant window openings.

Milky knew this because, at Zellwood's suggestion, he'd slipped down on foot with his job-issue night-nocs and watched them for a few minutes.

Zellwood pointed and Milky kept going.

"Where to, sir?"

"Ride some."

Milky cruised slowly around lazy roads through spoiled lawns—chemically addicted water hogs.

Zellwood clapped his hands, said, "Hooey. Opulence abounds. What you guess that one went for, Milky?"

Zellwood indicated a glistening white pile of stucco. What it lacked in taste and imagination it doubled for in square footage. To Milky it looked like the credit union building in his hometown. Three predictable stories with undersized windows at predictable locales. Minimal overhang, low roof.

Milky guessed: "Two million? Three?"

"Lot and a half, on the lake? This lake? In a boom town like this? Double your low number." He thought. "Maybe five if it's strong on appurtenance out back: dock, boathouse, pool-house and all."

A Jaguar sedan, a dark shade, slid by in the oncoming lane like a whisper. Zellwood's head swiveled with it, eyes locked on the Jag like radar.

Milky said, "What is it?"

Zellwood turned back, chewed the inside of a cheek. "Either that's the third time I've seen that car or there's a hell of a lot of Jags in this neighborhood."

"Could be, this hood."

Zellwood wasn't convinced. "Go park where you were. Let's see how many European luxury automobiles we can count."

In an hour, they counted five. Three of them were a dark green Jaguar driven by a hollow cheeked blonde.

Zellwood put an ankle on a knee, seat back to max again like he preferred it. "She doesn't find a parking spot, she's gonna have to go for gas before the fun starts."

Fourth pass, the Jag slid over not two hundred feet ahead of Milky's rent-a-heap.

A door opened and the light didn't come on. Zellwood sat up.

"Gimme those nighttimes, Milky."

Zellwood put the glasses up. "Damn, son. Nice piece of womanhood. Wonder what she's up to in her black clothes."

Milky didn't respond.

"Son, do I have to give you direct

instructions every single time here or you wanna try some initiative?"

Milky jumped into action, popped his door.

Zellwood said, "Shit," and shot a hand over the interior light. Some spilled out through his fingers.

Milky pulled the door shut. "Sorry."

Zellwood showed some disappointment, flicked a button on the light. "Here. You might need these too." He held out the night vision glasses.

Milky took them, added a contrite nod.

Before he slid out Zellwood said, "And remember, son, we ain't trying to steal anybody's shoes. Just see what she's up to."

Milky paused, fretting over something, wondering whether to ask or let it go.

"Get moving, son."

"Yes, sir," half-turned to go, then, "Sir, what if she's a hitter? What if she pops them?"

"Let her."

"Sir?"

"I said *let-her*. De-complicates things."

Milky bobbed his head a few times and closed the door.

When he was gone, Zellwood spoke to the windshield. He said: "Right there it is. Right there's why we had our asses handed to us in a bag in the Cold War. Recruiting dumb fucking choirboys when we shoulda been after reform school grads." Big sigh. "Ah, Granny's tired." Zellwood laid his head back and closed his eyes.

He may have dozed. When Milky popped the door, out of breath, it didn't make Zellwood jump. He didn't wake up like that. He did it one eyelid at a time.

Milky's excitement was untethered. "She put a bug on their vehicle."

"Yeah?" Zellwood got interested. "You sure?"

"She put something she could hide in her palm under their back bumper."

It pushed Zellwood off into a long stare.

Milky broke the cat stare with, "She's getting back in her car."

"Lemme see those." Zellwood's hand went out.

Milky handed the glasses over.

The blonde sat for a few seconds, feet on the curb, using a cell phone. Brief communication. She closed the door. The car's taillights flared white in the green field of the binocular's lenses.

"Shit. Get out Milky."

"Sir?"

"Get the fuck out. Trot over, get my car, get your ass right back here. The dickheads leave, you go with them."

Milky seemed to realize he was again looking slothful and inattentive. He opened his door as the Jag pulled off the curb.

Zellwood was out, coming around the car. Over its roof he said, to the retreating Milky, "Hey, son. You may need these."

Milky turned and Zellwood's car key hit him in the chest and fell to the ground.

Zellwood never looked back. He climbed in Milky's car and went after the Jaguar's taillights.

Zellwood found his cell phone on the seat, pushed speed dial, pushed one. The phone went to his ear, he said, "Bones. I'm gonna need a hand. I'm tailing somebody a little more professional looking than the rest of the cast."

He paused to listen

Then: "I *am* good. But not that good. I get off the interstate behind her, if *she's* any good, I'm made."

Pause again.

"Yeah. She's a her. Hey, Bones, I'm in a white rice-mobile of some sort and she's in a green Jag you'll appreciate."

Pause.

"I expect we'll come back to town. We don't, I'm fucked."

Pause.

"Yeah. Stay loose."

He lost the connection and tossed the phone back on the seat next to him.

Zellwood's reasoning, that if he looked like the girl looked he wouldn't be using the back door, was on the button. She went straight to the main gate.

Ahead, a delicate wave was tossed from the window of the Jag as it slid by the guard shack.

Zellwood picked up the pace, hoping to make the tollgate. It looked good right up to the point he had to slam on brakes. Something slid out from under the seat and hit his heels. Then the arm came down on the nose of Milky's car.

Zellwood had his buzzer out by the time the guard walked out with hands on hips, high school principal style.

The guard zipped over, moving like a manatee, took a look at the buzzer, took a look at Zellwood.

"Federal boy, huh?"

"Yeah. Raise the gate."

"Well, we'd appreciate it, when you gotta come in here . . . "

Zellwood pointed a Browning automatic at him, maybe crotch high, so the guard stammered to a halt.

"I won't kill you, but I'll maim your ass for life. Now you raise that fucking gate."

The guard's head went up and down with

sincerity. "Yes, sir." He went to the gate's mechanism pillar, bent. Before he stood, the arm was jumping to attention.

Zellwood said, "Thank you," but kept the Browning on the window's edge.

As he went by, the guard gave Zellwood an ugly face, said, "And you or somebody needs to pay for those two security bars you broke the other day too."

Zellwood told the guy to send him a bill and went to look for a dark green Jaguar.

He made the turn and the object under the seat migrated and was again under his feet. He reached for it. It was a hard cardboard notebook with a mottled cover.

Zellwood glanced at it and tossed it on the passenger seat—the Jag had stopped at the four-way ahead and required his attention.

[28]

"YOUR LAWYER'S A boring motherfucker, bread." Dupree walked the cheeks of his ass around to a new position on the concrete slab and leaned back against a bare block wall, legs out, crossed at the ankles, can of beer in a hand on his lap.

Marty sat on his own piece of the concrete a few feet away, pretty much the same pose as Dupree. He leaned against a skeletal wall framed of two-by-fours, beer on the floor beside him.

The commandeered house was in the rough-framing stage, translating to: slab, bare cinder-block exterior walls, bare interior wood-framed walls, roof trussed and plywood-sheathed, but only a felt-paper cap as yet. No windows, no doors—only holes where they would be.

From where Marty lounged, he had a

clear and full shot of Tony Wayne's digs. A few lights were still on at one thirty.

"I expect we all look boring, you were to do a twenty-four seven study." Marty crushed the empty can and skidded it across the floor. "You ready to call it a night?"

Dupree drained his beer can and sat it down beside him, "Yeah. You think the girl's gonna come up with anything?"

Marty shrugged. "I don't know, cuz." Resignation in Marty's voice. "I keep thinking eventually something's gotta break in our direction. What's it gonna hurt she doesn't?"

"You sound like you're losing heart. You ain't givin up, are you?"

"Can't. *One egg, one basket*, remember. Nah, I'm just tired." Marty could feel Dupree watching the side of his face.

"Cuz, I'm sorry it was you did those three years. You know that, don't you?"

"Forget about it."

"You forget about it, Marty?"

"No."

"Then don't tell me to. I appreciate you not rollin when you were in flames. I admire you for it."

"Forget about it."

Dupree smiled mildly, picked up the empty can and tossed it at Marty; Marty batted it away.

"You're a hard motherfucker to say thank you to, you know it?"

Marty sat the can upright. "Maybe I was looking out for me, not you."

"Have it like you want it, baby." Dupree stood, dusted hands and seat of pants. He walked over to the void that would get to be a window one day and looked at Tony's house.

Marty stood slowly, talked to Dupree's back. "Where you at, cuz? Right now?"

Dupree shook his head a little. "I still think we could beat it out of him, get it done."

"No."

Dupree turned, "Why not, Marty? We beat long enough, knock the wind out of im enough, he'll be glad to tell."

"No he won't, cuz. The size of the pot? He'd stick it out. I would. So would you. Think about it." Marty grabbed the cardboard sleeve the twelve-pack came in—two cans left. "Only way that works is he's gotta be scared for his life. Tony knows we won't kill him so it won't work. It's Eddie and a finesse or decide to kill Tony."

"I'm not too far away from that second option right now, bread, not too far at all."

Marty thought about how far he was from it and didn't like where he found himself.

"You got her, Bones?"

Pause to hear the response.

"Yeah. Green Jag. Like it?"

Pause.

Small laugh. "Un-huh. Second time she rode by, I thought you'd lost your mind."

Pause briefly.

"Un-huh. *Just like* the one you're driving. Aw right, take her on home. Call me if you need. Otherwise, see you at the ho-tel."

Pause.

"Nah. She'll put the receiver on the bug in the morning. She's done for the evening. I just wanna see where she's sleeping."

The Jaguar that Zellwood had followed out of the burbs put on a signal.

"Lookit this. We're all getting off at my exit."

Another green Jag, same model, came by Zellwood like he was backing up. The glass was smoked but he knew it was Bones positioning up.

Zellwood made the sweeping exit and saw the twin Jags bumper to bumper at a red signal ahead.

The signal went green and the parade continued. The Jags went left. Zellwood went right.

He put the cell back to an ear. "Bones, you still in there?"

Pause.

"Good. Call me when you're done."

Pause.

"I don't have the foggiest, Bones. She looks like a million bucks and moves like a panther. Scary woman."

Pause, then a smile.

"Nah. But I *was* to fall in love, she'd be a good candidate. Call me you get done. I got a bottle of Bas Armagnac 1893 I lifted off our friend Charles Taylor."

Pause.

"Shit. We've seen way worse bandit kings than old Charles. Hell, he may end up completely civilized—you hardly ever catch him eating his enemies' innards anymore. See you, partner."

Zellwood let a valet boy have Milky's car at the Bohemian, shuffled across the lobby. In the elevator, he watched himself repeated in the mirrored walls. All of them looked worn out.

Time to get out, Tommy. Don't let the game lull you.

Remember: amateurs are harder than pros. The pro, you know what he's going to do next. The amateur doesn't even know himself from one minute to the other.

Keep telling yourself retirement fund.

He looked at the many selves in the mirrors. He said to them, "Retirement fund, Tommy."

Later, in his room, on the bed in undershirt, pants and sock feet, Zellwood had almost let the thoughts of retirement rest in his head.

He was watching a rerun of Dharma and Gregg, thinking how Jenna Elfman was a genius, doing the quirky, goofy thing but doing it sexy somehow. He realized he must be horny, tried to remember when he'd gotten laid last without him or someone paying for it.

His thoughts went straight to the woman in the Jag. She was young, twenty-lates to thirty-earlies, but he couldn't think of her as a girl. He'd known women, and he'd known girls. This one was a woman.

The sure-footed way she moved. The self-confidence out there, even in the phosphorous glow of the night-nocs. He tried some other words for her but they all seemed corny. Old-fashioned. Words people were using during the Cold War.

Listen to you, Tommy.

Thank God, the hotel phone squalled.

"Yello."

Pause. Eye roll.

"You put them to bed, huh? Well, go on home, get some sleep."

Pause.

"Yeah. Pick em up in the morning."

Pause.

"What?"

Pause.

"No. No. Don't worry about it. I'll call you in the morning. Take my car on home. We'll swap out tomorrow sometime."

Pause.

"Yeah. I'm sure. Bye."

Milky was still talking when Zellwood dumped the connection.

He sighed, picked up the remote and pushed the up arrow a few times. Bull riding came up. Silvano Alves, the Brazilian boy, was getting his ass pureed by a big rank bull named Bushwacker. The bull won about three seconds into it.

Zellwood reached over, grabbed the receiver off the phone on the bedside, hit zero.

"Yeah, could you get somebody—a carhop or somebody—to get something outta my car for me?"

Pause.

"Good. A notebook. Lying on the passenger seat. Thanks."

Pause.

"Yeah. Send it on up. Thanks."

Zellwood drifted, eyes closed for a bit. His cell phone rang; someone knocked.

"Shit."

The phone: "Yello." Pause. "Hold on, Bones."

The door: a bellhop with a notebook and a hand out. Zellwood made the hop's hand happy, let the door click shut.

The phone: "Hey, Bones. Room service at the door. Where you at?"

Smile.

"Yeah? She's staying right here, huh? How convenient."

Pause. Perplexity.

"Yeah? Private airport? What'd we do there?"

Pause.

"Hmmm. Just window shopping, huh?" Some thought. "Okay. I got it: dollar to a doughnut, she's advance guard for the South African."

Pause.

"Yeah. Mueller. That *would* make her a pro then. Damn, Bones, easy money just got scarce. I believe we're in for a tussle here. Hey, how about we do that bottle of Armagnac another time? My ass is dragging." Pause. "Good, I'll see you in the daylight, partner."

Almost hangs up, then, "What's that?"

Pause.

"Nah. Let's see what tomorrow brings. I'm a little reluctant to break out that kinda tactic in this country. Right now, shit goes south, we're still investigating crimes against the government. We got a hall pass long as we don't hafta explain room-temperature civilians."

Pause.

"The lawyer? Oh, hell, you could make him squeal like a pig without drawing blood, but we start that shit the rest of the herd'll come rushin in. That happens, we'll have to buy a backhoe to plant folks."

Pause.

"No, Bones, I'm not getting sentimental. We may end up there yet. I'm just trying to be halfway quiet about it is all. See you in the daylight."

[29]

THE MAN WASN'T hard to spot. Nine o'clock in the morning on a Saturday, nobody much at the airport. Didn't matter—Peanut would have spotted the man at the county fair.

Little herringbone hat with a little red feather. Tweed overcoat over an arm. Italian suit an ugly-ass gray color, and look at the man—fine pair of calfskin shoes but the man's pants leg didn't even hit the shoe. High-water britches like a nigger in the projects.

Peanut hauled a lot of people around in his stretched out Lincoln limo and had found Europeans pretty much squarer than a box full of right angles. Some of them thinking they had it going on, showing the Yanks how it was done, and not even close. Others, get off the fucking plane, got on those little athletic shorts with the slits up the side, the ones nobody but women and sissies wore anymore. Maybe have on black socks and a pair of Nikes looking so old they could have come from Salvation Army. A T-shirt looks like it belongs to his kid, faded, skin tight, and always says something like *Mountain Dew* on it. There they are, thinking how American they look.

Foreign people just had no style for the most part. Nope, no real style. Just like the motherfucker coming at him.

Peanut did his standard introduction, putting his best Uncle Remus out there for the man's pleasure: "Yessir, Mr. Kaiser, sir. I'm Peanut, sent out by O-Town Limousine Services. I'm gone be yo driver on this fine Flawda day. You got luggage, sir?"

Motherfucker had luggage. Three good-sized cases.

He said he was staying at the Grand Bohemian downtown—did Peanut know it?

Peanut told the German sounding gentleman he knew it well. Gave him another courtesy *sir* free of charge.

But first the man wanted to go to an address at a swank hood out in the north burbs, away from the theme park trash. Way north. Good—the meter was running.

This was Peanut's first trip to the rich-boy club up at Alaqua Lakes but it was hard to spot like a Rolls Royce would be in the Washington Heights projects—made the fine sections around it look like trailer parks.

They were expected, got zoom-in directions on a Mr. Wayne's house from a security shack.

Peanut was told to wait with the car, and the man had his rap on the door answered by what Peanut thought first was a naked girl. It wasn't. Its dick was too long to be a girl. Mr. Herringbone hugged the naked boy and closed the door.

Fuck it—meter's running. Peanut leaned on a fender and fired up a Tampa Nugget It's-A-Boy he'd been saving for when his luck changed.

"Well, hey, Peanut. Ain't seen your ass in a while. That could be cause you owe Shady Grady four thousand and a lotta fuckin vig."

Back in the shell of a house across from Tony Wayne's, back at the future lake-view window, Dupree watched the little limo driver.

Marty was wandering around the house like he might be considering a purchase. "What? You know the limo driver?"

"Oh, yeah. Know him quite well. Owner-operator rents himself out to whosoever. When he ain't got cargo, he might call Grady for a gig. If he's gotta few bucks, he may lay a bet, lose a bet."

"He fucked up on a big bet?"

"Un-huh. Not a big player as a rule, but one time he fucked up large. Niggah's mama died, left him a five thousand dollar policy. He bet his heart not his head with four of it. Hear what I'm sayin?"

"He's stupid?"

"Nah, Peanut ain't stupid that way. He went in to it plannin on losin. See it?"

"Yeah."

Dupree must have thought Marty didn't see it. "Had he been bettin with his head, plannin on winnin, he woulda bet it all. You know the odds, you accept the numbers, you put the pile down, baby. Otherwise?"

"You're planning on loosing. I hear you, cuz." Marty rambled some more, checking out studs, top and bottom plates. "This Peanut thing may be the first break we've had in this deal. Whatchu think?"

"Yeah. I'll be talkin to Peanut. Who you reckon the hat was?"

"I'm thinking that was Tony's Eddie."

"Un-huh. That's what I figure." An emphatic beat. "His Eddie looks like he could kick our Eddie's ass."

"I hope it doesn't come to that, cuz."

Zellwood waited, notebook under an arm, and eventually the hop found Milky's car and brought it around.

A couple of bucks later, Zellwood had the car moving on asphalt, tucking the notebook back under the seat.

He pushed some numbers at a red light, got Milky on cell. Asked Milky's location; got told Wayne's.

He also got told about a limo full of a guy that looked Swiss. Zellwood had smiled. Mueller was in the wings. As was his pantheress.

Zellwood told Milky to break off, wait for him at the back gate. They could trade cars there. He fed Milky some bullshit about the woman in the green Jag, told him he was to meet her, get a folder.

A half-hour later Zellwood was sitting in his Lexus a few hundred yards down from the main gate at Alaqua Lakes. Milky's rental was rolling through the stop sign at the highway then it was going the other way.

Zellwood got comfortable, found a decent jazz station on the box, lit a cigarette and dialed Bones.

"Hey. He's on the way. You ready?"

Pause.

"Yeah. It's under the driver's seat. I didn't want him to miss it, get funny. You know he went for it soon as he got around the corner. Call me when you're done."

So the woman in the Jag was on their team.

Zellwood ran her, found out she was Bureau too. Called her last night he said, asked what her business was. Overlapping task force watching Margot and she stumbled across their guys. Good—someone from Milky's home crew to give him a corroborating story.

He'd been nervous as shit about this thing from jump. He'd meet this Bureau woman, get this folder she had for Zellwood, then talk to her, express his concerns, cover his ass. Good.

There was the Jag, like Zellwood said, sitting in the grocery store parking lot. Windows up.

Milky checked himself in the mirror, readjusted it. He found his friendly smile, wanting to be viewed as a regular guy, a fellow agent, but, hey, if it went beyond just business—say a drink or two—so be it.

The Jag began to pull away slowly, waiting up on Milky. Ah, looked like the woman was taking Milky to a quiet locale. Good idea, getting away from prying eyes. He dropped in behind and the Jag led him around on some county-maintained road until progress fell behind the horizon.

Another turn or two had him on a sandy dirt road. Pasture spread out on each side. A few cows were doing what cows do to content themselves. The Jag pulled off the road, crossed the narrow shoulder and parked under a couple of trees.

Milky pulled up behind, got out, sucked stomach, filled his chest, and walked to the car. The windows were heavily tinted and it could have just as easily been the Pope in the car as the woman.

The window came down. It wasn't the woman. It wasn't the Pope either.

The long narrow gun in a hand the color of caramel jumped, the noise no louder than a textbook slamming shut. The noise again, and Milky was on his back on the road. The trees looked peaceful moving in unison back and forth like that.

The Jag's door opened, and Milky knew someone stepped over him but he didn't care to look—the trees were too fascinating. Back and forth, swaying. Back and forth.

Milky heard his own car's door open, then close. Someone was near him again. He didn't look at the someone. It didn't matter. All the light was being sucked away, closing in, diminishing his eyes' periphery.

Milky's field of vision became only a point of light, maybe the size of a quarter, but shrinking. The trees were swaying back and forth in miniature like they were far away.

Bink—the light went out.

[30]

PEANUT COULD SMELL a hundred-dollar bill ever since he picked the man up. Took him the hell out to the edge of civilization, now back to town—to the Grand Bohemian. Peanut planned on being stern with the bellhop about taking care of Mr. Kaiser, look out for his needs.

He played it cool, he might even get another gig or two out of this man in the back seat. Peanut could see him back there, checking out the bar. Holding up bottles, reading labels.

No, no chartreuse, thank you. Pass on the Southern Comfort. Study on the Tanqueray bottle half full of Gilbey's cheap shit.

Hey, the Johnnie Black. Good choice. Wasn't really Johnnie Black, but it was civilized scotch in the bottle. Peanut couldn't remember, but it was a classy green bottle and had lots of plaid shit on it. Plaids were Scotch, weren't they?

Peanut caught a couple of lefts to get right on the one-way in front of the Boheme. He slid the limo around the arched drive and caught some curb under a stuccoed porte-cochere.

A bellhop beat Peanut to the back door. Peanut gave the bellhop some attitude, eased him aside.

"The Grand Bohemian Hotel, Mr. Kaiser."

The man finished his scotch, grabbed a valise and stepped out. A three-second appraisal of the hotel looked fair.

A search in a pocket gave up a money clip. Peanut watched his man fan through some colorful stuff that could be Monopoly money to some good old American green.

He looked at Peanut. "How much weight would a vehicle such as this tolerate?"

The oddity of the statement, the Deutsched-up accent, the formal speech—whatever—it floated on Peanut for a bit before it sank in exactly what the question was the man was asking.

Peanut shrugged, "I on't know, boss. I've had eight big men—professional football players—in here at once. I b'lieve she's rated at a ton." Peanut was perplexed.

The man peeled off two C-notes. "Splendid."

The treasury promises were coming at

Peanut. He said, hand coming up like a trout to a fly, "You mind I axe you why you axin?"

"No, not at all. I have some equipment I may need to move tomorrow evening. I could double what you are holding should you be interested and should repossession become a necessity."

Peanut looked at his hand, folded the bills, hid them in a quick pocket. He didn't want to wish bad luck on anybody, but he hoped to *hell* repossession became necessary. "Sure, boss. What time I'm pickin you up?"

The man asked Peanut what time it got dark. Peanut told him: "Summer's end, daylight savins? Pro'ly bout eight, hard dark bout eight thirty."

"Then make it seven, here. I'll be in the bar."

"Sure, boss. Sure as hell." Peanut put his head to work doing a good, responsible nod job. "I'm here, six-thirty."

"No. Seven is good. Please arrive with a full tank of petrol. Good day, Peanut."

"Yessir. Seven o'clock." To the bellhop: "Mr. Kaiser got three bags in the boot. Nice leather stuff so you don't be knockin it around, hear me?"

The hop, a short broad Hispanic man, gave Peanut back his attitude, put a little extra on it.

Peanut said. "Well get the man's bags."

Thc hop interrupted his trip to get the man's bags, turned to Peanut, said, "How about you let me handle Mr. Kaiser from here."

Peanut saw the ha-ha's tug the corner of the German's mouth as he turned and walked away abruptly. Okay, the man's got a sense of humor. Good.

"See you, Mr. Kaiser. Seven. Tomorrow evenin." No response from his man.

The bellhop raised the boot lid, grinning at Peanut.

Peanut said, "What?"

"Yessir, Mr. Whitey, sir," low enough no one but Peanut could hear. The hop found it way more amusing than Peanut did.

Peanut's hands went palms up, out at his side, drama prop to a perplexed face. "You a fuckin bellhop."

The bellhop lost the giggles, closed the trunk lid, "Yeah? So?"

Peanut held the pose, said, "I mean . . . you a fuckin bellhop, and you feel you got room to be dissin somebody?"

"Come on, Peanut, don't get on the interstate, now."

Peanut didn't. He turned away from downtown into Thornton Park, still mostly residential but for a few young lawyers and old architects spilling from downtown, doing business in ex-houses. The offices still looked like houses to Marty. They just had big wooden signs and bark chip parking lots instead of kids and front yards.

Dupree turned behind Peanut, closed the gap. "All right, Peanut, make a full stop. Mmm-mmm. You reckless-drivin little fuck, look at your ass float through the stop sign."

Dupree went through the stop sign faster than Peanut had. When Dupree wig-wagged his head to check for oncoming, Marty tossed out a grin.

Dupree gave Marty some eyebrow. "The fuck you find so funny?"

"You're a yacky motherfucker, you know it?"

"Got a nervous constitution is all."

"Mmm. I thought it was the tight shoes. Your boy just turned in 7-Eleven up here."

"I can see. Even tight shoes, I can *see*." Dupree bounced the truck into the parking lot.

According to several signs, if you weren't here on official 7-Eleven business, you would definitely be towed. There was a number you could call to get your vehicle back. There was a wrecker parked beside the store to back up the threat. There wasn't a tow driver in it and the lot was jammed with empty cars.

It took a wait and some angry honks to nab a spot. The gap was so tight Marty couldn't have gotten out had he needed or wanted. Dupree barely made it out alive.

Marty watched him walk over and lean against Peanut's money machine and suck his teeth.

The guy driving the car on Marty's side—a low slung ricemobile with tires as fat as rubber bands—came out, surveyed the situation, judged it hand on hip, exasperated I-can't-believe-it face going.

Marty gave him a smile, a nice cordial how-you-doing job.

"Is this a joke? Tell me this is a joke. Who's driving that thing?"

Marty's smile went to the you-won't-believe-it side. He pointed to where Dupree leaned against Peanut's limo.

The guy looked at Dupree, his face went funny, he looked back at Marty, he looked the truck over good, rebel flag and all. He looked back at Dupree who was now looking at the guy.

The guy went around and wrestled his way from the passenger side to the driver's side. He fired up the car. His window came down.

Marty looked down, grin remnants still around the edges of his mouth, but trying hard at civil in the face of unabashed asshole-ism.

The guy looked up, said, "Tell your friend he's a jerk, in case he doesn't know."

Marty said: "He knows. Be careful backing out."

"Fuck you."

"Hey, shouldn't I tell my friend he's lucky you didn't have time to wait, talk to him directly? Something like that?"

A middle finger came up as did the guy's window. He and the finger drifted. He showed it to Dupree on his way out of the parking lot.

Dupree looked at Marty, shrugged up some the-fuck-was-that-about.

Marty shrugged back some dunno.

Peanut showed with a six of cheap shit. He was looking lucky until he saw Dupree draped on his ride.

Marty thought Peanut might have dropped the malt liquor and run if he didn't think Dupree would run him down anyway. Marty felt sorry for the little guy in an unattached way.

Peanut was maybe five four, maybe go a buck ten wet and wealthy. A little round-bowling ball of a head served as perch to a diminutive Ralph Kramden peak cap. Black coat a little long in the tails and sleeves. Once white shirt, string bolo tie with a silver dollar clasp bobbing quick time with the Peanut's Adam's apple. The seat of his pants was a little shiny, the backs of the cuffs a little frayed.

Flight not an option, Peanut looked like he could collapse, like bad luck had picked him to drag a cotton sack five miles long.

He pulled himself together, found a heavy ornamental grin. "Shad Dupree." Not bad. "The hell you been? I was sayin to somebody th'other day: *the hell Dupree been?*"

Marty watched Dupree put on his bone-snapper face. He made a show of unveiling his eyes from behind black-lensed shades, taking his time with it. The eyes were good. Marty thought the whole package was good—your standard sports-book collector straight from the movies.

A big work van pulled in the vacant slot next to Marty, blocked his view of the limo and the two men.

The van driver opened his door and squeezed out, his door doing a job on the truck's door.

The driver, a skinny, shirtless construction guy with his hat on backwards, said, "Sorry."

Marty said, "Don't worry about it."

Marty put his head back and closed his eyes. Edy came on the eyelid show. Edy on beat with the White Stripes. Edy caressing Eddie's hand, impish grin for Marty and Dupree, her saying: *Gramps, I don't think your friends know what the fuck they're doing,* or *don't know what the fuck's going on* or something like that. Having fun with it.

He felt around for his cell phone, found it, held it in front of his face, opened his eyes. He shoved in a few numbers.

Anna said: "Margot residence." It came out almost a question in her Annie Mae voice.

Then: "Hello, Martin."

Then: "Yes. She is expectin your call, I believe. Let's find her."

Anna put the phone to her breast and went from the kitchen to Edy's room. She said, "It's him," no island in it now.

Edy was in the swivel chair at her work center, legs crossed, feet tucked away. She wasn't happy.

Eddie sat in a similar chair a few feet away. He wasn't happy.

In a light-tan silk shirt, linen pants in a little darker shade, the oil gone from the silver hair making it soft and fluffy, Eddie didn't look so old. It didn't hurt he had a decent set of choppers in, one that looked almost real. "Well, talk to him."

"I'm not into this."

Eddie bored into her with the ice-blue eyes. The eyes went to Anna. "You believe this shit? Pick this lot urchin up, teach her something, now she don't wanna play no more." The last came out mocking, a tone with a threat in it.

Anna put on a motherly face, phone still buried in her breast, said, "Edy, we're into the setup, we've got to play through with it. We're running out of money."

Edy stared at and through a screen saver running on a mummed monitor.

"Edy, honey."

"Don't call me Edy."

Anna deep breathed some patience. "Edy, talk to him." She pushed the phone at Edy.

Edy shook her head but unlocked her legs, letting her feet flop to the floor, and took the phone.

"Hi." Monotone even for one syllable.

Pause. Eye roll.

"Yes. I've got it." Still doing one tone.

Pause.

"Yes. Come on over." Same one tone.

Pause.

"Bye."

Edy pushed a button, sulked.

"What's wrong with you? Hey, I'm fuckin talkin to you, here." Eddie had drifted his line of sight to Anna, but was speaking to Edy.

"Hey." Eddie popped Edy on her shoulder with the back of his hand. She jumped, put a hand where the slap landed.

Anna said, "Eddie, stop it."

Eddie didn't appear to hear. "Hey, I'm fuckin talkin to you." He swiped at Edy again.

Edy swiveled in her chair, rose and right hooked Eddie in a single, quick move.

Eddie went over in the chair as much from his own defensive reflex as the blow.

Edy grabbed the glass globe of a lava lamp from its stand, gray eyes going almost green. The lamp globe came back. "I've told you to keep your hands off me, Eddie. You keep them off."

Anna's eyes sealed shut then opened. "Put it down, child. He'll keep his hands off you. He will or I'll cut his business off when he's asleep."

Eddie sat up, but on the floor still. "Jesus Christ. Leave me the fuck alone. Both of you." He rubbed his jaw, wriggled it around with his hand.

The globe relaxed; Edy said: "I'll do this—play these rubes—then I take my cut and leave. I'm done with this shit. I'm over it." She sat the globe back in its cradle. "I can't do this anymore. I don't even remember who I really am."

"You're either a player or a rube, sweet pea. I taught you that, I know I did. Help me up." Eddie put a hand at Edy.

"Fuck you, Eddie." She went for the door, stopped, turned, said, "I get my cut, I'm done."

"Yeah, yeah." Eddie flapped the ignored hand.

Anna turned to Edy. "When's he coming?"

"He's on his way. Why don't you two leave?"

Eddie: "Why? You gonna fuck him?"

"Eddie, hush." Anna shook a finger at Eddie still down on the floor.

"Yeah. I'm gonna fuck his brains out. Fuck him on your bed. Leave a wet spot."

"Christ. Stop it. I don't wanna hear that shit. Help me up, Anna." The hand came back up looking for Anna's attention now. It got none.

The women turned and walked out.

Eddie propped forearms on knees. "Goddam women—you don't fuck em they get pissed, you fuck em they get pissed." He shook his head. *What the hell was God thinking?*

[31]

THE VAN THAT had blocked the view backed out and the limo wasn't there.

A big guy with long hair and a beard, greasy pants and a good pose was looking like a car-towing fool. He was looking at Marty like Marty was Christmas dinner.

Marty slid over, fired the truck up and pointed it at Edy Margot's.

He thought about it. He wasn't even sure that was her last name. He'd ask when he got the chance.

Dupree had a little fun on Peanut's tab, Peanut looking like a deer in the headlights back at the 7-Eleven. Nervous small talk, tight-shoe chatter as Marty deemed it. Dupree leaning against the driver's door of the limo like he owned it, quiet, enjoying it more than he should.

Peanut eased up when he asked Dupree

if he was still working for Grady because Peanut heard he wasn't.

Dupree said no, but he needed to talk to Peanut about a dog and Peanut said he'd catch up with him later, he was pushed right now.

Dupree asked him had he squared up on the four large he owed Grady. Peanut said no but he was saving up. Dupree gave him a good low chuckle.

Peanut had grabbed the door handle, standing facing Dupree but off to the left a bit.

Peanut popped the door and Dupree's right hand was on Peanut's neck. Dupree's left came up with a cell phone, said, "Number three on speed dial, Peanut. Shady Grady's private line. I hit it? You're worth—let's see, I get ten and ten. Hmm. That's about eight hundred dollars, ain't it? You want me to push three?"

They had an understanding of where everybody was so they got in Peanut's long car to talk about that dog some.

"Look here, somethin I wondered when you lost that bet."

"Un-huh?" Peanut looked even tinier behind the wheel of the big car, privacy glass down and it going on forever back there behind them. "Hey, bust the head off a couple for us, blood."

Dupree twisted, handed a drippy malt beer across to Peanut.

"You had the money. How come you didn't pay Grady then?

Peanut put some gray cells on it. "I on't know, blood. Jes didn't seem right, me givin my mama's policy money to Grady's cracker ass."

"But it seemed all right to bet it, just not lose it? That what you sayin?"

"Aw, come on, dawg. That ain't how it is. You know it ain't."

"I ain't your dawg, Peanut, but you listen good while I tell you somethin, and you might end up makin up some on your debt." Dupree looked over, deadpanned Peanut. "Maybe even a little left over to put in the back of your underwear drawer. You interested?"

"I ain't nothin but ears over here."

"I just watched you just drop off a man with a funny hat at the Bohemian. Whatever you could share with me about him would tickle my generosity bone no limit. You dig?"

Maybe Peanut didn't dig. Not fast anyway. He nodded slowly. It reminded Dupree of one of those plastic dogs the Mexicans put in their back windows.

"I picked im up at the airport. Took im out to gloryland, back to the hotel. That's it, my man."

"You got future engagements with the gentleman?"

"Oh yeah." Peanut looked happy. "I'm pickin im up tomorrow evenin bout seven."

"Un-huh." Dupree got interested. "Where y'all goin?"

"I on't know. He say he gone repossess some equipment. Wanna know how much weight one a these bitches totes."

"Whatchu tell im?"

"Tole im maybe a ton. It oughta, you don't hit no railroad track nor no speed bumps too fast."

"But you don't know where he's thinkin of goin?"

"Naw. Mus be a ways. I'm scoopin im up at seven an seem like he want it to be dark by the time we get there. And he say full-up the tank." Peanut had a shrug that said he wasn't an atlas, he didn't know where they were going.

Dupree smiled anyway. "Peanut, you're alright."

Peanut got happy about being alright, killed his beer, asked for another. Dupree opened another beer and held it between two fingers; Peanut took it.

"Tell you what, Peanut, you just made a grand."

The good news worked on Peanut's Adam's apple.

"You wanna make three more just like it? Wash yourself clean with Grady?"

"Hell yeah. Whatchu need, blood?"

"You figure out where you're goin, you call me, tell me about it. You handle that for three big pieces of cheese?"

"Yeah, I reckon I could." Even dumb people can go wary. "What it is make where this man goin so expensive?"

"I tell you? I only give you two grand. Okay?"

"Naw. Naw. I'm awright. I jes like to know is all. Long as I ain't apt to hit no trouble."

"Nah, won't be trouble involved. Somebody wants to keep tabs on the man. Hired me to keep a notebook on his travels. For you hookin me up, I pass you on four of the big ten I'm gettin. Uh-oh, Peanut, I've fucked up and told you about it."

"Uh-un. I tole you I didn't care to know, now. You tole me on yo own volition."

Dupree twisted a cap off one for himself, tasted it. It made his face pucker. "Goddam, Peanut, that shit tastes like horse piss." Dupree put his window down.

Peanut said, "Uh-un, blood, don't throw it out. I'll drink it."

Dupree passed it over. Peanut seemed to drive okay with two malt beers cooling his balls.

"This thing got a bar?"

"Un-huh. Reach back behind you. They's some good Johnnie Walker Black in there. Where we goin, blood?"

"Holiday Motel by the airport." Dupree came around with the Walker bottle and a spotted glass. He polished the glass on his shirttail and poured himself a handful.

He sniffed. Another sniff under a suspicious brow. He tasted. Again. Said: "Peanut?"

"Yeah, Shad?"

"If that shit's Johnnie Walker Black, I'm Winnie Mandela."

Peanut sniggered over it a little.

"You been haulin girls in here?"

"Yeah. Why? You smell pussy?"

"Uh-un. I could smell vomit back there."

"They always vomit, don't they? Them white girls?"

"Seems like it."

Marty knocks on the door; Edy answers wearing a man's dress shirt, sleeves turned back a couple of turns. She wiggles a finger, he comes in, she leads him down the hall. Edy is barefoot and, from Marty's view, the shirt could be all she's wearing.

The bedroom is immaculate, the clutter probably hiding under beds or in closets or somewhere. A can light toned down to a murmur is the only light in the room but for the soft blue glow of monitors on the bench and a silly lava lamp sending luminous green blobs endlessly through a sea of red.

Edy sat in one of two swivel chairs and Marty knew the shirt was all she had on.

He used the other chair, worked on keeping his eyes on Edy's face.

Edy didn't help—she said, "The fiancée? She ditch you when you got sent up?"

Marty felt himself flush but believed it was more from the surprise tactic than anything. He smiled. "No. She ditched me when I got indicted."

"It surprise you?"

"No."

Edy grinned. "Her family was a big deal, huh?"

"In a small pond sort of way, yeah."

Edy nodded like she got it, stood and began working a mouse. Music came up slowly.

Marty recognized it as Iron and Wine, a nouveau-hillbilly outfit out of Miami. Said, "You do that with everybody you meet? Run their life up on a monitor?"

"No. Just people who interest me."

"Yeah?" Playing cool like Edy wasn't flat-out coming on to him.

"Yeah." Edy turned and faced Marty.

"I interest you? Or our business interests you?"

"You." Edy stepped over, straddled Marty's legs and sat on him. She put her hands on Marty's face, kissed him deeply, head tilted so she could get in there and feel it.

No one said anything for a while then Edy said, "How are those tastes developing, Marty Pell?"

"They're coming along."

"You been laid since you got out?"

Marty was smart enough to know the correct answer and the truth weren't always interchangeably applicable. He said: "No."

Edy went back in for another kiss, put herself into it.

When she came up for air, she said, "Put me on the bed and fuck me, you liar. I need to be bounced around, Pell."

Marty bounced her. A couple of times.

The second show ended slowly, soft and warm. They uncoupled and Edy withdrew to her side of the bed.

Marty lay there a bit, put a hand on her hip. She pushed it away and Marty pushed up on an elbow.

She was crying silently.

"Hey. What's this?"

Edy drew herself into a ball. "Get out of here, Pell. Your shit's on the bench. Get it and get out."

Marty sat up. He couldn't rotate this

Rubik's-Cube situation to a view that made sense so he said, "Okay."

As he slid across the bed a hand came back and grabbed his wrist. The grip was steel. He stopped.

"Pell, I'm sorry."

Marty nodded slowly, inadvertently looking down at his limp dick. "Don't worry about it. We'll work that part out. Good as the first part was, I'll work with you on the afterglow thing."

"That's not what I'm sorry about."

Marty nodded some more, looked at his sad unit some more. "You still want me to leave though, right?"

"Yes."

Marty stopped nodding, put on his clothes, grabbed a thick folder from the corner of the computer bench.

To his back, her back to Marty, Edy said, "Check out the farm."

"The farm?" Marty turned.

"Un-huh. He's trading pieces of real estate like a dime-store Donald but for that one property. A four-hundred-acre horse farm. Check it out."

"Okay." Marty's lips fretted, got out: "You okay?"

"Yeah, I've never been better. Marty?"

"Yeah?" Marty noticed he'd gone from being *Pell* to being *Marty*.

"I'm sorry."

Marty shut the door. He wanted to know what Edy was sorry for, but he just shut the door.

[32]

TONY WAYNE'S MIDDLE garage door grunted, shuddered and hid in the ceiling. A four-stroke engine came to life inside the garage.

The engine got coaxed to the upper range of its RPM capabilities and Toy fired from the opening, front wheel of a dirt bike unemployed under him.

He wore loose brown pants and a full-face helmet, black with little yellow smiley-skulls pasted on it. That was it. No shoes, no shirt, no serviceable signs of intelligent life inside the helmet.

Toy let the bike eat the asphalt, unbaffled exhaust pipes bragging, knobby tires singing against the street.

A few turns and shortcuts, Toy zipped along the sidewalk past the guard shack. The guard stood and shouted at the glass. Toy couldn't have heard if the guy'd had a bullhorn, and the guard looked like he'd had dealings with Toy before. He sat again.

Maybe thirty seconds: another scooter. This one a sleek rice-grinder, the driver lying forward in its seating. Another full-face helmet, the rider in black and yellow leather bike gear. His bike was noisy like an owl's wing. The guard never looked up from his fair and balanced news show.

Stanley Woo braked hard at the highway, saw the nearly naked kid on the dirt dauber hammering hell down the road. He gave the kid a half-mile or better and turned the crotch rocket loose.

A buck forty, Stanley clutched and coasted while the dirt bike swung right, in the direction of the interstate. Stanley tucked himself in about a half mile behind again.

The way the kid treated the interstate—in and out, jump a few cars in the breakdown lane now and again—begged the question why the foolish fuck even bothered with the helmet.

Stanley stayed smooth, sliding between cars in adjoining lanes occasionally, but just hammering the hollows in traffic pretty much kept Toy in sight.

A few miles, Toy took a spiraling exit into downtown.

Stanley lost him momentarily, then

listened, had Toy again. Had him all the way around to the Grand Bohemian Hotel.

The kid tossed the scooter in an alleyway half a block down.

Another half block, Stanley found some legal parking and fed a sentinel meter a few coins. A hotfooted half-trot got a glimpse of bareback Toy as Toy disappeared into the hotel.

Stanley got to watch the staff watch Toy. Shirtless, shoeless, helmet in hand, pants low enough to show signs of cracking. Only black eye goo today—Marilyn Manson-style. Dark hair hanging like cables across his brow.

Toy tossed them a look. Nobody seemed to have a problem so Toy took the lobby in. He processed the data, changed tack and moved to a door that led to a pool, the pool not much bigger than Manhattan.

After Toy, Stanley could have been Count Dracula and not garnered a glance from the registration desk. He moved to a gift shop that looked over the pool.

Tourist kids screamed and contorted sunburned faces, tourist moms honked like geese at their red-cheeked goslings, tourist dads checked out other dads' teenaged daughters' asses. Seemed all was well in Less-Than-Real-World.

Stanley browsed the gift shop wares like he gave a shit, like he might have a brain flop and entertain the idea of actually buying something.

Sports shit: alligators, Indians, aquatic mammals. Inclement weather was represented. Mouse shit—all you want. Some Grandma-went-to-LaLaland-got-pumped-by-a-Dominican-busboy-and-all-I-got-is-this-lou sy-T-shirt T-shirts.

Popular paperbacks, popular novels and self-help books. Magazines, crossword puzzle books, gossip rags.

Stanley passed on the exciting-as-oatmeal books and drifted to a T-shirt rack at the poolside of the shop. A scan didn't produce Toy at first glance, then there he was.

At a table with a couple. Scratch couple. Make it a man and a woman. Toy smooched the man smack on puckered lips. He looked at the woman like she was a sack of garbage. She wasn't.

Babe. Long and lean, blonde and fair. Maybe thirty. She was lounged out in a pool chair, her bathing suit looked like an Ace bandage across medium breasts. Same material below but less of it. Brown sandals and a brown net bag finished it out.

The man was older—twice at least. Silver hair, silver trunks, silver thong sandals, silver beach bag of the same material as the swim trunks. Hair went across his chest and over his shoulders like snowfall, like a silverback.

He was a serious man, guarded even through his obvious joy at Toy's arrival. He pulled out the chair next to him and Toy slouched, bouncing the helmet on the pool deck as he sat.

Stanley had a clear shot on the man and woman. The man's attention was on Toy. The woman's attention was on the man. She wasn't as happy about things as the man.

Stanley couldn't see Toy's face after he sat but figured Toy was pretty much stuck on pout. He was a hustler who worked it well, knew his stuff.

Some conversation, the woman leaned on the table and spoke to the man. Toy interjected and the woman put the displeasured face on Toy.

She wagged a warning finger at Toy, said something and rose. She wrapped a loose garment of pure white around her and picked up her bag.

She spoke to the man, who had a hand out now, palm up. Toy interrupted again and the woman gave him a four-beat stare, spun and moved away.

The woman came to the lobby door. A man in a blue button-down oxford-cloth shirt and relaxed jeans over good tan loafers held the door for her; she smiled for him.

Stanley remembered him standing across the glass hall from the gift shop in the coffee shop. Watching, as Stanley was, out the window and at the pool.

Stanley remembered because the guy had on a pair of Wayfarers just like a pair Stanley had lost recently—the ones like the Blues Brothers had worn. And there he was, a doorman now.

The woman moved to the center of the lobby, past the registration desk and on toward the elevator bank and here was the guy in the Wayfarers again, coming back in.

The guy walked out into the lobby, did a good Jack Nicholson take-it-all-in.

The woman was going in the elevator; the man moved toward the front exit. Elevator door closes, the man changes course, goes to the elevator bank, watches the floors count off on the elevator the woman took.

Stanley couldn't see that far, but at about halfway, the light stopped. A few seconds the numbers began to illuminate in descending order. The man seemed satisfied. He turned and came back toward Stanley.

Shit. He was coming in the gift shop. Stanley changed his mind about the bland bestsellers, stuck his face in one with a blithe cover. The guy breezed past Stanley close enough for Stanley to smell the Old Spice and then the guy went T-shirt shopping at the same rack Stanley had perused, the one by the window over the pool.

Stanley made the traffic hole in the glass and went across the lobby tiles, head down.

Head down, he didn't see Gretchen Gertz watching him use the exit. Didn't see her at the stairwell in a jogging outfit the color of twilight. Didn't see her turn and move quietly to a view of the gift shop. He didn't see her watch Tommy Zellwood with a smile in the game blue eyes.

[33]

THE RED BUBBLE on the phone was winking for attention. Marty followed the instructions and got Dupree's voice times four, Stanley Woo's once.

Marty cradled the receiver, grabbed the folder he got from Edy, walked next door and knocked. Knocked twice more.

Dupree answered sleep drunk. Dark socks, silk boxers that were as big as boxing trunks, a thin undershirt, the kind with the straps like old men wear. "The fuck you been?"

"Good to see you too."

Dupree moved over and Marty used the space. Dupree clicked the door shut, said, "Stanley Woo's goin fuckin crazy lookin for your ass."

"Yeah? He wasn't the one left four messages on my machine. You think you don't leave four messages, I might forget you?"

"Fuck you, bread. Whatchu got?"

"Tony Wayne's life reduced to an inch, inch and a quarter."

"You look at it? All the time you had?"

"No."

"Un-huh. Eddie and the housekeeper gone?"

"Un-huh."

"I see. You too busy lookin at that fuzzy thing between Eddie's grandbaby's legs?"

Marty shrugged. "You jealous? If I *was* looking? You are, then we're spending way too much time together."

"May be some truth in the part about *too much time*. You want me to look at the man's paper, interpret what's in there for you?"

"Absolutely."

Marty handed the folder over and Dupree took it to a blonde desk and dealt out some pages. "Hand me those eyeglasses on the table."

Marty picked up a pair of wire-rimmed glasses. "You wear glasses, cuz?"

Dupree paused to look peeved and take the specs from Marty. He wrapped them around his head.

Once on, he looked at Marty. "Go ahead on. You got something to say so say it, get it outta your system."

Marty pointed at the stack. "Nah, I'm good. Go ahead."

Dupree looked at Marty over the specs, went back at the papers, dealing a sheet onto this pile or that. He said *un-huh* a couple of times, went through it all a couple more times, segregated and integrated some more, sat back.

"The girl's good."

Marty agreed silently. Good as hell. Fucking fine.

"Looks like he's moved off a few hundred pounds, hard to tell the way he shuffles shit around. Motherfucker picks up real estate and dumps it like he's playin Old Maid. And he ain't done bad either." Dupree nodded his head once. "Not bad at all considering the condition of the market."

"Yeah? Good for Tony. What'd Stanley say?"

"Oh. He says there's a woman hangin with the plaid hat looks like a supermodel."

Marty's face went funny.

Dupree said, "Stanley followed Boy-Toy to the hotel. Him and the hat had em a kiss or two."

"That's interesting. Maybe Toy's got wandering eyes. Maybe Tony's getting dry gulched." Marty thought some. "That doesn't necessarily complicate things. The hat gets it from Tony, we take it from him."

"Well, this complicates things. Stanley says there's somebody else watchin too."

It caught Marty cold, played a finger up his spine like it was a xylophone. "Who?"

"Goddam, cuz, I don't reckon Stanley recognized him."

"Shit." Marty put a hand on his jaw, spun 360. "The cops?"

"Good guess. It wasn't fat boy. I asked Stanley. This guy's older."

"You call Eddie? Tell him?"

"Why? You're over there and I can't get you, why'm I gonna call him?"

Marty said *shit* again.

"You interested in what Peanut told me?"

Marty was interested, but he was equally interested in this other watcher. "Good news or bad news?"

"Compared to what?"

"Stanley's piece."

"Good. I guess good. Peanut's gonna pick the man up about seven tomorrow evenin." Nice smile to go with it.

"Yeah? Why's that good?"

"Peanut says the man wants to go repossess some equipment. Wanted to know how much weight Peanut's limo hauls."

"*Oh really?* What'd Peanut tell him it'd haul?"

"Maybe a ton."

"And the man said?"

"The man says *perfect fit*. Whadda you say?"

"I say *perfect fit.* You say Tony's moved how much?"

Dupree shuffled a stack, mumbled lips across each other. "He's got three transactions with a Hamburg outfit calls itself *Kimmel Diversity Group*, all identical. I expect this Kimmel Group would be our buddy in the hat. Let's see. It's in marks here. That'd be . . . ." Some ciphering, then, "Totaled, I'd say about eight, eight and a half mil, maybe less. You understand he's gotta be paying these Kimmel people a pretty persuasion fee?"

"Yeah. So he's probably slipping it out a hundred pounds at the shot, huh?"

Dupree nodded a shrug. "Close. The bars go twenty-seven and a half pounds, so I'd say he's doing four a shot. So what did we get for our money besides we *think* there's maybe twelve hundred pounds layin about somewhere?" Dupree lost the glasses. "Cause, unless you got eight, nine thousand dollars' worth a pussy, we overpaid considerably."

Marty sat on a smile, only his eyes giving it up. "Check for Old Maids. See what looks funny about a horse farm."

Dupree didn't ask, he just picked up a pile. Search. Find. Re-search. Again. A positive nod. "The girl's good. She found the Old Maid."

"What is it?"

"You don't know?"

"No. Got clued is all."

"Like I say, the man plays with real estate like he's tradin Beanie Babies. Buy a piece, sell a piece—hot-potato tradin style." Dupree nodded. "Not this one piece. Bought it, kept it. No animals, no nothin—it ain't a workin farm."

"How do you know that?"

"No agriculture exemption. If he had a couple a cows like the theme parks keep on the land they got out behind em, he doesn't pay tax."

"So whatchu think? About this farm?"

"I'd say it's where we're goin tomorrow night, blood."

"Yeah, I do too. I wanna go look at it. We need to call a meet, get a playbook together, cuz."

"Make the call." Dupree pointed at the phone.

Marty called. He spoke to Eddie softly for a few minutes, filling him in about new players, then asked for Edy.

It got Dupree's attention and Marty could tell he put his ears in Marty's vicinity but Marty wouldn't look over.

"Hey. You gonna make it tonight?"

Pause, smile.

"Cool. See you in a bit."

Pause.

"Yeah. See you." Marty cradled the phone, sat and looked at nothing.

"You in love, Romeo?"

"Love? What's love?"

Dupree studied Marty through the granny glasses a bit then grunted out: "Un-huh."

[34]

TOMMY ZELLWOOD BIT one off the neck of the bottle and put it back in the paper bag. Bones was headed this way to spell him, let Zellwood run by the queer's house and see all's well over there. Then he'd go by the hotel, clean up, eat and sit around his room some more, make his back even stiffer.

Maybe he should leave Bones with it, go introduce himself to the woman in the Jag. Tell her she needed to walk off, not get hurt here. Be chivalrous as hell about it. Ask her to some dinner and some whatever.

Not bad thoughts then, speak of the mean old devil, there she was.

Zellwood didn't see her Jag pull in and park, but she was walking to the stairs, bold as daylight. Sheer black sheath, black stilettos. Less was more. Less was everything.

She used the stair, moved to Dupree's

door and knocked. Zellwood found Milky's binoculars on the seat and focused.

The door opened. Dupree stood in the gap, nice long silk robe, drink in one hand, the other behind the door.

The woman must have spoken: Zellwood lip-read Dupree saying, *what*, to her.

Next, Dupree smiled, nodded some then shook his head some.

The woman used her hands to indicate something about her body. Dupree shrugged, wagged his head, sipped his drink.

The woman shrugged, grabbed the hem of the dress and peeled it off. She wore only the black fuck-me pumps now. Zellwood watched and didn't know how it made him feel.

Maybe he couldn't feel anymore. Maybe he was too far-gone already. *Tell yourself: Retirement, Tommy.*

"My, my," was all Dupree could get out. He had way better lines, but, goddam, this was one to tell the grandbabies about.

"Are you satisfied that I am harmless?" Gretchen didn't seem to mind the way Dupree was looking at her.

"Mama, there's nothin harmless about you."

"You are going to make me stand out here naked in the cold?"

"It's colder in here than outside."

Gretchen tossed the dress behind her, over the balcony. "Would hopelessly naked suffice?"

"God Almighty, woman. Whadda you want?"

"I want to make you a proposition."

"I thought that's what all this . . . " Dupree used the drink to point to Gretchen's nakedness, " . . . was. Come on in, *fraulein*, before you get us arrested."

Zellwood watched the doorway go from the nude woman's backside to a blue door. He absently set the spyglasses on the seat next to him.

To no one but a windshield he said, "This shit gets anymore tangled, I'm gonna have to get me a speckled notebook like Milky had just to keep up with who's fucking who."

He fired up his car, pulled out.

Once on the street he called Bones, said *let's go get drunk.* Told Bones how everybody save Tony Wayne and Eddie Margot was fucking somebody else in the game.

Bones said maybe Zellwood should introduce Tony and Eddie, daisy chain up the whole crew.

Bones also said he'd met a couple of real cute Puerto Rican titty dancers who were coming by later—why not hang out, get some private dances, drink that Armagnac?

Bones was his man. Bones was a fucking psychic.

[35]

SHAD DUPREE HALF-SAT in bed propped on a couple of pillows, legs splayed under rumpled sheets. He was whipped. A two-hour nap today and he was still fried. Gretchen. Scary motherfucker.

He felt like he'd stood up next to the railroad tracks and let the train lurch by.

When he let her in, he'd kept the pistol he had hidden behind the door in hand. When he got okay, he dropped the mag, cleared the chamber and put it in the top of the closet where he hoped she couldn't reach.

Buck-ass naked, she still scared hell out of Dupree.

Like if he was fucking her from behind, her head might swivel around and eat his head while he was poling her.

But, goddam, dad, somebody had seen about her education down under the covers.

Goddam.

THE BIG NOTHING

Marty Pell sat in bed, head on the wall under a sad and pointless framed hotel print, knees up under rumpled sheets. Edy Margot was putting her wardrobe back together. Marty watched.

"Sorry for what?"

Edy finished situating a wide studded belt, looked up. "It took that long to sink in? You seem smarter than that."

Marty shrugged. "I thought maybe it'd come to me." He put some serious eyes on Edy.

She looked away.

"Look at me."

Edy wouldn't look.

"All I could think of, all that made any sense, wasn't nice stuff. You wanna ease my mind?" Marty watched her, said, "Edy, look at me."

Edy chased a clog down, rose on it, put the other foot in the other clog. She turned, grabbed her light hoodie. She still wouldn't look.

"Edy? You gonna say something?"

Edy was busy with the hoodie's zipper for a bit. Satisfied, she looked at Marty.

"We're not who you think we are. None of us. We're . . . jeez, we're high tech gypsies or something, Marty." A headshake, a shrug. "I'm going to say something and don't say a word. Okay?"

Marty nodded.

"Don't get taken, baby." She stood a moment in the doorway, looking off, out the door. "Bye."

She was gone.

Marty scratched his crotch, shook his head. On the opposite wall was a mirror. Marty's face was in the bottom of it, the bad motel art above him.

He told his reflected self, "Well that certainly cleared things up, eased *my* mind. How about yours?"

Haas Mueller lay sprawled under a rumpled sheet and light blanket. The boy lay across the bed, snoring softly. The door clicking and a light from the other room of the suite told him Gretchen was home.

Water ran and Haas drifted into sleep. He was a boy again and his friend, the village bully, an older boy named Ernst, was sitting on his young chest, holding Haas immobile. Haas could feel himself becoming aroused and Ernst saw his embarrassment.

Now he and Ernst were naked and Ernst reached back and took Haas's penis in a firm hand and manipulated it slowly.

A light came on and Haas moved his hand from his erect penis to shield his eyes.

"Oh, Gretchen, turn it off. Wait until morning. Whatever it is, please wait." Haas rolled his face into a pillow, rolled back with it over his face.

"Turn the light off, bitch." Toy seemed to be awake.

"Shut up, boy. Haas, tell the boy to get out."

"Gretchen, Gretchen, Gretchen. In the morning." Haas moved the pillow, squinted at the sudden light.

"Turn the light off, bitch." Toy was sitting, sleepy-eyed, sneering at Gretchen.

He screamed the five words.

Haas looked at Toy. "Please, Toy, no shouting."

"Tell the cunt to turn off the light."

Haas tsk-tsked Toy a little.

Toy found Mueller's pocket piece, a small caliber semi-automatic. Toy had been fascinated with it so Mueller unloaded it and allowed Toy to play with it. Mueller had forgotten until Toy pulled the pistol from under his pillow. "Turn-the-light-off-bitch."

Gretchen put a bland look on Toy, turned and walked out. When she returned she had her preferred piece of hardware, an efficient looking Browning semi-automatic. It was up and on Toy as she entered. She had attached an even more efficient looking silencer to its serious end.

Haas rolled his eyes. "Children, please." He picked up the clip that belonged to the gun Toy was brandishing and held it up to Gretchen. In his other hand was the pill from the chamber. "Gretchen, I may be jaded, but I'm not insane."

"Still I should shoot this urchin." Gretchen pushed the thumb-latch safety.

"No, Gretchen." Haas knew Gretchen. "Please."

Toy pulled the trigger, dropped pin on nothing.

Haas sat, palms out at Gretchen, the moment gestating rapidly. "Please, Gretchen, please."

Toy must have realized he was on the fence and it made his face go from lights-out to dim. He said, "I'm leaving."

Gretchen's chest rose and fell in cadence with the moment. Toy stood, grabbed his baggy pants, eyes on Gretchen all the while.

Eyes still on Gretchen, Toy stepped in his pants, buckled up. He found his helmet and stuck his head in it.

Toy paused at the door and, past the face-guard of the helmet, muffled out, "I'll get you, bitch." Nodded the helmet. "Wait and see I don't get you."

Haas said, "Please, Gretchen, love. I have so few pleasures at my age."

Gretchen let the door close on Toy. The gun relaxed its grip on her. It came down in anger.

"Because you are a jaded old pervert, I have to also do stupid things? Is this what we have become?"

Haas smiled, patted the bed beside him.

Gretchen sat heavily, full body pout going.

"This is what we have always been, child." His hand caressed her back tenderly, up to neck, then ears.

Gretchen dodged her head sideways. "Stop it, Dada." She laid the gun on the nightstand and snuggled under his arms. "Can I sleep with you tonight, Dada?" Playing an old game.

"Of course, child."

"May I keep my clothes on?"

"For a while, my child. Now hush and turn out the light."

Edy could feel Eddie waiting on her when she put her hand on the door from the garage. Knew he'd be sitting at the bar in the kitchen. Knew he'd be pissed.

She hesitated, took a deep one, blew it out slowly, noisily and pushed the door open.

No Eddie, but the feeling of him waiting still with her.

Only some shy under-cabinet LED lighting going in the kitchen. She dropped the dim lights and felt her way down the hall to her room and into the odd harsh crimson light from her lava lamp.

Edy closed the door and pressed the light. The lights came up and Eddie was on her. A punch to the face. A punch to her kidneys when she put her back to him. A kick in the tailbone when she went down.

The door sprung open and Anna was on Eddie like a banshee, clawing at his face, a gurgling noise in her throat.

Edy screamed, "Stop it. Stop it, goddammit."

Anna called off the dogs.

Eddie remained in a defensive pose.

Edy sat against the wall, balled up, arms around knees-up legs. She hid her face in the knees.

"Jesus, Anna, the hell's wrong with you? You think I'm in here rapin her?"

Anna didn't answer directly; she watched Eddie, breathed deeply, then said, levelly: "No, Eddie, I didn't. Because I think you know I'd kill you dead."

"Jesus. Don't forget or forgive, you two. Jesus."

"Shut up, Eddie. You alright, child?"

Edy looked up and nodded. Anna didn't see her—Anna was all eyes on Eddie.

"Answer me, child."

"Yes. I'm fine. I'm perfect."

"Eddie, you've got something to say, you

go ahead and say it. You don't have to beat the girl senseless to do so."

"Yeah, I got somethin to say. You don't go fuckin the mark like you was a couple of marsh hares. You fuck *with* him, you use what you got for the game. No freebies. No secrets, no pussy. What's so hard to understand about that?"

"Eddie, watch your language."

"Ha. Language? What does she care. Fucks the rube here. Goes to his hotel, fucks him some more. What'd you get for it?" The last to Edy.

Edy put her head down, mumbled into her knees, telling Eddie he didn't own the pussy.

"What? I can't hear you."

"Eddie, stop it."

Edy looked up, said, "I said you don't own the pussy," followed by a hard stare.

"Oh yeah? I own it all, toots." Eddie moved over to Edy.

Anna moved in on Eddie.

"I own you from the top of your head to the soles of your feet. All of you. Tits, ass, cunt and navel. I own it all. I took you off the streets, remember? You were sellin eight-dollar blowjobs and livin in a car in a junkyard. Remember?"

Eddie moved in aggressively; Anna clocked him with a ceramic lamp.

Eddie said *Jesus* a couple of times, holding his head like it might fall off and then he sat down abruptly on the floor.

"Get outta here, child. Go spend the night with the boy."

Edy stood, eyes on Eddie, mouth closed, anger heaving her chest.

"Go, child. I'll see you in the morning. Everything'll be fine."

"It won't ever be fine, Anna. Ever." Edy gripped the hoodie's cuffs in fists; her chest reflexed a shudder.

"I know, sweetheart. That's why you need to go."

Eddie tried to stand and did okay but tilted sideways and Anna caught him.

Edy heard Eddie ask Anna why she hit him.

Anna said she didn't. Said he hit himself.

Tony Wayne sat up in bed, feet propped on cushions, TV on a food channel rerun. A bag of Doritos was beside him, a plastic container of dip sat on his stomach.

The rat-tat of a motorcycle ripped the early morning in half. The bike revved unnecessarily a few times two floors below, then died.

Tony was up moving. God-damned Toy.

The door slammed hard downstairs and Tony folded his arms on the landing between floors and waited.

Toy came from the kitchen light, bounding up the stairs. He didn't see Tony until he was on him.

"Well. You decide to come home?"

Toy looked at Tony for a couple of seconds then slapped him hard across the face. Tony yelped a little surprise and winced.

"Toy." A shout.

Toy slapped him backhand, harder, and Tony could taste blood.

"Toy, stop it."

Toy grabbed Tony's face, fingers down in Tony's jowl, a thumb in Tony's mouth. Toy slapped Tony again with a free hand, spun them both around and kicked Tony down the stairs.

Toy looked back at Tony, motionless at the foot of the stairs. A few seconds, he turned and went up the stairs, got in the warm spot in Tony's bed and fell directly to sleep.

[36]

9:00 A.M.

"What you reckon you're worth?"

Odd question, odd hour after a long night—an odd night.

Edy leaves at eleven. Edy comes back about one.

No matter, Marty's awake when she knocks, sitting in bed watching himself in the mirror across the room, some sitcom flicking on the tube, stiff delivery and canned laughter putting up a good fight against a tough young silence.

Soft knock, search for pants, Edy's back, upset but uncooperative on how she got the smoker on the jaw. According to her, all she wants is to sleep. Good story but for the sniffs and silent tears on Marty's arm after she thinks he's asleep. Maybe two o'clock he is asleep.

Then eight o'clock, here comes Dupree,

knocking, being too loud out there. Dupree comes in, sits in silence, hair pulled back this morning, natural linen pants, peach silk T, two strands of brown wooden beads, the beads clicking as he looked from Marty, getting dressed, to the bathroom door. Behind the door the shower's going, some other shower noises coming through.

Dupree finally says he thought Edy had left last night. Marty asks how he knew she left. Dupree heard the door, heard her walk to the stair. Marty says: *yeah, but she came back.*

That's where they left it. Marty shot a toothbrush across his teeth at the vanity outside the bath door. He opened the door, tossed in a, see *you.*

He told Dupree he believed they needed to talk before the meet with Eddie. Dupree said he believed Marty was right.

The plan grew a sack full of gut grenades—coffee for Marty and soda for Dupree—at a fast-food drive-thru. Dupree landed the truck at a park by a lake. The lake had an interstate on concrete stilts running through its center. The interstate had cars creeping along it, regular people going regular places. Marty thought about it, thought it must be nice being regular, but he wasn't sure—he'd been irregular for a long time now.

Dupree chose a concrete table under a concrete roof. The table became a bench, the concrete bench a footrest. The view stretched out over the small lake, over ripples from a lone boat bobbing near the lake's center and away from the highway's pylons.

A guy was leaning over the port side, his hand on a girl of about ten or eleven who floated beside the boat. Dad's free hand was teaching: out flat, planing back and forth—probably in mimic of one of the skis floating nearby.

The girl pushed off, retrieved the skis and began the tough task of fixing them to her feet.

"Why're you asking?" Marty used a napkin on some grease, looked at Dupree's profile.

"What?" Marty hadn't answered the question when asked and looked like it had slipped Dupree's mind he'd asked it. "Oh. What're you worth. Yeah. What you reckon?"

"I reckon I'm wondering why you're asking."

Dupree shrugged. "I had a chance to sell your ass last night. Just wonderin, had I took the deal, what I shoulda got."

The boat started up and rope played out as it moved away from the floating girl.

"Bet she's cold."

Marty shrugged. "It's not that cold."

"I bet it is after you get wet, get up out of it."

The boat jolted, its front end rearing up, eggbeater on the stern roaring up.

The girl sprang from the water, moved okay for a bit, steadied up. She was doing something with a ski Marty couldn't see. The boat made a slow turn and headed back across the lake.

The girl dropped a ski, put the abandoned foot behind the other. All was fine for a bit, then the lone ski began a side-to-side swing, like a pendulum, increasing its arc until the girl hit the water headfirst.

Dad wheeled around, coasted beside the girl, grabbed her life vest. A little conversation, he lifted her by the vest and sat her on the motor cowl.

She seemed to be crying and he hugged her, hand stroking wet hair.

"She's got on a wetsuit." Marty uncapped coffee number two, blew at its surface, sipped, grimaced at the low pH.

Dupree had double napkins going at the grease. "She's got more'n that." Sip of coke. "She's got prime position. She's got daddy-baby status. You think she'll try again?"

Marty grinned, looked at the lake. He'd known Dupree six, seven years and never saw any of what the man was about until lately.

"Yeah, cuz, she'll try it again. He'll tell her she doesn't have to and she'll do it."

And she did. Eventually. The boat fired up and headed in. Then it came about and stopped. The girl bailed out; skis got tossed at her, then a rope.

"Who thought you were for sale?"

"The girl Stanley saw with the German yesterday."

Marty nodded.

The boat revved, the girl was up on two.

"She come see you last night? That who you were dancing with over there?"

"Yeah." Dupree took a peek in a bag. Chose another bag to put his hand in, retrieved a yellow paper-wrapped breakfast treat.

"How'd that come about?" Marty looked over. Dupree had more to say but he wanted Marty to work at it.

Dupree gave Marty a good grin. "You wouldn't fuckin believe it, cuz, if I told you."

"Try me."

Dupree tried him.

The story made Marty grin and wag head a good bit.

Somewhere in there, the girl behind the boat had dropped a ski and was on her second lap of the lake in the slalom mode.

Dad's fist pumped air. The girl tried to mime Dad's enthusiasm, almost spilled and got two-hand serious again.

When Dupree was done, the version literally more blow-by-blow than Marty felt he needed, Marty said: "She left naked? Just walked out into the night? Naked?"

"Naked as the truth, cuz."

"So what was the offer?"

Dupree shrugged. "Wasn't real specific. More like: I side with her and the German, I get to live and get a piece of change for my trouble. No set amounts. I don't side with them, I'm dead."

"This *banker* and this *girl*? They're gonna kill us over this?" Marty didn't believe it, didn't believe bankers and girls killed people. "Come on, Dupree."

Dupree tossed the remainder of the sandwich down for the local wildlife who had come to the picnic. Across the lake the boat hummed, the girl in tow.

"Well, here's the deal, blood. The man ain't really a banker. And the girl ain't just any girl. You dig?"

"No." Marty turned to Dupree.

Dupree looked over. "There was a lot of cute talk and some bullshit, but near as I can tell, this right here's what they do. Find somebody with somethin—particularly somethin like Tony's situation, somebody can't complain—and they take it."

The boat made a turn near the dock and the neophyte slalomer let the rope fly. She slid in on a spastic wobble, graceful balance unattainable, but stayed upright until lack of speed gave her back to gravity. She slowly sank, knees, hips, body, stopping only a few feet from the dock.

"Goddam, Dupree." All Marty could find beyond that was a headshake.

"Tell me, cuz. Makes you feel downright homegrown, doesn't it?"

The lake was glass again.

Marty slid off the table and went into a spastic stretch. A nice yawn accompanied. When it was done with him, he said, "You want the bad news or the good news?"

"You got good news?" Dupree glanced over.

"No, I was just getting your hopes up. I got only bad and worse."

"Ease me into the bad shit."

"I talked to Stanley. The guy he saw watching the hat and the chicken at the hotel? Sounds like the guy on the elevator. You recall?"

"Un-huh."

It didn't seem to move Dupree so Marty stuck more on: "He's government."

Dupree came out of his lake view revelry. "Yeah? Why do you say that?"

"The gold was going to Ghana. Some jungle boys involved."

"Yeah, I recall—I was there, remember?"

"When the Feds had me, grinding on me, one of them said the CIA wanted to get their hands on me. It was their shit and one of their guys took it real personally. They kept threatening to give me to him, to this guy who had the bone on. Now here's the kicker. How much you say we got that night? All totaled?"

"We always figured fifteen hundred pounds, but that was a guess. Was actually four ninety-five a crate. While you were gone with the second crate, I had time to count the third. Eighteen bars in the sawdust packing. Why?"

"The whole time the Feds are at me, they're talking about a ton. Nineteen hundred and some odd pounds. Four crates. They showed me the bill of lading." Marty backed up and sat on the table.

"Of course, you don't mention anything about how we only emptied three crates."

"Nooo. I didn't feel it'd help my fragile situation. So after my trial, while I'm waiting on transport, this new guy comes to see me. I'm in a room looking at a wall, he comes in, stands behind me, asks me questions. He's a smart-ass, knows it was me. Admired my being able to hide fifteen hundred pounds of gold under their noses like that. You heard me, right, Dupree?"

"Yeah. The man knows it ain't but fifteen, not a ton."

"He told me to go do my time, he'd be waiting when I got out."

Marty began putting wrappers and cups in bags. He did an overhand flip at a trashcan. Two points.

"That's been almost four years, cuz, and I couldn't say I'd remember the voice, but something about the guy in the elevator cued me. Then this guy turns up in the game? I got to wonder." Marty nodded. "Could be the same guy. Same odd soft southern accent in there somewhere."

The boatsman had his little craft trailered, plug out and was strapping down before Dupree spoke. He said: "What's he waitin on?"

The boat pushed an SUV out of the parking lot.

"Same as what we're doing: waiting for the stuff to float to the top, then take it."

"I'm missin somethin. You don't mean confiscate evidence, do you?"

"No."

"You think he's on his own time?"

"Yeah."

"Where do you get that?"

"He's talking to the back of my head, I ask him why he's taking it so personal."

"What's he say?"

"He said it happened on his watch. He had gotten off the plane in Fort Stewart up in Georgia. It was to wait on him in Jacksonville at the Naval Air Station but weather didn't allow it, couldn't land in Jax. He drove on to Orlando, jumped on the plane and took off for Ghana."

"Man seems to take his job serious."

"Un-huh. He said something else. He said I was fucking up his retirement. At the time, I'm thinking he means getting fired or busted down in grade or something. Now I don't think so. Think about it: this CIA guy didn't tell the other Feds shit about fifteen hundred pounds; let them think it was a ton like the paperwork said. I think he got off in Georgia with five hundred pounds—four ninety-five—stashed it and was gonna do the same in Jax and maybe Orlando. I think he was gonna take it for himself—his retirement fund—but the weather fucked him."

"Ummm," was all Dupree had for a bit.

A cop rode through the parking lot, tossed a wave. Marty tossed one back, like regular people do.

Another, *ummm*, then, "And that's the better news?"

"Yeah."

"Shit, I'm not sure I want the bad one."

"Eddie's setting up to fuck us." Marty turned his head to Dupree.

"That's news to you?" Dupree gave Marty some funny eyebrows.

"Call me chump."

"Chump? How about double-chump? The girl tell you?"

"She tried. Couple of times. How'd you know?"

Dupree shrugged. "Too much coincidence: him latchin on to you inside, showin up here, bein the expert at what we need. That and the fact I don't trust anybody I don't know. You dig?"

"Yeah, I dig."

Marty held up. Dupree was going to say it anyway. Let him go ahead.

"But him showing up here says something."

Dupree left Marty a hole. He put, *yeah, I know*, in it.

Dupree said it anyway. "You know Eddie had the girl run you and probably everybody else he met while he was in jail?"

"Yeah, I know—I was farmed, I'm a mark, I'm a patsy—kill me. Where are we, cuz? Right now?"

A blue heron shuddered in on heavy wings, pulled off an ungraceful, high-stepping approach and went straight for the trashcan. It speared Marty's ringer, opened the bag deftly and went through the debris one item at a time, tossing any stray morsel down the chute.

"We're way out our game here." Dupree

tossed a tidbit at the bird. The bird nabbed the morsel from the air.

"Yep. *Homegrown* somebody said."

"Everybody but me and you and Tony're professional."

"Yep."

"We can still walk off, Marty. No foul, no gain." Another tidbit for the bird, another perfect catch.

"Yep"

"Or we can see if we can't get around in front of everybody, seein we're the only ones know about everybody else."

"Yep."

"You're thinkin the last option, ain't you?" Tidbit—catch.

"Yeah."

"It won't be pretty."

"Nope."

"Maybe some shootin and such." Dupree tossed the rest of his sandwich and the heron all but grinned.

"I expect so."

"You ready?"

"Yeah."

"Un-huh."

Dupree studied the side of Marty's face long enough Marty asked: "What?"

"You think we can take this thing? The whole shebang?"

"Yeah. I look around, we're the good

guys—in a relative sort of way—and the good guys always win."

"Or die young."

"There's that too." Marty stuck out a fist. Dupree bumped it with one of his own.

[37]

TOMMY ZELLWOOD SAT on the small balcony, the morning sun friendly and warm already. The Times, the Journal and the local rag lay on a table with a room service tray of coffee and pastry.

He wore trench coat over underwear, a little bleary-eyed but pumping coffee in to flush last night out. A laptop was on his outstretched thighs. A picture of Gretchen was on the screen. A click, he was reading about her.

Jesus Christ, lady.

Gretchen Gertz was born twenty-eight years ago last October in Johannesburg. Mother died in childbirth. Twelve years later, Gretchen killed her father with a letter opener.

Seems the authorities thought he deserved it. Adopted at thirteen by Haas Mueller and his wife, Halla. Halla dies suspiciously two years later. Mueller and Gretchen are both suspects at different times. Then suspects together. Then they're gone for nearly five years from South Africa, no word on them.

Belgium, both picked up in an arms-for-poppies deal gone bad. Six Armenians executed in a bookstore basement. No mention why Mueller and Gretchen were only questioned, but that's all they got.

Algiers, the next year, Gretchen is arrested passing funny Deutschmarks—ones that had already been processed out by the German government to make way for the euro. Cut loose in days. Gone. Below the radar for a while.

New Chapter: Mueller and Gretchen chased out of Toronto two years ago—platinum bullion, dead Iranians, more dead Armenians.

Then the pair went quiet. Only a footnote. The note said: *There is a high probability Gretchen Gertz is an active hired assassin.*

The agency didn't say why they PS-ed that bit but it was something to keep in mind.

Zellwood fed the motel phone a few numbers.

A couple of purrs: "Bones. Got it? Some gal, huh?"

Pause to listen. And a smile.

"I don't believe I'd stick it in her mouth. Even if I got the chance."

Pause.

"I hear you."

Pause.

"Nah. Not yet."

Pause.

"Yeah, I know. Sooner or later, but she is nice to look at."

Pause.

"Un-huh, I agree. She is indeed the most deadly, but let her breathe on for a while. She improves the scenery considerably."

Pause, smile, head wag.

"Nah, Bones. Only thing about me getting soft is my dick. We take anybody out of the game, we may queer it—no pun intended."

Pause.

"Yeah. Let's just keep on watching. Nobody knows we're out here. Let's just let it happen, cut down on players at a couple of bottlenecks."

Pause.

"Yeah. They'll start thinning each other out here shortly. There ain't that much to go around, way things cost these days. Greed's the great motivator. We'll get to it soon enough. Hey, where you at?"

Pause.

"Breakfast in the park. Ain't that sweet? Y'all heading back to the motel?"

Pause.

"Huh. Must be cutting through to Margot's place." Zellwood killed the laptop; Gretchen's life evaporated. "Well, let me wash my ass and I'll see if the other team's holding court today too. We're closing in, Bones."

Pause.

"Yeah. Take it light."

Pause, grin.

"Yeah, you're right—nothing wrong with the dark stuff either."

Pause, more grins.

"Oh hell yeah. I believe that young lady could suck a bucketful of golf balls up a drink straw. Talents like that, makes you wonder why she wastes her time titty-dancing."

Pause.

"Get out. They make that kinda money dancing? No wonder I gave her a couple of hundred, she wasn't impressed. Hey, I appreciate it—she did hit the spot. I'll call you in a bit."

Zellwood racked the phone. He hit the power button on the laptop, hit another button and got Gretchen's face again. Another click it went full-screen Gretchen.

Zellwood loved the picture. A mug shot.

Slightly blackened eye, jail smock hanging from shoulders. Missing was the usual either surly or contrite expressions you most always find in mug shots. Replacing it was a foxy grin, like she was allowing herself to be arrested. Like it was all temporary. Like all she needed was a little audience with the head jailer.

No, not the slightest bit of fear or embarrassment or contrition. And certainly not surly. She wouldn't be able to do surly. Wouldn't have to resort to such base emotions.

She'd smile as she put the blade between your ribs. Infatuating goddam woman.

[38]

FOUR BALCONIES UP and four suites over, Gretchen and Haas sat at an identical table in identical chairs on a balcony identical in minutia to the one Zellwood was using. Even newspapers, pastry tray and coffee were duplicated.

Mueller wore the hotel comp robe. Neither length nor width was appropriate. The robe came well below Mueller's knees but barely transversed his broad chest. Gretchen wore a man's silk robe—mostly opened—sunglasses and nothing else. Legs propped in another chair, pastry poised at ready in a hand propped up on an elbow. A newspaper was four-folded in the other hand.

Mueller was describing a meal he'd experienced in Vienna last fall. The meal, though handsome, was utterly over spiced. The whole affair was a flop, and the garlic breathed Duke and Duchess didn't have a clue about the food or the flop.

"Maybe they didn't care, darling. I know I don't." The story had become muffled ya-yas about three courses back in Gretchen's mind.

Mueller dropped the news section he'd been speaking through and viewed Gretchen. "Oh my. The tiger between your legs didn't get satiated last evening? The swarte? He's not . . . " Haas held his hands about two feet apart.

Gretchen reached over and moved one of his hands to mark out another foot. "Long on body, short on spirit. I think he was distracted by my presence."

"No. You don't mean it. Well, dear, if you were left wanting, you should have mentioned it before I went to sleep."

"Please."

"What?"

"After the swarte?" She tossed a glance at Mueller's crotch. "You could only have annoyed me."

"That seems to have become part of our relationship: *annoyance*."

Mueller was looking for sympathy but he was at the wrong well. Gretchen had long ago quit nourishing such useless emotions.

"That's why we don't live together anymore, darling. You're inadequate yet jealous—a tragic combination to someone with my personal urges."

Mueller smiled kindly. "You are just trying to hurt me, Gretchen, because that is what you enjoy."

"No, Haas, trust me—it's true. Besides, you have your boys."

"Yes, but boys are only boys for so long."

Gretchen placed the ignored pastry back on the tray, rubbed the sugar off and flicked the fingers. She lowered the shades and put her gaze on Mueller. "What about this new boy?"

"I should have let you kill him last night, while I was spent of seed."

"Yes, you should have. I shouldn't have listened to your silly emotions. I should have shot the little bastard."

"Maybe—he's far too volatile."

"Don't forget unpredictable. Haas, the boy is insane. Look at his eyes. He is in there somewhere but barely engaged with the world."

Mueller's hands came out, palms up. "Then kill him."

"No. Now I am going to use him. We have to do something about the government agent. And the boy does seem to want to shoot someone."

"Gretchen, do you think the boy could take the agent?" Mueller's tone said he didn't believe it.

Gretchen shrugged. She didn't care who

took who. It was time to begin the winnowing.

[39]

CAN WE JUST call a truce? Till this thing's finished? Can we? The rubes'll be here soon. How about it?"

Anna shrugged. "Don't look at me, Eddie. Look at Edy."

He did. "How about it?"

Edy shrugged. "Just till this thing's finished. Then, like I say, I'm outta here."

"Fine. Good. Goodbye and good riddance in advance. Now let's get in character." Eddie turned to go. He wore a golf shirt and white tennis shorts, boat shoes, his good teeth. He didn't look so old again today.

Eddie halted his retreat, looked at Edy. "Just say yeah and nod, okay. Don't blow this. I need it. I lost my ass in the market while I was inside. I'm hurting, doll. I need this." Kind fatherly smile. "Okay, princess?"

"Stuff the cotton candy, Eddie. I'll play it like you say. Don't insult me though."

"Sure, princess. Thanks. Anna, you changin?"

"What? I don't look like your average Jamaican domestic in this old thing?" Anna had a long flowing gown, aqua with white hibiscus flowers on it.

Edy smiled, her first in this house in a while. "I'll miss you, Anna."

"I'll miss you too, child."

Soft looks. Sad-eyed ladies of the low-life.

Eddie tossed out, *Jesus*, and a hand flap, went down the hall to get into costume.

From down the hall, he shouted, "Don't use all the hot water either. I'm gonna need a shower after I trim my hair."

Edy looked at Anna. They harmonized on: "Good Luck."

Tony Wayne wasn't speaking this morning.

His lip was swollen and he made sure Toy got a good look at it. Put it out there when he brought Toy's bed tray with the required bowl of Nut 'n Honey plus two big spoonfuls of sugar in the milk. Walked around to the far side of the bed so Toy could get a good shot.

Toy didn't seem to care. He was grinning a nasty grin at Will Robinson. Will was ignoring the robot with dryer vent-pipe arms, the robot attempting to warn Will of the inevitable. Will was predictably getting duped by Dr. Smith into doing something that would surely result in lots of sparks and lots of squeals from Dr. Smith—girly little yelps of pain and fear.

Tony put the tray down and almost spoke, but it hurt when he was revving up his lips. He left Toy out in space with the Robinsons. It occurred to Tony on the way down the stair, on his way back to the kitchen, that Will Robinson might well have ended up married to either Dr. Smith or the robot. Mom had dad. Sister Judy, or whatever her name was, had the young, intelligent yet impulsive pilot. Who'd Will have? Who'd Dr. Smith have? Who'd the robot have? Who'd poor nubile Penny have?

Who'd Tony Wayne have?

Tony was pretty sure Toy was with Haas yesterday and half the night. He'd called the hotel until Haas answered about five. Haas said he'd been at the pool. Then the spa. Then he was getting a massage. Tony thought he heard Toy's giggle through the phone then and again later when Tony called back.

He trusted Haas with his business, his money, maybe even his life, but not with Toy. He loved Toy like he never loved before. He needed Toy, needed the youth and the vigor. The passion.

And Toy needed him, Tony believed. Toy was a child upstairs. A fine strong body, but imperfect. Seventh grade education. Learning disabled. Toy could neither read nor write. Socially promoted year after year. Product of the foster home.

Tony had gotten Toy in a deal on a property. A friend of Tony's had eyes bigger than his wallet but the friend had Toy. Tony and the friend struck a deal and Toy was sent to Tony's house. Toy was fifteen then. He was nearly eighteen now.

Tony decided having control of the goods put him in the driver's seat. He'd tell Haas to lay off Toy in no uncertain terms. Do it as soon as Haas got here, get it out of the way and off Tony's mind.

Okay: a few adjustments and the *casa* would be ready for company. Haas was on his way and bringing someone. A friend. A woman. Gretchen. Please.

Bringing a woman in on this kind of deal seemed a little tacky to Tony. Oh well, whatever.

Haas swung both ways. Tony knew that. Maybe she was a new distraction of the vagina-ed kind. Tony could only hope so.

He'd already set out wine, juice, fruit, cheese and sliced bread pieces. Ready but for the goodies in the fridge. Maybe he'd go up, forgive Toy. Play one of Toy's pretend games. Maybe the convict and the guard one. Tony kind of liked that one himself.

Tony hoped Toy wouldn't want to play *poochie*. Toy was a little scary when he had something around your neck and was behind you. He'd choked Tony unconscious twice playing *poochie*.

[40]

SO WE GONNA play this straight-face?"

"Yeah. I think that's best."

"You don't feel it's a good idea tellin Eddie should he try and fuck us, we're subject to beat him stupid?"

"I don't think it'd matter. He'd grin, play good old Eddie, try and fuck us anyway. This way we know something he doesn't."

Dupree braked at a light. He looked at Marty. "Surely we ain't still plannin on usin him to move the shit. We ain't, why're we playin with him like this?"

"Keep him from coming at us blindside. He flipped me once, Dupree. Last shot. I'm tired of being fucking odd man out. I'm gonna out-think these people. All of them. The light's green."

Dupree moved off. "Okay. How do you control him?"

Marty grinned. "Age."

"I need some explanation on that."

"How's he gonna move twelve hundred pounds of anything, Dupree? He's what? Seventy something? Nearly eighty? We just don't let him get too far outta view is all." Pause. "And we don't let him split us up. That'll be his next move: try to get one of us off somewhere so he can get the drop."

Dupree grinned, said, "Look at you talkin like a thug. We still got the government man."

"Stanley thinks he's a Mongolian bad ass. Let him tangle the guy up for a bit when it counts." Marty punctuated with a shrug.

"When's that?"

"When the Fed goes to take Eddie and the tow truck." Marty dropped it on Dupree like that, knowing Dupree would appreciate it.

"Tow truck?"

"Sure a tow truck. How else you gonna snatch and grab a limo full of gold?"

Dupree grinned up. "I have said it before and I say it again: Marty, my man, you are fuckin beautiful."

Annie Mae answered the beck with perfect island accent, black dress, pilgrim plain. Sturdy shoes. Starched apron today and no jewelry—very domestic.

"Allo, boys. Come in. The old sinner awaits you. Martin and Shadrack, isn't it?"

Yes'ms and nods went out from heads.

Annie Mae led them through the house, out French doors beyond the kitchen, down steps to a trellised patio, bougainvillea vines in perfect disarray overhead.

Eddie and Edy sat at a table under the trellis, Eddie in something like a morning suit, Edy in a long velvet dress about the color of dried blood. It made Marty think of Alice, Edy sitting there awkward legged in the dress and low heels. Eddie played the Mad Hatter, leaning on his cane, back straight, off-colored dentures filling his smile.

"Gentlemen. Sit."

The gentlemen sat. Marty looked at Edy. Edy looked at the tablecloth.

Some hey-hello-how-are-yous got tossed around, some coffee got poured, some breakfast items got turned down. Annie Mae drifted inside.

Eddie wanted to know: "So what'd your coon limo driver have to say."

It was out there. Eddie reacted poorly, looked less comfortable than Ed Sullivan for a moment. Edy laughed. Marty laughed. Eddie tried but it sounded more like a kid's machine gun noise: *hah-hah-hah-hah*. A staccato bray.

Dupree said, slowly, levelly, "I'm gonna let that pass on the benefit of the doubt that you don't think of me bein a *coon* cause you know and love me so."

Eddie put on a peacemaker, started to speak. Dupree held up an interrupting finger.

"Just don't do it again. You're a bigot, keep it to yourself. We straight on that?"

Eddie said, "Yeah. Come on, kid. Like you said, I don't even think a you as bein a . . . as bein colored."

Marty grinned, winked at Edy. She grinned back.

Dupree watched Eddie for a beat or two, let whatever he had to say go, said, "The *coon* said he and the man're goin trick or treatin this evenin about seven."

Eddie liked it. He said so. He asked, "You get to him? The colored driver?"

"We're meetin him in a bit, put this under his fender." Dupree pulled a small electronic device from a pocket, held it between fingers. "I got a reader with a GPS for it. Tell you within a couple a hundred feet where the sending unit is."

"He know you're puttin it there?"

Dupree shrugged. "Depends on how it goes talkin to his ass."

Eddie liked that too. He smiled kindly. "What else we got?"

Dupree looked at Marty. Edy looked at Marty. Eddie looked at Marty.

Marty looked at Eddie, then at Edy.

Marty shrugged. "Haven't heard a thing new."

Poker faces looked back.

Eddie said, "How about the paperwork? I hear somethin about a farm or somethin?"

"You might have. I'd say it's the spot." Marty was talking to Eddie but he was looking at Edy when he said it.

"Say again?" Eddie cocked an ear.

"The farm. It's it. It's where we're all going tonight."

"Yeah? Tell me about this farm." Eddie slopping it on, doing it straight-faced.

Marty stayed on the game despite the almost overwhelming urge to tell Eddie what a lying old sack of shit he'd turned out to be. He smiled at Eddie, said, "Thirty, thirty-five miles outside town. Tony's held on to it. Not up for offers. Everything else? He rolls quick. Not this piece."

Eddie played thinking about it. "Makes sense." More play thought. "Perfect setup." A nice convincing nod. "Edy, you find this?"

Edy didn't want to play. She just stared at Marty.

Marty said, "Yeah."

"Good work, kid. So, we gonna put all the chips on this one square?"

Marty shrugged. Dupree said, "Bet the farm."

Marty added: "We'll have the bug on the

limo; they head somewhere else, we'll know."

Eddie looked from Marty to Dupree, back to Marty. "What about they go in the other direction?"

"We're fucked if Peanut can't slow the show." Marty looked over, had eyebrows that said, *oh well.*

"Peanut's the stretch driver, right?"

"Yeah—the colored. If they move funny, he calls and we haul ass that way." Marty put a piece of a shrug on it, looked at Edy again, went back to the other game she and Marty were playing.

Eddie did a head dodge, loosened his collar. "I don't know, boys." More head wagging. It looked like it was an effort. "Maybe one of you sets up midway, the other goes with me to the farm."

Marty could feel Dupree looking at the side of his face. He kept his eyes on Edy's. "No, we all set up at the farm. Edy watches Tony's. I got it down like I want it to happen. We'll do it that way."

Eddie looked up; Marty looked over at him. A hammer blow of silence shook the trellis overhead.

Eddie's finger came up, his mouth opened to speak.

Marty said: "Eddie, it's decided. We do it my way. My shit, my way. You don't like it, get out, find yourself another . . . " Marty stopped his mouth. When he started it up again, it said, " . . . gig."

Eddie sat back. "Sure, kid. It's *your* gig."

"Yes it is. You wanna hear about it?"

"You ain't gonna have to make drawings, use the cups and the salt 'n pepper shakers to demonstrate or nothin, are you?" Eddie'd gotten friendly again—good old Eddie was back.

Marty let Eddie's eyes go, put them back on Edy. "No, Eddie. It's not that complex. More like a brick through a pawn shop window."

Eddie: "I like it already."

Edy put on a puck grin, shook her head so Marty grinned back.

[41]

TONY WAYNE'S FRONT STOOP:

"We seem to have interrupted a lovers' spat. Shame on you, Haas."

Gretchen Gertz wore roping boots, pressed jeans, a dark blue cord jacket over a designer blouse that was no more than a man's plain white T-shirt. Sunglasses and some eye shadow but very little makeup otherwise. Stunningly dressed down.

Mueller wore camp khakis with big pockets over hiking boots, a frail yellow collared cotton shirt and a light canvas jacket.

Together, they looked like slumming gentry, Euro-trash indulging ne'er-do-well country relatives in the colonies.

From within, the sounds of an argument bounced against the glass door: shouts, some breakage, doors slamming.

Gretchen reached over and pressed the

bell again. The chimes leaked onto a lull in the war upstairs. Silence.

Gretchen added more chimes to the break in the storm.

Toy shouted something unintelligible that sounded like it involved some stray spittle. A door slammed, slammed again.

Gretchen turned to Mueller. "Homewrecker."

Mueller put innocent hands out. "What can I say? Even I find me irresistible."

Tony Wayne's legs and torso appeared on the stairway. He adjusted his outfit on the second tier, one of those matching shirt and shorts sets. This one was green like a greenlight with white floral silhouettes on it. His feet slapped in big industrial looking sandals. He smiled when he saw his guests.

"What a reptile," through mannequin lips.

"Be nice, Gretch. He knows where the end of the rainbow lies."

"Watch me smile, Dada."

"Good girl."

Tony opened the door, added a deep bow, hand sweeping in invitation. "*Mi casa, su casa.* Come in."

Tony uncurled, snagged Gretchen's hand as she passed.

"Gretchen. Love that name." He must have—he said it again twice.

"Good to meet you too, Mr. Wayne."

"Hey, no misters here. Call me Tony." Tony gave her the eye. "Matter of fact, call me anything you like—just call me."

"She knows you are gay, Tony." Haas moved into the foyer.

Tony went limp like he might fall down. "Oh well." He flapped a gay hand. "My secret's out. Good to meet you, babe. Come along, people."

Tony turned away and Gretchen looked at Haas, placed a finger to a lip in reference to Tony's battle scar. Haas shrugged, put on innocent eyes, put out innocent hands.

Gretchen took in the décor on the way to the lanai. She'd seen worse in better houses. Unfortunately, Tony Wayne had spent a considerable amount of money on a decorator who couldn't give Tony the touch of class he was after. But who could?

Beyond the banality, a screened area held a round patio table with a crisp white cloth on it. On that was an assortment of caviar, nova salmon, truffles and appropriately expensive baked items to corral the goodies. The smell of chlorine from the pool swirled around uninvited.

All sat. Tony couldn't hide his exuberance. Gretchen could. Mueller looked amused.

"This is all so cloak-and-dagger. Like a

spy movie. A plane swoops out of the night sky to fly us out of the country." Tony's hands were busy this morning. "So who's the pilot?"

Mueller nodded in Gretchen's direction. "Flies like an angel."

Tony made double pistols with his hands. "So, you're a pilot?" His face didn't believe it.

Gretchen opened her purse, found cigarettes. She searched for a lighter, found it, used it. Said, "Yes."

"You gotta plane?"

Gretchen blew smoke over Tony's head. "Almost."

Tony looked at Mueller but got no clarification. "Okay." He gripped his little finger. "We go to the Bahamas." Another finger, the ring finger. "Then to Hamburg for business." Index finger. "To wherever my heart desires. I got it right?"

"Absolutely, my friend. How does the song go?" Mueller put his hands up in a dancer's pose, pumped them alternately and sang, "*Two tickets to paradise,*" badly.

Gretchen flipped ashes, rolled eyes. "Could we move along? How do I find this place in the dark?"

Tony searched his outlandish outfit, came up with a folded sheet of pastel paper. The paper unfolded to become a crude sketch.

"Here's the interstate highway. Right here it joins the Turnpike—the Turnpike goes northwest. Follow that to a big landfill on your right. Can't miss it. Looks like Apocalypse Now out there at night. You know Apocalypse Now?"

Gretchen blew smoke at Tony's pointing finger. "Yes."

"Okay. Big pinkish-orange sodium lights, covers maybe a thousand acres. That's your benchmark. A road runs along the west side. Follow that about three miles. You'll see a cell phone tower winking at you." Tony pointed, "That's us. The barn's lit but not too well. This piece here is the old exercise track, hard as a monk's dick."

Gretchen looked for an ashtray, made it obvious. Tony didn't catch it. She dropped the butt and ground it out. "And what am I using for lighting?"

"I'll have Toy go out and run a string of lights."

"Toy? That makes me feel better." Gretchen shook her head, folded Tony's sketch a couple of times and put it in her purse.

She stood, said, "I'll leave you gentlemen to your business. Shall I send the driver back?"

Haas waved a hand. "No. Have him pick you up this evening at the hotel then come here for us."

"Goodbye, darling. Goodbye, Tony Wayne."

"Don't rush off."

"I must. I have to go take a flying lesson."

It got Tony's attention. "Yeah?"

Gretchen put the blue shades on the blue eyes, said, "Yeah."

[42]

PEANUT COUNTED THE ten Franklins again, folded them tenderly and slipped them in the pocket of his shiny black jacket. "Preciate the business, gents."

Marty believed he meant it.

Dupree leaned against the back of the limo, Marty against the front of the truck. Peanut was between them.

The park was no more than a big smelly lake with a hundred-foot band of landscaping ringing it like a green lifesaver. Very downtown. Kids screamed at a playground. Bums and *au pairs* watched from park benches. Moms in Gap shit and Banana Republic shit yacked nonsense at each other. You could see a chicken hawk, a chicken or two, you looked close enough. Most anything, you looked close enough, looked just beyond the bright white light of civility—it was a city park, after all. It didn't look to Marty like anybody seemed to mind the place smelled like algae and duck shit. Too busy communing with this rare piece of manufactured nature in a metastatic sea of concrete.

"Peanut, you wanna make half that again, standing here? Before you ever drive off?" Marty waited for Peanut's monkey eyes to light up.

"Brother, you talkin my language now. You got them five Franklins on you, white bread?"

Dupree was rolling the dingus in his hand. "He doesn't, I do."

"Un-huh." Sometimes the dimmest lights cast the longest shadows. Peanut studied a bit, worked on a thumbnail with his rabbit teeth. Spit the debris, said, "Why this shit so important? I mean, you don't mind my axin."

Dupree looked at Marty. Marty shrugged, made a hand sign: he held his index finger about an inch and a half from the thumb.

Dupree said, "What you're askin's not why it's important, Peanut. What you're *askin* is how likely is it you might get skinned up. Am I right?"

Peanut shrugged up to Dupree like Dupree was the man, not another brother. "I reckon." Pause. "But it might help my determination I knowed what was what." Apologetic pause. "I mean, jes a little bit."

Dupree nodded. "The man you're haulin? The German? You took him to a house in Alaqua belongs to a fairy name of Tony Wayne."

Dupree held up, let Peanut catch up.

When Peanut caught up, he said, "Un-huh. Sure did now." Peanut grinned at Dupree. "Man got im a nekkid boy stay there."

"This Tony Wayne, out in Alaqua? He took somethin belongs to me and my partner here. You dig?"

Peanut dug but it took awhile. "And y'all gone take it back?"

Dupree said, "Un-huh. But that part? That's me and my partner here's business. We need you to help keep tabs, make a phone call or two. Shit, Peanut, look at yourself. You think I needed somebody could kick somebody's ass, I'd call you?"

Peanut grinned. "Nah. I on't reckon you would, blood. Say the man stole from y'all, huh?"

Dupree looked at Marty, said, "Yeah. Stole somethin valuable, Peanut. You in?"

He nodded, grinned to show some gold, said, "Good nough." Big animated, full-body nod. "Sure is. Man stole from you, you want it back, I'll sure help out. Sure will. Yeah, Shad, I'm in. What I need to do?"

Marty grinned at Dupree and Dupree

said, to Peanut, "Look over at the lake for half a minute."

Peanut's face became confusion. "Say what now?"

Dupree nodded at the lake, artificially colored an unlikely aqua-green to hide the brown stagnate hue it preferred. "Look right out there, count fifty for me."

Peanut shrugged, stepped up on the curb and began to count loudly but not too accurately after fifteen or so.

Dupree dropped to one knee, stuck a hand under Peanut's car.

Tommy Zellwood focused dead Milky's binoculars. Best thing about the boy, the nocs were.

The little limo dinge was ignoring his company, looked like. Uh-oh. Dupree down on a knee. Re-focus. A box? A locator. Ah yes, a fucking GPS. It went under the car, behind a leaf spring.

Zellwood had it. That nirvana moment when knowledge, experience and intuition collide and you got it.

Good, boys. Not bad. Lookit us wising up here, getting out in front of the game.

Zellwood traded nocs for cell, punched Bones up.

"Hey, boy."

Pause.

"Bones, when you're eighty and I'm a hundred, you'll still be a boy to me." Grin. "So fuck you—boy. Anything popping on your end?"

Pause.

"Yeah? She leave Mueller there?"

Pause.

"She ought not've left that poor innocent child alone with those two reprobates. They get done with the boy, he'll be able to sit on a fire hydrant and not touch the sides. Where'd Ms. Gertz get off to?"

Pause.

"Ah. Her little airport. The limo driver leave her there?"

Pause.

"Yeah, he just hooked up with my boys. Sounds like the lady's about to steal an airplane, doesn't it? My kinda woman. Listen, we're all positioning up here. Get ready."

Pause.

"This evening. I'd bet on it."

Pause.

"Yeah. Going first class. Stretch limo."

"Un-huh. I'd say about sundown the snakes'll get moving. I'm gonna let you stay on the boys. They got something up a sleeve."

Pause.

"They may surprise us, Bones. They keep coming on."

Pause. Laugh.

"Yeah, I know. They weren't even in the gate when the race started. Look at em now. Got their own guns and everything."

Pause.

"Huh?"

Pause.

Headshake Bones couldn't see. "I don't know, Bones. Never can tell. Some of em you don't think'll shoot'll fool you. That's the ones'll kill you. And these two, I mean you've seen em—homeboys. You ask either one of them why they took that shit in the first place they couldn't tell you, don't have a clue. It landed in front of them and they took it—can't say as I blame them. They'd had a half-assed plan they'd be in Monaco pulling cards out the shoe right now." Zellwood stopped himself, then said, "Listen to *me*—I had a plan involved counting on Florida weather. Point is, for what I call a couple of blue-collar opportunists, they ain't doing half bad. Hell, I'm almost proud of them."

Pause.

"You know you keep saying it so I keep thinking about it. Maybe I am getting soft, but I'm gonna see if I can get around it. I've grown kinda fond of em, in a couple-of-lost-puppies sorta way. Hell, I may even give them a piece, it's all over."

Pause.

"I'm not kidding. But I'll kill them both it comes to it. Won't think twice about it."

Pause.

Smile. "Nah. They live to talk, I'll give them a bone. Call it a bird-dog fee."

Pause.

Sigh. "Cause I'm tired of killing every motherfucker who steps in front of me, Bones. All right? I'm tired, I didn't sleep; the economy sucks, the world's fucked up hopeless." Pause. "Hey, sorry, partner. I'm tired of sitting in cars is all. Take it light."

[43]

PERFECT. The flight instructor was a cowboy. He should have put his hand under his dropping chin when he came in the office and saw Gretchen. Then somebody in the room would have believed the uninterested act that followed the clumsy entry.

Next, a thorough and serious inspection of the paperwork Gretchen had filled out. A smile and eyes up. And, "Ms. Kaiser? You ready for the wild blue yonder?"

Gretchen put, *I can barely wait*, out there honeyed up with plenty of accent.

The cowboy pilot nearly came in his slash-pocket slacks.

The lady who had initially taken Gretchen's paperwork turned, read a computer screen and looked weary, like she'd been witness to such nonsense before.

"Well, let's go. Two hours?"

"Yes, sir." An appropriate smile followed.

"Hey, make it Alvin."

The woman sat at a desk, and under the chair squeak she said, "Please."

Gretchen heard, but the pilot said, "Say what, Vernice?"

The phone rang and rescued the moment. The woman grabbed it, ignored him.

The pilot smiled, held out an indicative hand at a door and said, "Shall we?"

"Yes. Alvin." Gretchen winked at the woman and slid by.

The woman rolled her eyes, blew out her breath in a nearly imperceptible *pooh* sound. The pilot held the door.

The office appended a small hangar with a few planes in it. Most appeared to be in some stage of repair. Beyond, connected by concrete to an apron of more concrete, were three more aircraft. A small Piper that could have been in World War II, a slick bi-wing thing done in canary yellow with an angry, hands-on-his-hips Tweety Bird painted on the fuselage and a nice Beechcraft turbo job.

The cowboy went for the mosquito.

Gretchen said, "Could we take that one?"

The cowboy pilot stopped, turned. "That's a lot of airplane for a beginner, little lady."

Gretchen shrugged. "It's just that when I was little, my father would take me flying. He had an airplane exactly like that I think. He used to let me fly it. Of course no take-offs or landings." Some coy stuff from blue eyes topped it. "It is a Beechcraft turbo-prop, correct?"

"Hey, you're already familiar with that particular aircraft, good. We ain't gonna make you take off and land today neither." The pilot put enough friendly assurance in it to take the edge off.

Gretchen looked thankful. "Oh, you are so kind. Thank you. I am more relaxed now." She smiled appreciative relief at the ass.

"Well, let's get this bird in the air."

They did. But first, a little close contact gauge instruction. Seat belt buckle demonstration, on Gretchen of course. Then a power lift to the clouds, the cowboy pilot showing Gretchen his stuff. She expected him to flip a lever and start making contrail hearts in the sky, put little arrows through them.

He was pathetic. They weren't airborne two minutes and he asked her to dinner and a show. Used that word: *show*. He meant the cinema, Gretchen assumed.

Where his hand lay on the controls, a wedding band was winking. "Will your wife be joining us?"

The pilot watched the horizon for a full minute before saying; "You know, I figured you saw the ring and I was going to tell you how my wife died in a car wreck and I haven't been able to take the ring off yet."

"Do you use that often or did you read it in a magazine?"

He shrugged. "I've used it."

"Much luck?"

"Some."

"So is your wife joining us?"

"No."

"What time?"

"Seven sound good?"

"Sorry, I am busy at seven."

The pilot looked ill. "Eight?"

"No."

"Nine?"

"Sure. Could we go northwest for a bit, maybe look at a farm I am thinking of buying?"

"Lady, I'd go anywhere with you. You wanna try it?" The pilot pointed at the controls.

Gretchen took them past the landfill, up a road, flying low now, making the pilot nervous.

"Do I scare you, darling?"

"Nah. Ma'am, I flew choppers in Desert Storm. I been there."

"Me too."

The pilot looked perplexed. "You were in Desert Storm?"

"No, silly man. I've flown into Kuwait. And Iraq. Would you call that a horse farm, darling?"

Gretchen banked sharply allowing the pilot a view of the earth.

He stood on his nerves and Gretchen came out of the bank. "I'd say so. Someone's out in the pasture working."

"Yes? Does he have a shirt on?"

Gretchen had circled back and came in at an even lower bank. Toy put a hand up to shade his eyes, lights and wires strung out around him like mayhem.

The cowboy told her, no, the fellow didn't have a shirt on. Nor pants. He appeared to be buck-ass naked.

"Could we land?" Gretchen put a plea in her voice.

"We could. Way this bird handles I can put her down most anywhere. Should we? Probably not."

Gretchen pouted. "Why not?" Promising eyes. "Would you like to see the house? I hear it is furnished quite well." The promise lingered.

Alvin thought hard. "We didn't schedule a landing, but we're local. It wouldn't hurt. What about the little nekkid fellow?"

"He is the son of the real-estate agent."

"I guess a few minutes off the screen couldn't hurt. What the hey." Gretchen believed the pilot would have jumped out of the plane if necessary.

"Yes. What the hey."

Alvin took the controls and put the plane down on some hardpack, shut the engines down.

Toy hadn't moved. Mouth a little open, blank, like he wasn't really sure he was seeing a plane landing.

"Do not mind the boy, Alvin. He seems quite dim. And rude."

The pilot had no response, so he opened the door and followed Gretchen out.

A faint light flickered in Toy's eyes. He remained immobile.

Gretchen, not speaking, led Alvin by Toy.

Alvin said, "How you doing?"

Toy grinned.

"We're going to check out the house. Watch my ride. Okay?" Alvin seemed to think something was funny too so he grinned.

Toy grinned back more.

A barn was off a neglected paddock. To one side of that sat a plain farmhouse, fresh paint but of older construction—most likely *country* as interpreted by Tony. More wood rail fence in need of some paint trickled off here and there. The scape was treeless and the nothing ran unfettered until it washed into the dirt mountain of the landfill.

Gretchen blazed a straight path to the front steps of the house.

Alvin padded along jubilantly behind—Gretchen hoped he was enjoying the view.

Toy turned, squinted at the retreating couple, watched them enter the house.

He ground his teeth until they made popping sounds.

The crisp report of a pistol round rang from the house. Another.

Toy dropped the anger, smiled a new smile he felt like he'd been saving for a long time. It made his face feel good, made his cheekbones feel hollow like the feeling good heroin gave him. Made him smile some more of the saved-up smile.

Check it out: the bitch comes out, the plane dude doesn't. Toy nods, says, *way cool*, under his breath like a whisper.

Toy stood in the sun, naked, sweat glistening, hair in dank clumps over one eye. A coyote grin going.

Gretchen thought he might put his head back and howl. As she approached, his eyes came viewable.

The eyes said the relationship had changed. Like they now shared some secret knowledge or maybe power.

"We will not be needing the lights. Drive me back now, please."

The cunning went away some from the black eyes. The grin stayed. He looked back at the house. Looked at Gretchen, back to the house.

Toy dropped the tangle of wires and started in the direction Gretchen had come.

"Hey. Where are you going?" Gretchen stopped and turned to Toy.

Toy accelerated the walk to a trot, dust coming up in the afternoon heat around his bare feet, bare everything.

"Hey." Gretchen considered killing Toy. She didn't and didn't know why—she'd never get a better chance. She let him trot off. Perhaps he was some Ayn Rand character, unattached, primal and selfish for his own sustenance and pleasure—a pure, uncomplicated thing on an impure, complex planet. Tony Wayne owned a fine piece of art and could only fellate it, nothing more. Gretchen found it sad in a poetic sort of way but would lose no sleep over it.

She turned back and walked to the barn where Toy had parked Tony's car, a new BMW convertible. The top was back, keys in the ignition.

Gretchen sat in the driver's seat and pulled a small Walther from her bag. She dropped the clip, found a few pills in a pocket and pressed two into the magazine to replace the ones spent on the pilot.

The clip went back in the handle, the pistol and remaining cartridges got stashed in pockets. She turned the key, shifted, drove over to the house, circling around to put the passenger door by the steps. She honked. Again.

Toy pushed through the screen door. He'd found his pants, loose brown things, and was jamming something in a pocket. He stamped his feet down into the pilot's cowboy boots. Down the steps, step over the closed car door onto the seat, slide down into a sitting position.

Gretchen didn't look over as she motored up and pulled away. She could feel Toy looking at her, knew if she looked over she would see the conspiratorial grin.

"Like the boots?"

My, Toy had become chatty.

"Love them. They are so you. You should get a cowboy outfit to match."

"Got one. Silk shirt, Mexican pants, leather chaps, uh, leather vest. I wear just the chaps and vest sometimes. And the hat. Big hat."

"Oh darling, chaps, ostrich skin boots and a hat? Haas and Tony will be fighting like schoolgirls, yes?"

"Yeah." A few moments of silence

competed with the wind. "They're old aren't they?"

More jerky silence. Gretchen's curiosity was peaked.

"How do you mean, darling?"

Toy shrugged. "Like old. Like their junk's all wrinkly."

Gretchen smiled unintentionally.

"It ain't funny."

Gretchen agreed and said so. "Are you tired of Tony?"

Toy shrugged, sulking down in the seat. "He's stupid. Comes up with stupid games to play. So sometimes I get mad and hurt him." Toy noticed something on a hand, worked the hand across his jeans.

"How do you think about Haas?"

Another shrug. "He's got good dope."

Gretchen smiled, grabbed a wayward wisp of hair from her mouth. "This is why you like Haas?" Gretchen was thinking of Haas's ego—his old and wrinkly ego.

Another shrug from Toy's side. "Yeah. But he's cheap with money."

"Yes he is, darling. With everyone. But, as you say, he has the dope." Gretchen thought: *whatever your addiction, Haas finds it, feeds it, milks it.* For her, it was these adventures full of lust and adrenaline and violence. She pitied people who had no sex in their violence, no violence in their sex. Such a dreadful waste of both.

Toy fussed around, ripe with something he wanted to say. Gretchen waited him out. They were nearly back to the city limits before Toy got it organized.

"I wuz thinking."

"Yes?"

"Yeah. If you could get good dope like Haas, then . . . " Toy lost it in there somewhere.

Gretchen helped. "You are saying that you and I should team up?"

Hesitation. "Yeah, I guess. Like we take the stuff and go somewhere cool and live."

Gretchen was a little surprised, but it amused her. "You like to fuck girls, Toy?"

Toy put a stupid grin on, almost embarrassed. "Yeah, I like fuckin girls. I can fuck good."

"You want to fuck me, Toy, darling?"

More goofy grin, a bobbing nod.

"How much money do you want?"

"For what?" The grin dimmed away.

"For helping me take the gold."

"Is it gold?" Toy seemed truly amazed.

"Yes."

"Cool."

"How much do you want?"

Shrug. "I don't know. Some thousands."

Gretchen didn't understand. "Thousands?"

"Yeah. Some thousand-dollar bills. Maybe some hundreds too. If it's a lot, I want big bills."

Gretchen laughed, put a hand over her mouth. "Oh, Toy darling, you do not have a clue, do you?"

"About what?" He was dead serious.

A mile from her exit, Gretchen said, "Toy, I saw you put something in your pocket, then I saw you wipe blood off your hand. Okay? I do not know what you took off the man, but if you want to be on my team . . . " She looked at him warmly, like a big sister.

"Yeah?"

"You cannot go around with pieces of people in your pocket. You understand?"

"Yeah, I guess." Toy dug in a pocket, extracted a sock, a white athletic job with two red stripes at the top, fresh blood at the toe.

Toy wiped his bloody hand on the shaft of the sock and tossed it on the grass beside the freeway.

"Thank you. What was it?" Gretchen was thinking a finger, an ear, genitalia.

"His eyes." Matter of fact with it.

Gretchen gripped the wheel and took the exit ramp too fast. After a hard brake at the intersection, Gretchen said, "What if I let you have Tony?"

"Whadda you mean?"

"To do with him as you wish?"

Toy was still lost.

"Maybe you could use my pistol."

Toy: "Got one. A biggun."

"How does that sound?"

Toy liked the idea. "Cool. I'll do it when I get home."

"No, no, darling. We must wait until tonight. Once we get the gold loaded in the plane, then, my love, you may get your wish."

"Haas too?"

"No, darling. Haas is an old friend and an old lover. If someone must kill him, it should be me."

"Lemme know you change your mind. I wouldn't mind killing him too."

"I am sure you would not, darling. I have someone else for you also."

"Who?"

"A policeman."

"Cool. When?"

"Probably tonight as well, darling. Be patient."

Toy had his left middle finger in his navel, through his shirt, the finger traveling in a never ending circle, mad grin working overtime. He wobbled his head, said, "That back there, that was cool." Meaning the farm, the cowboy pilot. "I'm really wanting to try that. It's fun, isn't it? Feels good?"

"Toy darling, it's better than sex if you haven't done it in a while."

[44]

"A FARM, HUH? Way out?"

Pause.

"Ah hell, that ain't too far. You there now?"

Pause.

"No, me and the boys are at a tow yard, looks like. I'm across the street at a gas station."

From where Zellwood sat, he could see the tailgate of Dupree's truck beyond a hurricane fence. The fence had white aluminum slats in it. Through the gate, and even through the diagonal slatting, he could see cars. Not wrecks, just parked cars. All shapes, sizes and circa.

Bones had called back, told him about following Wayne's chicken-boy out to a farm. A plane lands, the panther gets out with a guy, takes him inside, leaves him. She and the boy leave in a sports car.

"Your end sure sounds like Mueller and

the lady are getting ready to go to the Carabee-an."

Pause.

"Whatever. Better not burn it though. Local gendarmes'll wrap you up in fifteen minutes out there. Forestry would call it in, then it's local yokel day at the fair. Tell you what though, that's the right idea, just fix it so it won't fly. Think you could handle that?"

Pause.

Laugh. "Yeah, I figured you could. Come on in. The whole deal's gone electric now—things popping. I'll stay on my boys till you get in, then I'll go to Wayne's, keep an eye on that crowd. Hey, hold on now."

Zellwood ignored the phone, watched a big wrecker rumble from the gates.

"Hey, Bones, let me call you back. My boys just traded mounts and took off."

Pause.

"No, they won't hardly lose me—they're in a fucking tow truck."

Pause.

"Swear to God. Big white and red job. You could tow a Greyhound with it."

Pause.

"What's that?"

Pause.

"Yeah, it'd grab up a stretch limo, I guess, no strain at all." Smile. "See what I'm saying, Bones? These boys ain't much more'n cavemen, but they ain't doing bad in a primitive, heavy-handed sorta way."

Pause.

"I hear you. Call me."

Zellwood folded the phone, grinned at what Bones had said. He said if they didn't watch it, Pell and Dupree could wind up wealthy men.

Not on my retirement fund, boys. Not a chance in hell.

"You're crazy, Marty."

"Listen to me. If the Fed was looking to bust us, he's there now. Everybody involved knows Tony's got the baloney. So if the guy was looking to score a bust, he'd grab Tony. Tony might let me and you beat him to death, but if the cops squeeze his light ass, he'll lawyer-up and start cutting more deals than a Jewish butcher on a Friday afternoon."

"So why doesn't he go get Tony?"

"Cause he'll have to kill Tony and everybody else involved if he wants to be quiet about things."

Dupree watched, said, "You notice fat boy ain't around anymore, don't you?"

Marty watched back. "Yeah, but the spook himself seems to be avoiding direct contact. We'll snatch and grab under his nose. I'm crazy for that?"

"That ain't the only reason you're lookin

crazy. You're also crazy for sendin Stanley out to tackle this guy."

"Best place to take him. There's one of him, several of us, you include both parties. He's waiting to enjoy some leveling out, waiting until one party owns the prize. Then, he takes it—uses his badge, whatever—and we don't ever see him again cause he's down in St. Croix spending our money."

"Why do you think he'll come after Eddie first?"

"It's not Eddie so much as the wrecker. He sees what's going down— sees Eddie drop us, go hide—he thinks about it, sees we're gonna disable the limo, tow it home. One of two things: either he'll drive the truck off, or he'll disable it so our play's fucked. But I don't think he'll disable the truck because he's got to haul the shit like anyone else would because he's thinking we're killing the limo for real. He'll take the bait."

Dupree must have been thinking about it some. He went quiet for a bit while the tow truck bounced along residential streets. Then: "What if Stanley shoots the motherfucker?"

"Then I hope Stanley kills him, he does shoot him."

"I don't know, cuz. I say we grab Tony, wrap him in a carpet, run with him. I believe I can squeeze his porky ass hard enough if I had the chance."

"You had the chance, remember? He kept fainting and you kept tossing water on his head. We're doing it my way, Dupree."

Marty knew Dupree looked over at him but he kept looking at the road ahead.

"Umm-hmm. And cause you did those three, four years, you makin all the decisions now?"

"Yeah." Flat out, no room for wobble. Marty turned to Dupree knowing Dupree would want to work it more.

Dupree's head bounced around in a nod, lips tight. "You know, I got thrown out. Wasn't any dishonorable discharge—a general dismissal, some shit. Marked my record all up. Seven years shore patrollin for the Navy and I couldn't get a job takin nine-one-one calls in Quincy. Or Yulee. And I tried."

"Where's Yulee?"

"Doesn't matter. And, you not knowin makes my point. You think I was enjoyin it, out there drivin one of Grady's yessir-mobiles?"

"I thought you enjoyed collecting." Marty was trying to lighten things up.

Dupree looked over, exasperated. "Yeah. Un-huh. I enjoy goin out, pushin some poor dumb-ass around, take out my hostilities on the wagerin public. Fuck you. I ain't kickin my karma around like that."

Marty never knew Dupree worried shit about his karma. "Look, cuz, I've been rolling this around, I can see how it goes—to an extent. I'm asking you: *roll with me.* I want everybody out in front of us. This way, we got everybody in sight . . . " Pause. " . . . but Eddie. Eddie we gotta watch."

Dupree's eyebrows jumped up and down once. "All right, cuz. So when you thinkin Eddie'll make his run?"

"He couldn't talk us into splitting up, so now he'll try and talk us into letting him take the stuff and meet up later."

"What about he may have an alternative plan?"

"I'm sure he does. That's why we don't let him get too far out ahead." Some noodling, then: "That'll be a good job for Stanley after he finishes up with the cop."

"What if the cop finishes up with Stanley instead?"

"Dupree, I'm plotting and planning as hard as my marginal brain allows, but I'll admit there's still gonna have to be a good shot or two of luck. But we're gonna do this, cuz, gonna win it all."

"I'm prayin to baby Jesus you're right, bread."

Some silence.

Then: "What about the girl?"

"What about her?"

Dupree looked like he was disappointed in Marty. "Come on, Marty. You're tryin to make my question sound dumb and you ain't hittin on shit."

"Yeah, I know."

Silence.

Then: "Baby, me and you still got our deal, right? Bust the dust straight down the middle, right?"

Marty looked over at Dupree, tried to put irritation on his face. "You know, you call me paranoid when I'm just doing my damndest to make sure we don't go to jail, and there you are, paranoid like a motherfucker. Damn, Dupree." Marty shook his head. "You don't owe Edy shit beyond your half of the ten grand she charged us. I decide to give her something else, that's my problem."

"Well, women got a way of doin shit to a man's head."

Marty was getting bored. "Dupree. Whatchu want? Want me to cross-my-heart-hope-to-die? I *like* the girl, okay? We're not picking out wedding sets, looking at Oneida patterns."

"I just had to ask is all. Let's drop it."

Marty looked across his eyes at Dupree. "Let's."

"You don't think it's better we just jack the limo once they got it loaded?"

"Yeah? How does that go?" Marty knew he was about to get some vague generalities. Dupree was good with paper and numbers, but micro-planning didn't really seem to house his wheel.

"We get the drop, appeal to their sensibilities."

"Dupree, the crazy-ass kid's gonna pull that revolver and start popping caps the moment he sees us, drop or not. I don't believe the punk's got any sensibilities."

"Why would they let the crazy motherfucker bring the piece. That shit ain't happenin."

"You willing to bet on that?"

Dupree conceded, wagged his head. "Un-uh."

"You willin to bet on Peanut faking up some car trouble, calling in a tow truck?"

"Yeah, I'd bet on that."

"A little practice, Eddie should be able to hook the limo. That's all we need. We take their wheels, they're stuck at the farm."

"When Eddie's hookin up, that'll be when it goes ugly."

"That's what I'm thinking."

"How's that go, cuz?" Dupree looked over again.

Marty deadpanned him. "That'll be break point I guess. You be able to do it? If it comes to ugly?"

"Baby, I believe it goes ugly, we won't be left with many choices."

Marty put on a funny grin, nodded. "Oh, it's gonna go ugly, cuz. Bet on it."

[45]

"I DON'T GIVE a shit, Anna. Pack what-the-fuck-ever. We're goin light, buyin new."

Anna—in their bedroom, two small cases open on the bed—was folding items, placing them in one of the bags. "When are you settling up with the girl?"

Eddie looked pained, sitting at a three-mirrored vanity in flannel shirt and old-guy khakis, unlaced work boots. He was whittling brows into disarray with a little pair of curved scissors. The hair was done, blued a bit and flat to his head. A hat advertising chewing tobacco sat ready. Redneck Eddie.

"Don't worry about it." Eyebrows done.

"I am worrying though. You *will* settle up with her, Eddie. I mean it."

Eddie stood, looked at himself, placed the hat on, slumped and humped into old Eddie, checked his reflection. Adjusted, checked the reflection. Satisfaction three sides. Unslumped, pop in fake hearing aids.

"I'll leave her somethin."

"A couple of hundred thousand, at least."

Eddie flapped a hand at Anna. "Stay low, the rubes are due. And don't forget my good teeth. These cheap sons-a-bitches are killing my gums."

The boys rolled into Eddie's, rappelled down from the tow truck and used the front doorbell.

Eddie answered dressed like Mr. Green Jeans. A little conversation on the stoop, a helping hand for Eddie into the truck, the tow truck rumbled out of sight, Dupree letting Eddie drive. Pell tugs pud for a half minute, the girl comes out of the garage in the big Mercedes, the two of them haul ass after the boys. Now that's interesting.

Tommy Zellwood turned back toward downtown, found his hotel.

He traded his car keys for a slip of paper at the valet kiosk, went up the elevator, to his room, then straight to the shower. Shave, Old Spice.

Khakis with a good crease, black microfiber jacket with a shirt that reminded you of the inside of an oyster shell. Pair of black Cole Hahn's and he was ready to go.

Stroll to the elevator, up to six, down the hall to six-eleven. Knock.

Gretchen. Cigarette in crossed arms. A tiny film of a shorty night jacket. Inhale. Exhale at Zellwood.

"I expected you sooner. Won't you come in?"

Toy came through the bedroom door and into the closet.

Tony and Haas looked at the closet then at each other.

"Hello, Toy." Tony leaned around, clutching the covers to his chest.

Toy came out with a cowboy outfit on a hanger. He held it up, admiring, displaying. The shirt was dangerously turquoise. It sported a mile or two of yellow piping and a yellow rose embroidered over each snap-button breast pocket, a bigger rose on the yoke. Yellow Vaquero pants with half the world's supply of silver buttons peeked out below the shirt. Some poor black and white piebald cow had given its all to be a vest and chaps. Alternating black and white tassels whished around when Toy swung in a circle.

"I'm gonna shower."

Tony did mock shock. "Is it Saturday already?"

Mueller punched his pillow up, placed it behind him, against the headboard, and leaned back. He smiled, said, "Very authentic outfit. Would you like for Tony and me to bathe you?"

"Nah. I'm gonna start fucking girls again."

"Ex-cuse me?" Tony was on the edge of the bed.

Mueller put a hand up massaging his eyes. "Have you been with Gretchen today?"

Toy smiled a big phony one, made a gun with his hand, dropped thumb on Tony, moved his sights to Mueller, dropped thumb again. He took the cowboy outfit and the smile into the bath.

Tony twisted around to Mueller, near nausea curling his face. "The hell was that?"

"I wouldn't pay much attention to it—youth and young manhood." Pause. "And, there is this: Gretchen could turn a dance troupe into a hockey team."

"Really? I don't see it."

"No, you wouldn't."

"And what was with the grin and the gun finger thing?"

"That, my friend, I would worry about."

"Why's that?"

"Did you hear what I said about Gretchen's particular sorcery?"

"You are asking me to betray my friends, yes?"

"Oh heavens no, sweetheart. I'm just

giving you a heads up on what's gonna happen. Nobody walks away tonight unless I say they do. So far nobody's on the guest list."

Gretchen pulled the thin fabric together. A useless gesture considering its density. The silky material sliding over her nipples excited them involuntarily.

Zellwood noticed—Gretchen noticed him noticing.

He excited her. A rugged man. No one thing remarkable but well constructed overall. Chiseled features. Yes, almost rugged. He would be a hard, demanding lover.

"What do I have to do to get on this guest list? I do not know your name."

"*Tommy*. Decide to live, sweetie. That's all. There'll be some confrontation. You're in a good position to help me out."

"Oh. So now I am to kill my friends?"

"Who's your friend? The chicken-hawk lawyer? The hustler kid? The guy you came to the party with? What is he, your step-dad?"

It caught her cold. Zellwood saw it, saw the pale skin flush ever so slightly.

The woman turned and walked across the room; Zellwood followed. She chose a large brocade chair, sat, gave Zellwood a bold, noble stare. "Where did you hear that?"

Zellwood sank uninvited into a cream-colored couch and smiled cordially. "So it's true?" He knew the truth but was enjoying having the woman off-balance.

The woman appeared to blow it off. "Once. He has been many things. Once." The blue eyes searched Zellwood's. "And what do I get as a reward? Besides my life?"

Zellwood appreciated the question. "What you want, precious? Run away with me? Be my kept woman? You don't look like the type."

"You do not look like the type to pass on a nice temporary interlude either. Are you?" No come-on in it, almost no sales pitch. Almost.

Damn, he liked her style. "There's more to it, but you wouldn't understand."

"Oh. There's someone else?"

"Un-huh. A big black guy named Dupree. I can't explain it but, see, I grew up in the South. The old South." Regretful shrug. "I saw you strip down and go in his room, that was about it." Zellwood wasn't even sure if he felt this way. He was pushing, seeing where it went—that's what he told himself.

A cool smile, a slight shrug of the delicate shoulders. "So you are a bigot? Why be ashamed? So am I."

"I believe we approach it differently, darlin."

More stare. "Your friend, the one in the car like mine. He is black, yes?"

Goddam, she was good. Bones wasn't much more than a rumor of a shadow and she'd made him.

Zellwood shrugged. "High yellow, I guess. I don't think of Bones that way."

"But you have fucked black women?"

"Oh, probably more than white woman. I've spent half my adult life in Africa."

"And that is excusable?"

Another shrug. "That's different."

"Why?"

Zellwood knew he was backing himself into an undefendable corner. "I don't know, sweetheart. It just is to me and I'm old-school selfish like that."

"What if I said I stripped because he was afraid of me—afraid I was armed—and we never had sex?"

Zellwood smiled some. "You go in naked, stay twenty-two minutes. Maybe I'm just professionally suspicious. And he should have been afraid." The twenty-two minutes was bullshit. He didn't have a clue how long she'd stayed.

The woman smiled, rose, peeled the cover back. "Are you afraid, Tommy? Does my nudity scare you too?"

"Not a bit, doll."

She went over, pushed Zellwood's legs

open and kneeled. She looked up, eyes bold, staring into his. "If I kill the swarte for you, will you take me with you?"

"We're not planning on taking your new airplane are we? Cause Bones fixed it so it won't fly so good."

"You bastard." The woman rose.

As she turned away, Zellwood slapped her ass hard enough to leave his handprint.

"Offer stands. And, yeah, you pop Dupree, I'll take you."

"You are a liar."

"That's true, lady, but you wanna run with me awhile, I'll take you."

She said, "Let me think about it," and rubbed the red spot on her ass.

Marty, and what he'd come to fondly refer to as his *crew*, had spent the afternoon in the parking lot of a vacant warehouse practicing snatch and grab. It had been tough on Dupree's patience working with Eddie on technique but Eddie got it close enough, and the bumpers were still on Edy's old Mercedes if only barely.

Edy left to go watch Tony's house. The tow crew lit out for the farm. Made decent time in spite of Eddie treating the turnpike's minimum-speed suggestion like it was the maximum. Four lanes fell to two and the farm came at them over a rise.

THE BIG NOTHING

The tow truck pulled onto the shoulder, off the grainy county road. Marty and Dupree, back in black, dropped down and walked up the road to the farm. They were vague silhouettes in the long-shadowed world of a dying sun.

Gears ground. Again. Dupree said, *Jesus*, under his breath. The truck jerked away into the coming dusk. Soon it was gone but for running lights across the top of its cab.

They knelt in unison for a predictably short wait.

The katydids, mummed by the tow truck's passing, fired off again then died in unison as a low green Jag eased by. The Jag slowed then went as the tow truck had.

"So far, so good." Dupree hiked an athletic bag to a more comfortable position as he stood.

"Yeah, well, keep your two luckiest fingers crossed though." Marty was up and moving.

"Stanley in place?"

"Yeah. You want, I can call, double check, be anal as you."

"Fuck you. Where're we squattin?"

"I don't know. Let's check it out, see what looks good."

What was in the house didn't look good: a man, pants down to his knees, oily hole parting the hair at the back of his head; the bridge of his nose gone; the eyes gone; one sock gone.

"Jesus fucking Christ, cuz, that's a soberin damn experience. Let's wait in the barn."

Marty agreed with Dupree but didn't have much to add beyond a nod and a shudder.

The mentioned barn was beyond a hundred feet of dusty paddock. An incandescent bulb, high watt but still inadequate, was mounted on a pole beside the house; it cast a harsh yellow glow against the fading dusk, but would light the place up well enough after dark—too well.

Almost there, Dupree keyed on something in the pasture beyond the barn, put his light on it. "Look here, bread." Dupree played the light down a plane's fuselage.

Marty squinted. "The tires are flat. Looks like somebody was gonna surprise somebody, fly off into the sunset, and somebody else decided to keep the game on the ground."

"Un-huh. Looks like our government boy's positioning up." Dupree pointed with his head, led Marty over to lean against the barn wall. "There may be somebody around here still." Almost a whisper.

Marty mimicked Dupree's head point, said, "What if somebody shoots through this very thin wall here." A thumb jerk to indicate the obvious.

Dupree said: "Just watch your ass and my ass."

"That I can do."

Dupree went around the doorway and found nobody and no bodies in the barn. No dead men with no eyes and their pants pulled down.

Only stalls with mangers of hay fed from a loft. The loft was at maybe half capacity on hay bales. At the far end, a set of big double doors like the ones at the front stood closed tight. To the left was a small room with a plywood door, probably a tack room.

Marty felt the wall up, found a switch and there was light. Tack room.

Dupree put the canvas bag on a crude handmade wooden chest, unzipped.

First up, a twelve-gauge auto with a folding stock. The stock got folded out. A box of double-0 for it.

Next, an AK-47 that needed a banana clip. It got the clip.

A handgun the size of Delaware.

"The hell's that, Dupree?"

"A Czechoslovakian ten-millimeter. I don't recall who makes it. Some synthetic shit. Feel it."

Marty felt it—it weighed nothing. "Mattel."

"What you want, cuz?"

Marty touched a hand to his waist. "I'll stick with my old Smith nine—I know it."

"Take one of the long guns. We don't need to leave anything layin around."

"That thing full auto?" Marty meant the AK.

Dupree looked insulted. "Of course it is."

"Legal full auto?"

"About as legal as a convicted felon's got a fifteen-shot Smith and Wesson down his dungarees."

Marty picked up the shotgun and the shells.

"Hang on, Marty." Dupree dug a couple of five-inch canisters from the bag. They were black with hexagonal ends. One end had a pin like a hand grenade "Here." He pushed them at Marty.

"The fuck's that?"

"Flash bang. When you toss it, please yell *fire in the hole*."

"It makes some noise, huh?"

"Dad, you don't put your hands on your ears and duck, the motherfucker'll stun you stupid for a few seconds."

"That's what I yell, huh? *Fire in the hole*? Could I yell something else? Like, maybe, *Geronimo*, something like that?"

"You're a funny motherfucker. Tell you what, bread, why don't you just get a microphone and crack em up with your razor sharp comedy? You get em down in the aisles laughin and I'll run up and grab the shit."

Marty wagged his head, grinned.

"Come on, man, be more serious here. This shit's the real deal now. Hold on."

Dupree dug again, came up with a couple of mini bottles of liquor. A J&B scotch and a Tanqueray gin. He passed the scotch to Marty.

Dupree twisted the cap; Marty followed.

The tiny bottle up in two fingers, Dupree said, "Me and you, cuz."

Marty bumped his own tiny plastic jug against Dupree's, said, "Me and you, cuz."

The J&B went down easy for mixed glen stuff. Marty smacked.

"I got a couple more, dawg, you want."

"Nah. I'm good." Marty walked to the tack room door, looked out. "Whatchu think, dad? Where's it going down?"

Dupree rustled behind Marty. "I wouldn't guess the house."

"No, me either. If so, the guy on the floor in there woulda probably met his fate out here."

"Who knows, Marty? These're some odd fuckin folks here. Maybe they don't mind seein a dead man in the hall."

Marty turned back, wagged his head. "The smell's enough to keep me out. Fresh brains."

"He shit himself too. You see that?"

"Goddam, Dupree, I was trying to get out

without stepping in the mess after one glance."

"You sayin in here?"

"If it goes down here, we're blessed. It goes down in the house, we're in the open for a bit getting there."

"With a light on us."

Marty fussed with it. "Yeah, let's try it here."

"Won't hurt to set up here first. We need to move, we got options."

"We actually agreeing here, cuz?" Marty grabbed the shotgun and shells. "Let's do it."

Dupree found himself a tall cabinet full of leather accoutrements for riding, tried it, liked it. "Where you goin, cuz?"

"Loft. If we do it here, I'm set. I can even cross over, either end. If I'm on the wrong side—and the chutes look climbable—I can ease down in one of those mangers, be on top of them."

"I wouldn't get too close. I believe my girl Gretchen'll shoot your ass just as quick as the crazy boy. Guarantee you one of those two did that deal in the house over there."

Marty shrugged. "I was planning on kinda watching everybody."

[46]

PEANUT FOUND TONY Wayne's circular drive and bent the elongated Lincoln around it.

Brake, hop out, quick step around, door open and: "Yes, ma'am, yes, ma'am," giving it to her with his Remus treatment.

He watched the woman do a good job of walking away. She tried the door. Locked.

She pressed the bell continuously until the boy came down the stairs. Look out, now. A cowboy tonight, big white Tom Mix hat, tacky black and white cowboy vest with chaps to match, good light colored boots with silver toe and heel things.

Peanut was beginning to think this beat the other night when the boy answered the door fresh-born naked. Then, while the woman checked him out, the boy turned and damn if he hadn't forgot his pants—pale, white ass hanging out there for the world.

Whoeey. Peanut got back in the car,

dialed Dupree. "Hey, blood, I had to go by and get the woman, bring her up here to Alaqua."

"What's the deal?"

"She tole me hang tight a few minutes, they was in a hurry."

"Keep me posted."

"Hey, Dupree?"

"Yeah?"

"These some funky-ass white people."

"They're all funky you get deep enough inside em. See you."

And Dupree was gone. Peanut checked the piece of fishing line that fed through the firewall and ran along the floor to his seat. It was there.

Earlier he had tied the far end of the line around a vacuum connection on the motor then ran the working end through a grommet in the firewall. A quick yank would disconnect the vacuum line and the idle would go erratic, then the motor would die with a hack and a wheeze. A couple of trial runs at home went like silk.

Plan Dupree'd put on him was to pull the fishing line as they turned into the farm road, limp in rough, go to idle, die. If he cranked it, it would run as long as he held the gas, but it would be rough. Then he'd call the number Dupree'd loaded into his cell phone's memory, a pretend tow company. Once the tow truck was hooked up, Peanut was to ease off on foot and get home as best he could. Dupree would drop the limo later.

Shit, four big fish? Plus five small ones? He could damn sure get his narrow black ass to the house on his own and get him back square with Shady Grady. Well, maybe give Grady a couple of G's to hold him, let Mr. Peanut enjoy a little of it. Seemed only right, now. Sure did.

Three houses up, on the curb, Edy was in the old Mercedes, the college station tossing out frail waves of new sounds. She punched a couple of buttons, didn't like what she heard, went back to college.

A lean and a click, she reached in the glove box, extracted a fatty, inspected it in the dark, licked it down, sparked it up.

The reefer was totally dank and regardless of how small a hit she nipped, she coughed.

Three hits, third cough, the back door opened and Tommy Zellwood slid in. Edy took another hit, passed the joint to Zellwood. He declined with a thank-you attached.

Edy put the joint in the ashtray and waited. She was good at waiting.

It didn't take long: "That shit's bad for you."

"Yeah?"

Zellwood shrugged. "So they say."

"Maybe *they* never smoked any good organic pot."

"I'd bet you're right. What're you to Eddie Margot?"

The question surprised Edy. She shrugged. "To Eddie Margot, I'm just a piece of shit he picked up off the street to use like he needed. A con, a shill, a beard. A couple of fucks till his wife told him she'd cut his dick off if he did it again."

"His wife?" Zellwood got it. "The maid. Goddam, you people are good—in a medicine-show sort of way."

"Yeah, I was just telling somebody that the other day. What's going on here?"

"Damn, my dates usually don't get bored until after dinner. You bored, little bit?"

"Fuck you, mister. Whadda you want?"

"You know who I am?"

"You're the cop, I assume."

Zellwood seemed to like that, leaning over the back of her seat, grinning, chin on seat top. "So my boys knew I was back there. Who was it got me, Pell?"

Edy nodded.

Zellwood grinned. "Damn, girl, smart boy like that, all that money he's thinking about running off with, he'd be a nice catch if he *did* get the goodies. How'd he make me?"

Edy shrugged. "Probably took one look at your cop ass."

Zellwood grinned some more. "You think I look like a cop?"

"That's all you look like, pal. You may have a fancier badge than the rest, but underneath? All cop."

"Damn, darlin, I believe you've hurt my feelings. What do you think I want?"

Edy drama-ed up weary with her eyes, fished the krypie roach from the butt dish and re-lighted it. Cough. Puff, cough. Puff, cough.

"Yeah, that's some good smooth shit. You hear me ask what you think I want?"

Edy gave Zellwood the weary look again. "I really don't wanna play cop games with you. Or anyone. So, how about you tell me what *you* want and split."

Zellwood turned sideways, laying his head on the seat top. "See, that's where your reasoning encounters the fatal little error, darlin. I'm not splitting. Not from you."

Edy exhaled, nursed the joint alive, coughed a little. "That's what I was afraid of."

"Nothing to be afraid of, sweet pea. In my club, I'm considered a nice guy."

Edy coughed smoke at Zellwood. She pushed the joint at him again. "You sure you don't want a couple of hits? You seem to need it."

"No, Toy, you have got to wear pants. You can't walk through the Freeport terminal bare-assed."

"I'll put on boxers."

"Over the chaps?"

Tony looked from Gretchen to Mueller, all smiling. Toy was at the kitchen counter polishing up on his shiny revolver. "Yeah."

"That'll look ridiculous, Toy."

"Who cares?" He brought the gun around across Haas to rest on Tony. One eyed, he said, "Ppkow. Ppkow." Making the gun jump in harmony with his sounds. Gun down for a quick inspection. "Gimme back my bullets."

"Un-uh." Tony shook his head.

Toy didn't like it. He looked at Tony, face contorting in frustration.

Gretchen said, "Toy, behave. I have a bag in the car with a holster that would be perfect for your gun. Will you have the driver get the bag, please? It is the blue suede."

Toy didn't look at Gretchen, but he let Tony off the cross. He slid off the stool, sauntered for the door. He stopped, looked at his hands as though he just realized he didn't have the gun. He turned back.

Gretchen said, "Not outside, Toy. The neighbors might not like guns outside."

Toy shrugged, turned, and went out empty handed.

Mueller watched Tony watching Gretchen and Toy. The scene hung a sly smile on his tanned face.

Tony made a *hmph* sound.

Gretchen glanced at Mueller then looked at Tony. She walked over, tits close to Tony's face, put a soft hand on his cheek.

Tony glanced up, sad-sack mug, looking for sympathy.

"Poor, poor, Tony. You should teach your children to obey. I promise you . . . " Gretchen leaned back, looking down into the shorter Tony's eyes, " . . . when this is done, the boy is all yours."

Tony brightened a little, then went suspicious. He pushed back a little, said, "Tell me you didn't fuck him."

"Oh, heavens, darling. You are too much. He is a boy."

Tony wanted to buy it. "Well, he's got some grownup parts."

Gretchen laughed, looked at Mueller. Mueller said, "That's not what she means, my friend. She means he is a hustler. Right, my dear?"

"Yes, Haas. You are always right. Are we ready to go? Is everyone packed?"

Tony nodded, still somewhat distracted by the previous scene. He came back into focus. "Yes. One bag each for Toy and me. Water heater off. Thermostat down. I called my friend Jade—she'll come by, check on things, water plants. How long should I plan on being gone?"

Mueller shrugged. Why waste a lot of commitment on his reply? "Who knows, Tony? A few months? A few years? Forever? Who knows?"

Tony looked around the kitchen like he was making memories. His eyes lit up. "My pre-Colombians." And was gone from the room.

Gretchen raised an eyebrow. "Pre-Colombians?"

"I sold them to him." A smile tugged the corners of Mueller's mouth up a bit.

The eyebrow fell. "I see."

[47]

ZELLWOOD FOUND THE Sig in its home under his arm, pulled it out, racked one, catching the live one from the chamber in the air over the front seat.

The drama was for the girl. He took it on a step farther, held up the 135 grain bullet then put the Sig against her head.

"Call them."

"Who?"

"Come on, little bit, don't make me be a bad guy."

"What? You're gonna shoot me if I don't?"

Zellwood huffed, said, "No, little bit, but I'll whack you pretty hard on the head if you don't." He tapped the barrel against Edy's skull. "Call em."

Edy picked up her phone. Some digits and a purr, she said, "The party's on the road." She killed the phone. "What now, officer?"

"Why, just act like I wasn't even back here. Follow them on to wherever it is Pell and Dupree are waiting with their tow truck. Your hero Eddie Margot's probably there too. Maybe a farm? Am I doin alright?"

Edy brought the engine to life, geared up and followed the limo out of the subdivision. "You're telling the story—go ahead and turn the page."

"Let's see, they got a bug on the limo. I'd say you got the other end in here somewhere." Zellwood looked in the front floorboard. "There it is, right there. Turn it on, you want to, little bit."

"I think I know where they are right this second."

"Un-huh. And you folks got a side deal with the limo driver." Zellwood put some thought to it. "The tow truck? The deal with the limo driver? I'd say we're planning a breakdown and a highjack. Close?"

Edy drove past the upraised guard arm, silent.

Zellwood had let the pistol relax, hanging over the back of the front seat at the end of a loose arm. "I'm thinking the plan is to wait till the goods're in the limo, right? But your driver ain't gonna be able to pull his shenanigan. Know why?"

"No."

"Cause everybody but Mueller and the woman are gonna be dead."

Edy looked quickly at Zellwood in the rearview.

"Oh. I see. You didn't know anybody in this . . . " Zellwood's free hand waved around out there, fishing for a word, caught: "Affair? How's that? You didn't know anybody was that serious, huh?"

Zellwood shook his head. "Lord, Lord, you carneys are way up out of game, huh? How about Pell and Dupree? They got respect for the Himmler twins? They realize they're not dealing with the pansy and his crazy-assed chicken?"

Zellwood leaned out to look in Edy's face in the oncoming headlights. "Mmm-mmm. What's Eddie say about falling for the mark? He get pissed? That where you got that boo-boo on the chops?"

"Shut up, you fuck."

"Whew. Bulls-eye, Tom-mee. I'm good, I'm good."

Stanley Woo sat on a mat of pine straw in a pine thicket drinking soda from a twenty-ounce bottle. He was a couple miles from the farm. He'd been here long enough to see how quickly the sun evaporates in the pines as it withdraws for the day. Long shafts of light slid under the pine tops making tall windows between trunks. Then it's gray. Then it's dark.

Then he heard Eddie and he was glad. The poetic moment didn't go with the evening's work.

The big truck rumbled by on a logging road that was no more than a couple of parallel ruts. It rumbled on around a bend and out of sight.

Stanley knew an open place lay ahead where Eddie could wheel around, set up for the wait. Faux wait.

Eddie was the tethered dog at a gator hunt. The Fed would drift in like a gator and Stanley would take him. Supposedly take him.

Then someone was walking up one of the ruts in the dappled dark. Stanley could see a crouched silhouette moving as the truck had gone. Perfect—the guy was on foot.

Stanley moved off in his own crouch as the silhouette had come. Not far, pulled off on an even more secondary trail, covered with a couple of leafy limbs, was a Jag sedan.

Stanley slid in the Jag's back door, found his phone. He pushed autodial, said, "He's on foot and I'm at his car. You can move out."

The truck came alive somewhere beyond the pines. In a few seconds, headlights came down the road at a fair clip. The plan was for Eddie to move fast enough so the guy couldn't jump on. Eddie was going at least that fast when he came by Stanley.

Stanley could hear the truck hit the pavement hard and knew it was off to the actual wait spot. The silhouette drifted down the rise after the truck. It could have been a ghost the way it moved.

The leafy cover was whisked away. The car door popped and a man slid in, the back of his head to Stanley slumped in the rear seat.

Stanley slid the power tab on the laser sight. A red dot popped up on the back of the front seat. Stanley sat up, put the red dot on the rearview mirror.

A reflected dot lit the man's forehead. His hands fluttered as though to raise them then went back to the wheel. One hand reached for the ignition and rolled the key.

The Jag hummed happily. Stanley put the red dot on the dash, about where he figured the engine was. He dropped pin. Again.

The Jag shuddered and died. The guy flinched a little each shot but got his hands up.

Stanley dug up his best Charlie Chan, said, "Please to be getting out of car."

The privacy glass dropped away in the limo.

Peanut turned, caught Mueller in the corner of his eye and said, "Somebody need to make that boy put that pistol up, quit pointin it at the back of my head. I see im doin it."

The boy pointed the Ruger and made his pistol sound. Then again. Pistol back in the nylon holster clipped on his chaps. Back out, quick draw move from a slouch in the back seat. *Ppkow*.

"I mean it now. I'll stop the damn car. Sure will."

Peanut watched the rearview. The man looked at the woman.

The woman leaned over, spoke quietly to the boy. The gun went to roost.

Peanut nodded. "Where to, boss? After we get off the turnpike?"

The sissy told Peanut to turn at the big lit-up garbage mountain.

In a bit, Peanut did. He asked for more directions. The folks sure were stingy with their directions. Peanut hoped it didn't fuck with the three long ones he still had coming from Dupree since he couldn't call and tell Dupree something.

Fuck it. Peanut found his cell, pushed redial in his lap.

Dupree said, *yeah*, down in there. Peanut said loudly, "We get on beyond the landfill, where I'm goin?"

Tony Wayne, the pansy one, said, "Two miles, take a right between the big white columns. Can't miss it."

Peanut said, "That where we goin? Tween two white columns? Bout two miles?"

A *yes* got tossed at Peanut. He put the privacy glass to work.

He lifted the phone to his chest, mumbled, "You get that, dawg?"

He could hear Dupree say, *yeah*, and click off.

Peanut followed suit.

He looked in the rearview.

The woman was watching his eyes. Hers were two holes poked in nothing. Cold-ass woman, now.

Dupree stepped out of the tack room. He looked up, saw Marty in the loft shuffling bales of hay.

"Hey, cuz, the funny company's almost here."

"Peanut?"

"Un-huh."

Dupree's cell chirped. He put it to an ear. A couple of yeahs a couple of pauses, then a, *cool*. The phone went away.

"Stanley?"

"Un-huh."

"He get the cop?"

"He says he did."

"Good man. He gonna put him in the trunk or what?"

"Stanley says he shot the man through

the cheek of the ass. He doesn't figure the man's gonna walk up here two, three miles, bein ass-shot and all."

Marty dropped a bale of hay on another, dusted his hands. "Stanley shot the man in the ass?"

"That's what he says. The motherfucker came into this thing dyin to shoot some-fuckin-body, know it?"

Marty thought about it, shrugged. "You best turn that cell phone mute. One of your ladies calls, we're fucked."

Dupree backed up into the source of the light and pushed some buttons on his phone. "What'd you tell Stanley to do, he got done with the cop?" Satisfied with the phone, Dupree looked up at Marty.

"I told him to sit across the road, watch Eddie in case he forgets we need a ride."

Dupree nodded. "You say it was somethin the girl said?"

Marty picked up the shotgun and box of shells. "Yeah. She kept saying she was sorry."

Dupree said, "For what?"

"Don't know—never would say. That's why I got Stanley watching Eddie Margot. Hit the lights when you get ready."

Dupree turned and the lights went down.

[48]

THE HEADLIGHTS caught a couple of tall white concrete things Peanut would have called columns. He pulled his little cord that ran under the hood.

The car coughed, caught up, coughed. He motored up and dropped the privacy glass. "This it?"

The sissy: "Yeah."

The German: "What is wrong with the car?"

"Sound like a little trash in the fuel line. We stop, I'll see cain't I tap the filter with somethin, unclog it."

Peanut made the turn; the car died.

He cranked the engine.

The car died again about halfway to the buildings. Another go made the rise.

"Pull in the barn." The sissy again.

Peanut aimed for the opened doors of the big wooden barn, pulled inside. The car died dramatically. "This good?"

The sissy: "Could you pull down a tad?"

"We'll see."

Peanut got her going, coughed on a few feet, died with a little wheeze.

He turned the key to off and pulled the hood latch. A look around said unless they were repossessing hay bales, somebody was poking somebody.

Peanut said, "We got lights in here?"

The sissy said, "Yes. Leave your headlights on a minute."

Tony climbed over people to a door.

The swarte beat him to it, swung it open for Tony.

Tony followed the headlights to a room, pushed the door open and a light came on. He disappeared from Gretchen's view and lights far overhead came up, flickered dimly, then jumped to life.

Tony reappeared, crowbar in hand, and joined the rest of the group disembarking from the car.

Toy stepped out, stood legs apart, slapped the cheeks of his ass and drew the big revolver—he was getting faster—and made his gun sound.

Haas assessed, nose wrinkled against the lingering smell of horseshit. "Peanut, my friend, will you pull the doors closed?"

Gretchen surveyed. Noted the tack room.

Noted the bales of hay stacked neatly in the loft. Instinct ran a cold finger up her spine. She unbuttoned her jacket. "We need to move. I still have to get another aircraft tonight."

Tony pointed with the crowbar and then hung it on his arm like it was an umbrella. He did a little penguin step into one of the stalls.

He stopped at the stall gate, leaned back, glanced right and left. The stalls all looked the same so Gretchen assumed he did it to make sure he was in the correct stall.

Tony penguin-walked to the chosen stall's rear wall and brought out the crowbar.

A couple of crude stabs, Tony wedged out a piece of wood siding. The next was exposed and easier.

Tony popped one end of the siding board by board, moved over and popped the other ends. Boards fell and stacked at his feet.

New felt paper was tacked to the exposed framing members. Tony ripped it away.

The little swarte—done with door duty—moved to stand beside Haas and began telling the inattentive Haas how the job was complete. He interrupted his report with: "Lawd Jesus." Only his shoes kept the swarte's jaw from hitting the ground.

Tony turned, proud of the dusty bricks

stacked in the wall cavity, made a frou-frou game-show gesture Gretchen would have expected.

Toy quick-drew and pretend-shot the gold bricks.

Gretchen glanced at Haas. Nothing passed, everything was said.

"A beautiful sight, Tony." Haas slapped his hands together. "Shall we load it?"

"Let's. Toy, you and . . . what's your name?" Tony put the last to Peanut.

"Folks jes call me Peanut, sir."

"Okay, Peanut, let's get this in the car. Come on, Toy." Tony mimed Mueller's handclap.

"Fuck you. Let the nigger load it." Toy was busy quick-drawing.

"Hey." The swarte stood up for himself.

Toy turned in a pivot, drew, aimed, made the gun sound.

"Stop it, boy. I mean it."

Toy fired more imaginary bullets at the swarte, hammer clicking.

Haas said, "Toy is right: Peanut is the domestic. He can load it."

The swarte was wagging his head. "I on't know bout that now. I on't mind helpin, but that a good bit of whatever it is. And it ain't gone ride in the trunk neither. Gone need to spread it out round on the back floorboard. That's gone be some heavy work for one man, now. We ain't bartered on nothin like that, no sir, sure ain't."

"How about a bonus, Peanut?" Haas's face was ruddy and full of mischief. He glanced at Gretchen, nodded to her.

"What kind a bonus we talkin?"

Gretchen knew where Haas was going. She stepped up behind the swarte.

"Gretchen won't shoot you in your head if you load our goods."

Gretchen touched the barrel of her Browning Parabellum to Peanut's neck, right at the nape.

The swarte jumped, then froze, hands up and out.

"Is that acceptable, Peanut?" Haas used a voice that didn't reflect the amusement his face did.

"Yessir. It sure is."

"Good. Tony, would you accompany me to the house, please? My prostate." Haas's hands come out, fluttered there. "I seem to piss every ten minutes." Speaking to Tony, but he looked at Gretchen.

She gave him a nearly imperceptible nod, glanced over at Toy. Haas returned the abbreviated nod, said, to Tony, "Shall we?"

Peanut slipped out of his jacket. He might be pressed into servitude at gunpoint, but he didn't have to act pleased. "What about the car? Who gone see to it?"

"You are, Peanut, after you've finished your first task. Hurry along now." The German did his little hurry-up handclap and turned for the doors.

The sissy fell in behind.

Peanut tossed a, *shit*, at the ground, rolled some shirtsleeve.

The chilly-ass woman sat on the lip of a hay manger and looked bored.

The crazy boy, ass hanging out for the world, crept toward the end of the barn, gun hand out and ready. At the last stall, he jumped into a roll, came up on one knee, gun pointed in the stall. *Ppkow*.

The boy got up clumsy, like he wasn't used to the boots, spun on the tack room door. *Ppkow*.

Then, gun up like a TV cop, he peered around the doorway in a quick move like a bird or something. Jump in the door. *Ppkow*.

Dupree could see the kid through a vent in the cabinet door. Watched him enter, sniffing like a dog—something wild and primitive and as un-evolved as tadpoles.

Watched Toy wander a bit, thump a puff of dust off a riding crop he found on a nail. A few swishes with it convinced Toy he might need it. He threaded his hand through its leather loop.

An encumbered quick draw attempt proved the quirt to be on the wrong wrist. It got switched.

Another try. *Ppkow* gun sound.

Toy sauntered to the row of tall cabinets. He used the crop to open a door.

His nostrils quivered. Something flickered in his muddy eyes. Another sniff; another cabinet door. Dupree readied up, wished he could tell Marty, *watch out, I'm about to pop this crazy motherfucker.*

Gretchen called out for Toy. He stood at the cabinets then, like an explosion, slammed one of the doors shut.

The entire of the eight-foot-long fixture shook. The abused door vibrated like a junkie in a three-day kick program. It swung back, striking its neighbor.

The neighboring door eased open. Toy turned to the voice repeating his name and didn't see Dupree's dark fingers grab the cabinet door's edge and pull it shut.

The adrenaline screamed like a freight train in Dupree's skull.

Gretchen could read Toy's mind as he approached with the crop dangling from his wrist, hand going for it, getting a grip.

She was right: he grasped it in a fist and

walked straight for the swarte, good fun on his face.

The swarte was moving two bars at a time, but was ready to drop to one it seemed to Gretchen.

"Toy, no. Come here." She stood on a smile.

Toy came there.

Gretchen reached in a coat pocket and came out with two shiny bullets. She bounced them in her palm, looked at Toy.

He liked.

Gretchen slid off the manger and crooked a finger at Toy.

They walked out of the stall and beyond the trunk of the car a few feet.

Gretchen stopped, turned to face Toy, Toy's back to Peanut loading the gold. She held out the bullets.

Toy grabbed them, hand grasping for his shiny pistola,

Gretchen put her hands on his face, said, "Toy. Look at me."

It took a few; Toy looked, engaged, his face smeared from the pressure of her hands.

"After you deal with Tony, come back and wait outside." Gretchen grasped his face more friendly. "I will send the swarte out." Blankness from Toy. "The nigger. Do not look at him."

Gretchen held Toy's face, his eyes trying

to roll to see the swarte. "Stop it, Toy." She slapped him lightly.

Toy brought it back to Gretchen.

She smiled, leaned her pelvis in. Her hands moved down Toy like he was a ski slope. She stopped at his bare buttocks, pulling his hips into her.

Toy's free hand fluttered around, hopelessly vagrant.

"Go, Toy. Tony is waiting."

"Haas too?"

"No. Remember? Haas is my friend. I deal with him. Come back, wait on the nigger."

"Okay. What about the cop guy."

"Be patient, darling."

Toy disengaged and moved off quickly, moving as if to something he was going to enjoy.

The swarte emerged from the limo's big side door. He was sweaty and dusty.

"That boy gone sure nuff hurt somebody someday."

Gretchen went to the car's trunk. "Yes. You are right." She was aware it sounded obligatory, distracted, but she didn't care—the little man was only a swarte.

She studied the trunk lid, didn't see a latch. "How does it open?"

The swarte came from the stall, dusted his hands as he passed around the front of the car. He leaned in, pulled a lever, the trunk rose.

Gretchen hurried the trunk lid up as the swarte went back to the stall. He said, "You welcome," over the low wall.

Tony was hungry. It had been a busy day without much food involved. The dead guy in the living room should have been enough but it had just been that kind of day. The fridge was turned off so that left it to the pantry, a big, country walk-in job. He perused the choices.

A tin of sardines got his attention. He snapped the key from the top and put the tab in the key's slot. A few turns of the key, Tony had yellowish-orange grease running down his chin.

The back of a hand fixed the chin. A swipe of the hand on pants fixed the hand. Another sardine. Another swipe and wipe.

His eyes shopped. Mostly vegetables. He and Toy had pretty much gone through anything snackable on their trips out here, checking on the booty in the barn wall some, playing some. Playing a lot.

Toy could go naked out here. Toy liked being naked. Tony liked Toy's nakedness too. Jesus, the evening sun shining on Toy's bare skin. Made Toy bronze up like a Greek statue. Perfect. Outwardly. But like a statue, inside he was dense as stone. Maybe it was good he was attracted to Gretchen. Traveling with the fuck would be like taking a child along.

Tony turned and Toy was standing in the doorway. His legs were apart, hand out for the draw. Haas was over Toy's shoulder, standing in the kitchen, but watching like more was going on than was.

"Go for it, pardner."

Tony tilted his head and dropped a sardine in his mouth. "Don't start, Toy. I'm not in the mood." Tony went back to browsing. He picked up a jar of walnut and toffee ice cream topping, studied it. He kept it, putting it under an arm.

"Pardner, you don't draw, I'll drill you where you stand."

Tony sat the sardine can on a shelf, found the nutty treat under his arm and tried to open it. Through gritted teeth, he said, "Drill away, honey. I'm having some . . . " Tony held the jar up, read, " . . . walnut-toffee-supreme ice cream topping. You can't wait, you go ahead, shoot me."

Toy did. A nice quick draw, gun steady in two hands, crop dangling from a wrist. He shot Tony in the side of the head, just above the right temple.

The topping broke on the floor and Tony danced in the mess for a few uncertain steps then fell in it.

Toy blew imaginary smoke from his gun and holstered it. He looked at Tony remorsefully. "You shoulda been on the six o'clock stage, pardner."

Haas Mueller applauded the performance richly, shouted, *bravo*, a couple of times.

"Well done, my young friend. The stuff Emmys are made of."

He lost Toy. A light flickered on in there somewhere. Toy ran out.

Mueller looked in at Tony. He lay on his stomach, legs and arms bent in an unnatural fashion as dead men will.

Mueller tsk-tsked Tony. "You should have been on the six o'clock stage, partner." Mueller shut the door on Tony Wayne and, for once, Mueller noted, Tony didn't complain.

"Tha's it, ma'am." Head wag, then, "Whew."

Peanut was whipped. He'd shook it up when he heard the gun shot off toward the house. It didn't seem like a good sign. Especially with the woman watching him when it popped off. Shit, it almost had her grinning.

Peanut got his jacket off the car's hood, almost slid it on, thought better and tossed it in the car. He walked to the trunk.

The woman looked up from a case she had put there when Peanut picked her up at the Boheme. She came up with a compact gun, all tubes and knobs.

She put it on Peanut. Peanut put his hands between them like that could stop the bullets from the mean looking little pistol. "Come on, lady, now. Don't *you* start."

She might as well have not heard him the way she acted. She said: "Know what this is, Peanut? No, of course not. It is called a Steyr. Nice fully automatic machine pistol. Very accurate, very dependable, very expensive. Nine-millimeter. It fires fast enough to cut a man in half before his heart stops."

The woman smiled at Peanut.

Peanut said: "Whatchu want, lady?"

She smiled. That could have been a good sign or not.

She said: "For you to tell me what you have going on."

Peanut was in motion to put a puzzled face on.

The woman beat him. "And do not insult me. You have a deal with the other swarte, do you not?"

Peanut could have asked what's a *swarte*, but he had a good idea. He could have said: *who*? Put some drama on it.

He said, "I come clean, tell you how to fix the car, you let me walk outta here fore the crazy boy gets back?"

The woman looked over a shoulder at the door. "Be quick about it."

Peanut was quick. Told her everything except the part about the money and the part about Dupree and his white friend already being here. Told her to follow the string that ran behind the fuel injectors to a vacuum line at the front of the engine.

The woman watched him. "How was the wrecker to be alerted?"

"I was gone call."

The way she watched him made Peanut nervous. "Make your call."

Peanut made the call, play-acted telling Eddie how to get here like he was supposed to. Did it perfect like a stranded limo operator should.

"I go now?" Peanut was grabbing his jacket and moving for the door as he said it.

The woman wished him good luck but Peanut didn't think she meant it.

He moved faster, stopped briefly at the door, slid in his coat. Looked toward the house, took a step.

The loudest sound Peanut had ever heard exploded in his left ear. A hand reflexively went up to protect it.

Something stopped the hand. It was the fucking ground. *What's the ground doing up here beside my head?* Damn, his whole face was numb.

THE BIG NOTHING

Peanut's left eye wouldn't give him shit. The right focused. The ground. *The fuckin ground way up here in my face like that.*

It made no sense at all.

[49]

IT TOOK PRETTY much all Marty had not to stand and shoot the kid when he came from the shadows and began going through Peanut's pockets.

He'd seen the woman give Toy the bullets but didn't get it then. He could pop her too. That would leave the German and Tony. That's if Tony was still available after the gunshot from the house.

No he couldn't—couldn't shoot the woman cold—for some primitive genetic reason he harbored. He could shoot the kid though. He sat, waited on Eddie and watched through openings between bales.

The German walked in, hands on hips, turned and looked at the woman. They watched Toy like he was a live-Neanderthal exhibit rifling through dead Peanut's pockets.

Toy stood, disappointed.

The German enlisted Toy and they dragged Peanut by the cuffs into the barn and on into the first stall. The German then re-closed the barn doors.

"Wonder why the chicken hawk didn't come back and help drag the chauffeur back in the barn, little bit? You don't reckon . . . " Zellwood made an *O* with his mouth. "Nah. They wouldn't a killed him. Probably just somebody slamming a door. Maybe a car backfiring. Swamp gas. Something. Whatchu think, little bit?"

"I think you like to hear you talk."

"Be nice now." Zellwood focused Milky's glasses on the barn, chin on the seatback. If the twin ruts constituted a drive then the car sat off the drive. "That's two won't be needin a cut. Wonder who else ain't gonna make it, little bit?"

"Peanut's dead, Eddie." A whisper.

Pause.

"Yeah, the woman's got our number. Fuck it. Come on. The doors are closed. Turn around and ram through backwards. We'll keep em pinned." A whispery, "You got one shot, Eddie. Hook it and run like you practiced, baby. Bye."

Dupree wiped a finger across his brow in the casket sized closet, slung the sweat down. He cracked the door. Peeked out.

Through a dusty window, he could see

silhouettes of everybody he figured was still alive but the crazy boy.

Dupree ducked under the window, went to the light bulb and unscrewed it until it flickered out.

Duck off, back in the cabinet.

A few seconds, the light switch did two long and several shorts. Gretchen's voice, close, said, "It must be blown."

Dupree couldn't catch what the German guy said—it wasn't English.

Gretchen replied in like tender.

They laughed. Dupree couldn't tell what they were saying; it didn't matter.

He fanned the door opened and closed a couple of times, said, fuck it, and went down on all fours, moved around the big wooden tack chest. It was cooler even if the floor was nasty.

Wait a minute. Something Gretchen said, something that didn't sound right. What'd she say? Fuck, all she said was: *it's blown.* Oh shit—in English.

Gretchen beckoned Haas with her eyes. She moved to the car's trunk.

When she spoke, it was the untranslatable mélange of German, Afrikaans and Dutch with the occasional English term she and Haas had developed over the years.

"The two fools are here." Gretchen

selected a pump action shotgun, Italian made. She loaded it, handed it to Haas.

"You saw them?"

Headshake. "I smelled the swarte, the faint odor of him. His cologne. He is in the tack room."

Haas nodded. "The other would be in the loft?"

"My guess, yes." Gretchen frowned. "I expected a more highwayman approach from them. Maybe this way is better. We deal with them here."

Gretchen got Haas acquainted with the Italian bazooka, a big ten-gauge.

Haas propped the gun in the crook of his arm, smiled at Gretchen. "What do you say to the idea we used in Istanbul on what's his name?"

"Basseem. Basseem Nadjir. The Palestinian."

"Yes. The Palestinian."

"God. The man died hard." It made Gretchen smile a little. "Deadly surrender. How sweet. Very good, Haas." Gretchen walked in a stall, laid the machine pistol on the manger. She returned to the car's trunk, extracted a twin to the other Steyr, checked its status. She looked at Mueller, said, "Do you think the swarte will die as hard a Nadjir?"

Haas smiled grimly at Gretchen, said,

"You are becoming a black widow. Breed with the male, then devour him. Yes, I like that very much." He studied her. "The Steyr looks like it was made for you, my dear."

A spin had Haas forty-five degrees to the tack room, his face tilted at the loft.

Back to English: "Gentlemen." Loud.

Niks.

Some disappointment in: "Come now, gentlemen, a word is all I crave."

Niks.

A look at Gretchen. She shrugged—she knew they were there.

"A deal, gentlemen. Some for the two of you, some for Gretchen and me. An even split."

Niks.

"Speak up, please." Haas searched the loft, then looked at Gretchen, a question on his face.

Gretchen moved around the car to get clear on the tack room door. The Steyr swung up from the strap to feel familiar in her hands.

Toy came from the stall looking guilty. He looked at Gretchen, put on a toothy smile. "I left them." Toy looked like he wouldn't mind a pat on the head.

"Hush, Toy." Haas was becoming irritated.

Toy drew his pistol, put it on Haas. Haas

looked at Gretchen. Gretchen shook her head dismissively. "Empty."

"Toy, we're discussing business. Please don't be impetuous." Haas turned to face Toy but still watching the loft.

Toy looked perplexed at the statement. He pulled the trigger, the hammer jumped and fell on an empty chamber.

Haas's face was something else now. "Don't do that again, child."

Gretchen thought, *Listen to Dada, child.*

Toy laughed, showed the toothy smile.

His finger came back, the hammer jumped. Toy made his pistol sound.

Haas shot him in the chest. He eased the shotgun down as Toy kicked out.

"I simply cannot tolerate impetuousness."

Gretchen leaned on the car and said, "I remember. Shall I try?"

Haas gave her a gesture—a turned up hand—supporting the idea.

Into the tack room, Gretchen said, "Dupree."

Niks.

Then, back to English: "I know you are in there. I smelled your cologne. What is its name?"

A silence then, "Don't worry about it," from the tack room.

Gretchen shifted, looked at Haas. He was looking at the loft, looking for the other one.

"Shall we barter? You cannot let us leave, we cannot let you leave. We seem to be at an impasse."

Again from the tack room: "We've been at an impasse, lady."

"Come on, darling. There are two of you, two of us, the government man outside. We consolidate and conquer."

Silence. Then: "You know about the cop?"

"Is he a cop?"

"Fuck, I don't know what he is, baby. What kinda deal we talkin? Fifty-fifty?"

"There's your daddy."

"He's not my daddy."

"Granddaddy?"

Edy rolled her eyes at Zellwood. She was a cute-as-a-button little thing, but, damn, she had an attitude on her.

Zellwood watched Eddie roll up slowly, headlights taking in the building ahead.

The tow truck rumbled on, balked at the closed doors. A three-point brought it

around to face out, big tow kit toward the doors.

"If all goes well, they let him in. They don't? The plan's to shit, I guess." Zellwood had the nocs back up though he really didn't need them. The truck was only a couple of hundred feet away. "Shit, where you at, Bones?" Fish out a cell phone, hit Bones.

He could make out a figure inside the truck but wasn't sure it was Eddie. Or anyone. An inside light flashed on. It was Eddie. No Bones on cell; he killed it.

Eddie dropped down, went to a control panel on the side of the truck. He pulled a lever and a cable lowered a long bar to lie parallel to the ground, about six inches above it. He took a look, came back around and climbed in the truck.

The truck's engine revved until it was humming like a jet turbine.

"What's up, little bit?" Zellwood dropped the field glasses. "Goddam, if it ain't a fuckin snatch."

The truck slammed into gear and disappeared through the void it made of the wood doors.

"Here we go. Game on. Come on. Get out."

[50]

MARTY HEARD EDDIE outside, heard him turn the tow truck, rev up. When he heard Eddie drop the clutch he pulled the pin.

Damn good timing on everything but the *fire-in-the-hole* part. And after the flash bang popped and Eddie came in like he did, Marty couldn't see yelling anything would help.

Instead, he stood and fired the twelve-gauge where Mueller had been. That seemed helpful.

But then Mueller wasn't there anymore and Marty shot the bed of the tow truck as it rolled in. He ducked and something the size of a cannonball hit the hay bale he was behind. He changed bales.

A quiet automatic weapon reverberated subtly in the rafters. Maybe the grenade wasn't the nazz it was claimed to be.

Marty moved down a few bales, saw Mueller backed into a stall, saw Eddie slide the metal tongs under the limo. Mueller ran forward.

Marty stood and fired. Mueller cried out and fell behind the stall wall. Marty pulled the nine-millimeter and dropped three into the wall where he thought Mueller should be.

A piff-piff approached from the left. Marty ducked off and the piff passed over him a couple of times.

The woman yelled something in their tongue. Mueller answered. He was winged—Marty could hear it in his voice.

The truck revved, the automatic piff-piffed again, then glass shattered.

Another full-auto with a lower voice barked, then wood shattered. That would be Dupree's Russian automatic.

The limo lurched upward in the rear. Eddie had it. Engine rev. Hydraulics raked the limo to the tow truck. A large shotgun blast, Eddie yelling, *Jesus,* through the shattered back window. The truck's power train moaned in complaint.

Marty jumped up again and dropped some double-0's in Mueller's stall.

The truck and its tractored car moved forward.

Marty tossed his last flash bang, yelled, "Fire in the hole."

He jumped on the truck and ducked

down in the metal boxes and equipment back there. The barn shook from the grenade.

"Come on, Dupree."

The truck was moving now, digging out ruts in the soft humus floor of the barn, picking up speed.

The deep full-auto barked and Dupree came through the sound, firing into the stalls off to his left.

Marty tossed a couple of pills that way.

A big blast took the paint off the metal support over Marty's head.

He put the business end of the shotgun at the sound and the pin clicked on air. Duck off, find the Smith.

Up. Fire, fire. Duck off. Up.

Dupree's on the hood of the moving limo. He's on the roof. The trunk. He balances clumsily.

Marty's left hand was out, his right firing wildly at the stalls.

Dupree slipped a little, lost the AK. The soft pop of the other automatic following him up the limo. Balance up, crouch for a leap.

As he came from the crouch, a pill hit the heel of his left shoe. The heel shattered, Dupree lost the shoe and fell, almost went between the two vehicles, but pushed himself out and rolled away to the ground.

Marty saw Dupree come out of his fetal

roll and run for the stall where Peanut was sleeping.

Marty dropped the last of his clip in the general direction of Mueller and the woman, or where they had been.

Missed the fuckin bus, didn't you, Holmes? Shit.

Dupree pulled the big Czech ten millimeter, knocked some dried horse shit off it.

He looked at Peanut lying face up in the center of the stall. Pants down to his knees, and what's going on with your face, Peanut?

Ah, shit.

Dupree closed his eyes, a reflexive move, Jesus, to seeing Peanut's eyeless sockets. He leaned his head back, rested against the stall wall. Eyes opened slowly.

Ah, shit.

Where Dupree's eyes were pointed, level with the top of the opposite wall, maybe five foot high, Peanut's eyes looked at him. Big orbs, looking too big to fit in anybody's eyeholes and damn sure too big for Peanut's.

Dupree looked away from the eyes.

"Sorry, Peanut. Goddam, I am sure sorry about this shit."

Peanut had nertz to add so Dupree took another turn. "Look at us, Peanut. Same ole same ole, ain't it? The white folks go to the bank, the niggers get stuck with the dirty."

"Does the idea of a deal sound more attractive now, darling?" The woman, Gretchen.

Dupree sat out, held pat, said squat. Why? These people planned on killing everybody but each other—that had become pretty obvious.

Same feminine vocalization in the mélange tongue. Masculine response, same tongue, but closer in to Dupree.

"Darling, if you do not cooperate, we will have no choice but to kill you. Is this what you want?"

"Bring it on, bitch." Dupree scooted around behind the stall's hay manger, wedged himself in the nook as well as possible. He still felt exposed but you played them like they hit the table.

Dupree heard soft shoe-fall in the stall behind him. Movement outside the stall gate, less soft. Dupree saw it coming.

Mueller would step clear, fire the big shotgun. Gretchen would lean over the top of the low wall and head-pop Dupree while he was keyed on Mueller.

Dupree scrunched in there sideways as small as he could, put the barrel of the big plastic gun against the separating wall. Wait now. Wait now.

Mueller made his move. Dupree fired three times through the wall, into the adjoining stall where Gretchen would be, as buckshot showered the exposed areas around him.

Now. Dupree swung and put two in the stall wall by the gate, the spot he expected Mueller to be. Nobody moaned in pain.

Gretchen's voice told Dupree she had moved off. Mueller's response showed he had done the same.

A wait.

The Steyr purring now. Shards of wood flying around.

Dupree went face down, next to Peanut. He tossed a couple of pills at nothing in particular. The breech on the Czech gat locked open.

Shit, shit, shit. Foreign piece of shit. Dupree had dropped seven. That left a dozen rounds available. Eighteen-round clip, one in the chamber, minus seven. Yep, twelve.

Mueller was coming in a hurry. Dupree expected a run by shot. He hunkered behind the minimal cover Peanut's body provided.

Then Mueller was there, the hole in the end of the shotgun coming around, then down as Mueller located Dupree.

Dupree put his face down, tightened for the lead bath he saw coming.

Four quick ones. Whoa. Not a shotgun.

Not the quick sound of the auto the bitch was using.

Dupree peeked up. Mueller's toes pointed at the roof.

"That you, cuz?"

"Bet your big dark ass it is."

Dupree rolled on his back, began working on the spent casing jamming his piece with a car key.

"Cuz, you're fuckin beautiful. You know that?"

"Yeah. You think I left you?"

"There was a rough couple, three minutes there." Yeah, Dupree did. He figured Marty and the girl and old Eddie were eating up asphalt, leaving his long, skinny niggah ass here.

"Did what I could. I couldn't get clear without showing myself."

"You did fine, baby. You just made me nervous like you always do. Where's the woman?"

"Got me. Hey, lady."

[51]

TOMMY ZELLWOOD LAY on his back. Lot of stars out. Maybe out in the sticks it just seemed like more.

He could hear intermittent pops and stutters from the barn. He couldn't look. He couldn't turn his head. He thought his neck might be broken. He could feel nothing.

He should have been feeling plenty. Eddie Margot had run him over with that big goddam wrecker. That was something you'd think you'd feel.

Par for the recent course, though. This fucking thing had been kinksville since the day he and Bones had decided to move on it. Seemed simple enough. The backwater warlord the gold was bound for wouldn't know one crate from four, and he damn sure wouldn't see a bill of lading on a deal like this. Started well: got crate number one off the plane and into a waiting storage unit up in Georgia. Haul ass to Jax and run head-on into a fucking full-blown tropical storm just dying to be a hurricane. No plane in Jax—had to go on to Orlando to refuel. He'd said fuck it in Orlando, figuring to drop the other two crates on the African coast before delivering the fourth to the jungle bunny. And guess what? The boys had pinched the golden goose, and away they ran.

Okay, no problem—the rabbit always runs in a circle. Zellwood waited, and the waiting paid off. All he had to do was pop Margot, wait on the young war in the barn to produce a relaxed and relieved victorious side, then pop them when they came out. No problems? Wrong.

The problems started at jump street: the girl bolts out of the car, takes a couple of strides. Zellwood yells, "Don't think I won't pop you, little bit." She hesitates, like a gazelle, unsure. Takes another couple of strides. Zellwood drops a cap at the ground. The girl freezes.

Zellwood walks over, opens the fingers of his left hand and slides the hand up her neck to the back of her head. He closed the hand into a fist, hanks of hair between clenched fingers. "Come on, little bit."

Zellwood's impressed with the girl's moxie. Never a hand coming up in protest to the roughness he uses to guide her to the ruts that led to the barn. Not a peep about pulling hair. No girl shit.

Pops in the barn. What sounds like a concussion grenade. More pops. Another boom.

The tow truck moves out of the barn. Lookit this: my boys're pulling it off. Looks like it, anyway.

Someone jumps off the back of the moving truck and runs for the barn. Plans going awry, boys? Somebody getting left?

Zellwood stands in the middle of the drive, girl out in front of him, held there by his left hand in her mop. In his right, the Sig.

A thumb comes up, drops the safety. He pulls a bead on the windshield over the left headlight, where Margot should be sitting. Zellwood can see shit but headlights.

He's working too many variables. He concentrates on his shot.

The girl squirms when the truck is a hundred feet away. She says, "He'll run over us."

Zellwood laughs, says, "Not his baby girl he won't, little bit."

"You don't know the bastard like I do, dude. He'll run us down." The girl is obviously nervous.

It gives Zellwood pause.

Fifty feet away.

Steadies up on the shot again.

Thirty feet.

The girl jerks around, getting frantic as headlights bear down. It throws the first shot wide.

The truck is on them.

Steady up.

The girl drops the support from her weight, goes down low quickly, then she jumps right, across Zellwood's path.

The unexpected change of direction, his hand laced in her hair like it was wound in a bull rider's rope, concentrating on popping Margot—factors stacked too quickly. Sum result: Zellwood goes sideways, stumbles, fires wildly.

He watches the girl lunge away. Headlights wrap around him like a blanket. He kisses the tow truck's grill. Lights explode in his face then dim out for a few.

See, Tommy? Easy as pie.

The jolt of pain in his right leg was welcomed like an old friend. It meant his neck wasn't broken. He wiggled the toes on his right foot, wiggled the fingers of his right hand.

He still had regions not reporting in yet, but several areas, his head on the left side, left ribcage, left hip, were all reporting loud and clear, hurting pretty good now. Nothing from the left arm or lower left leg yet.

Another wave of pain. Fight off the urge

to puke. *Come on, Tommy, you lay on your back and vomit, you drown in your own slime.*

Not today.

He forced his head to the right. Vomit ran from his mouth, into his right ear, onto the ground.

The fuck are you, Bones?

Stanley couldn't believe it. Matter of fact, it scared him some, seeing what kind of guy he'd been fucking with in the pine thicket.

Stanley does the Charlie Chan, the guy pops his door, like he's gonna be cool with it, play nice. Then, he drops like he cut a special deal with gravity. Gone, daddy, gone.

Next minute, holes are popping through the floorboard, banging against the roof of the Jag. Stanley yanks his feet up and hands the guy back a few pills, dropping them through the floor.

The guy grunts hard in the lull. Stanley hears him scrambling around, under the car. Then he's gone. Stanley reaches over, bumps on the headlights.

The guy's leaning against a tree, checking out the seat of his pants. There's blood there. A point, a bang. The windshield turns to giblets. Another. One of the headlights goes down. Stanley dives out of the car and the other headlight goes out with a bang. Stanley pops off a couple in the general direction the guy was last seen, belly-slides his shaking ass to his scooter, coasts the fuck down the hill and outta there.

All that shit, kill the guy's car, shoot him in his ass, and now here he comes limping up the shoulder of the road about the time Eddie pulls in the farm's gate.

Stanley sits tight, balanced on his scooter. It's backed into a thick place across the road—perfect seat.

Guy ducks under the white rail fence. Stanley lets him limp on undisturbed.

Then Eddie crashing in the barn doors, it looks like. A car's interior light comes on in the pasture, more in front of the house, off to the right of the action going on now. He'd not seen it—dark car, dark night.

Two people get out of the car, walk coarsely, like connected drunks, stumbling to the long drive.

Eddie comes out of the barn in a bit, a lot of shooting behind him, more sporadic and lumped than in the movies.

Eddie is picking up speed, two figures in the headlights. Stanley gets it. The cop. He's got the girl—the granddaughter Marty's fucking—by the hair. Who the fuck was in the pines, then?

Eddie guns the engine.

From the corner of his eye, Stanley sees

the guy from the pines. He's limping, running stiff-legged on his hobbled side, but making good time in a half-jog now.

Shit. The truck's not stopping. It doesn't even slow down.

At the last instant, the girl goes down and springs out of the way. The other figure, the cop, almost makes it but the front of the truck swerves and catches him.

His head knocks the headlight out and he flies in a manner Stanley never imagined a body flying. The form hits the pasture rolls twice and stops.

The girl runs for the car. The limping man intersects the truck, manages to hook an arm in a big rearview-mirror frame on the passenger side. Some really fast gimpish footwork and he's on the running board.

Holy shit. Eddie's aiming for the big old concrete pillar the gates are mounted on. Last minute he swerves, raking the far side of the truck, scrapes the guy off like he's shit on a shoe, rubs the limo behind him on concrete. Sparks fly.

Eddie brakes hard, makes the turn onto the paved road.

The man who was hanging from the truck is lying in the drive face down. Stanley hits the starter, the bike comes alive. Stanley revs it, still looking at the inanimate lump. Knowing the guy's roadkill, right?

Stanley catches a gear, weaves to the road, takes one last look at the dead guy.

The fucking dead guy rolls over, sits up, looks at Stanley across the road.

The guy raises a hand. A gun's in it.

The gun flares and barks. Sparks fly from the asphalt between them. Not even close.

The gun hand drops; Stanley moves off.

Eddie squinted the oncoming headlights away.

Yeah. There his road was.

Blinker on, slow, turn.

He found the cell phone beside him, punched up memory, hit one.

"Hey, doll. I'm coming in."

Pause.

"Nah. Better'n expected. I lost em at the farm. The white guy made it but I guess he went back."

Pause.

"Yeah. They're stooges, both of them."

Eddie cast a glance in the remaining rearview. "But hang tight. I believe I got a motor scooter tagging me."

Pause.

"Who knows." Thought. "Nah. Ain't cops. Probably a friend of the rubes. It ain't the German. It was, he'd a come on, got it done, him or the cops either one."

Pause. Shrug.

"Just hang tight. We'll see."

Stanley sat at the turn and watched the truck and the limo get smaller.

Some gray cell time. Maybe Eddie was playing fair. This was the changeover spot, the place they'd left Eddie's Cadillac. Off in the trees a bit, down the dirt road a quarter of a mile or so.

Stanley eased out, keeping the grinder quiet as mechanically possible. He low-tached about half the quarter mile and slid the bike against a water oak in the final throws of heart rot.

Ahead, he could hear Eddie hostling the limo with the tow truck.

A bit farther, when he saw the red of taillights flickering, Stanley took to the trees that lined the road.

He maneuvered close enough to see Eddie in person. The tow truck and limo were parked on the side of the dirt road, Eddie's Cadillac backed up to the limo's doors.

Eddie was hustling metallic bricks like somebody else just outbid him on the last tomorrow.

Stanley stepped out, the HK visible for Eddie to appreciate. "No need to move it. The limo runs fine."

Eddie looked up. Fear, surprise, maybe

even a little shock registering. His mouth moved like a fish on the sidewalk.

He recouped, said, "The fuck're you?"

"Move away from the car, Eddie." Stanley doing it serious for Eddie, pointing the pistol at Eddie's chest.

Eddie looked at his heart. There was a tiny red dot on it. He swiped at it like he could wipe it off. "The fuck is this? You gonna kill me?"

"Not if you move off."

"Who the fuck're you?"

"Move off, Eddie."

"Un-uh." Eddie almost smiling

Silence. Stanley was out of moves.

Eddie: "You don't know what to do next, do you?"

Silence. Stanley thought: *I could kneecap you.*

"Well, I'll go first, although it woulda been good you'd a started with something stronger like: *Hey, pal, you may not know who I am, but you're about to find out who you're messin with.* See how I did it? Not a question. Like matter-a-fact, like, okay, you know what sorta individual you're messin with, go ahead and be foolish."

"I like it. What happens next?"

"Okay, then maybe I do the old talk-to-someone-over-your-shoulder. You laugh, say somethin about the oldest one in the book. I say, *Oh yeah*?"

Stanley fell for it. "Then what?"

Eddie shrugged, "Either I'm bluffin or you get cracked on the head, cucumbered."

Stanley opened his mouth to speak and something hit him on the back of the head so hard he bit his tongue. The way it landed, it could have been the space shuttle.

Stanley lost his gat when his hands went to his head. He bent in pain, said, "Goddam."

Stanley raised his head a little with his hands, saw a well-dressed black woman behind him holding an old blue steel revolver in both hands. Her face was wrong—it should have been malice. Should have been a head-knocking woman's face. Her face was horror-stricken, eyes and mouth wide. "Goddam, lady."

"Oh, baby, I'm sorry. Oh, Eddie, why did you make me do that?" More anguish. "Oh, my baby."

The woman moved to Stanley.

"Stay the fuck away from me, lady." Stanley still bent partially over, hands on head, moved away.

The woman turned to Eddie. "Here, Eddie, take this damn thing." She held the long pistol out by the barrel.

Eddie stepped over and took it, then bent and retrieved Stanley's piece.

The woman went to Stanley, arms open. "Come here, baby. Let Anna see what she did."

Stanley looked at her. There were tears on her cheeks. Eddie was laughing over her shoulder.

This was the strangest night of Stanley's strange life. Even stranger than the nights he spent in jail, stranger even than the second night when he finally got tired of it and nailed the biker, busted the guy's eardrums. He'd left the biker screaming in the shower, bleeding from both ears.

Stranger even than the night the U.S. Marine grabbed Stanley's outstretched hand and the helicopter took him up, out of Stanley's mother's arms and to a new life with the Marine and his wife.

Now, after *The Gunfight at the OK Corral* meets *The Great Train Robbery* and a little ass-shooting, some motherly black woman hits him on the head with an antique pistol and then coos and mm-mm's over his wound.

Days like this always made Stanley think maybe he shouldn't have grabbed the Marine's hand that day.

[52]

YOU KNOW WHERE she is?"

"Un-un." Dupree didn't sound like he cared.

"Talk to her."

"You talk to her."

A beat. Marty again said: "Hey, lady."

Repeat the beat. "The name is Gretchen." From about half way down, back in a stall to the right.

Marty chanced it, zipped around to the stall opposite Dupree. He could see Peanut, his bare ass, the top of his head. He couldn't see Dupree.

Dupree leaned out, deadpanning Marty.

Marty said, "Lady, you wanna walk off?"

"Of course. Do you?"

A beat. Marty hadn't done this a bunch and wasn't sure where he was going. "Sure. How do we do it?"

"You throw your arms out. Then I throw mine out."

"Un-uh. Two of us. You toss first." Marty looked at the half-prone Dupree.

Dupree looked unconvinced.

"Okay."

A machine pistol came over the stall wall.

"Come on, lady. I know you've got a handgun. I saw it. You forget, look on your left hip, sitting cross-draw over there." Marty leaned out, saw the pistol fly out, nestle in the dirt and fibered debris of the barn floor.

"Your turn, gentlemen."

"Why? You threw yours out. You're clean, come on out." Dupree was standing.

"Glad to see you get involved, cuz."

A pair of slender hands came up, arms snaked up in pursuit. A blonde head. Blue eyes. Aryan nose. Nearly amused mouth. Gretchen stood behind the stall wall, head and shoulders showing. She dropped the hands, walked up to lean on the low wall, rested one of the hands, the left, on the stall wall.

The mouth twitched, said, "This looks very much like surrender, yes, darlings?"

Dupree rolled his eyes at Marty as Marty stood.

A little dusting, Marty walked into the long center run, pistol dangling like it had gotten heavy.

Dupree turned to face Gretchen.

"Hello, my darling." For Dupree.

Marty looked over at Dupree. Dupree looked at her, gave her nothing.

She glanced at Marty, smiled. "Did your friend tell you how I prove I am disarmed?"

"Yes, my friend did mention it."

"Shall I?" All for Marty now.

Dupree raised the big Czechoslovakian pistol and shot Gretchen through the left eye. She was gone before the sound soaked into the walls.

"Goddam, Dupree." Marty looked from the spot where Gretchen had stood to Dupree. "The fuck's wrong with you."

Dupree turned. He looked at Marty and walked out of the barn, stopping to retrieve his heelless shoe.

Marty turned to watch Dupree go away. When Dupree was part of the greater dark, Marty walked down and looked in the stall at Gretchen.

With an eye gone, she was still angelic. A broken statue, limbs tangled in death, her hair a halo around her head.

She had a smile on her lips. She died happy, Marty guessed.

It must have looked good right up to the end. She'd lured Marty out in the open. If Dupree'd fallen for it she could have used the gun in her rigid right hand, a machine pistol exactly like the one she'd tossed out.

Marty believed Dupree was fucking beautiful his-own-self.

Tommy Zellwood heard the survivors coming. Weary footfalls on the dirt drive, low chatter, men laughs. Well, well, his boys made it. Good thing too—the woman or Mueller either one would put a bullet through his head.

A voice said, "Look. It's Edy's car."

Pell's voice.

The other one, Dupree, grunted.

Pell said, and they were within fifteen, twenty feet now, "Why the fuck did she leave her car? What the fuck did she park there for?"

Dupree told Pell he didn't fucking know.

Zellwood tried to tell them Edy flooded the car in the excitement, drained the battery then lit out on the hoof.

What he said was just noise. He didn't know his jaw was broken. He followed the noise with an unsolicited moan.

Dupree said, *Goddam*, jumped about three feet.

When Dupree came down, he showed Zellwood what could have been the world's biggest pistol.

Teeth locked about a half-inch apart, Zellwood tried: "The hell you get that handgun, son? Buck Rogers?"

Pell said, not to Zellwood, "The cop."

Zellwood mumbled, "I see you're quick becoming the brains of the outfit."

Dupree said, not to Zellwood, "Whatchu think?"

"I think he's a smack talking mother, laying on the ground, arms and legs poking every way but right and us walking around, nothing but dirty. You want I should kick him?" Marty nudged Zellwood with a toe.

Dupree turned, looked at Marty, big grin going. "Nah, ain't no use in kickin im. He's down. He's just makin conversation cause he can't send anybody to jail."

Dupree walked over, leaned over Zellwood. "You say somethin about the car?"

"I said she flooded it." A grimace, a difficult swallow. "Try it. It'll run. Just don't flood it."

"Un-huh." Dupree stood. "We get it running, I guess you gonna expect a ride somewhere?"

"That'd be white of you."

Dupree turned for the old Mercedes, said, "Go ahead on, kick him, bread."

Marty didn't kick Zellwood. He straightened Zellwood's twisted appendages while Zellwood passed out. Then he and Dupree spread Zellwood out on the back seat.

Marty popped the passenger door and

Dupree said, "You drive this foreign motherfucker. I couldn't even get the lights up."

Marty slid in, said, "Gimme some light." Dupree obliged with his flashlight. Marty studied, rolled the key: the dash lights came on—the battery had recouped. He fired the car up, brought up the lights and pulled out.

A little bumpy pasture, a double bump onto the double rutted drive made Zellwood moan back there.

"You feel him up?"

Marty pulled Zellwood's wallet from a shirt pocket, tossed it at Dupree.

Dupree opened the wallet. Marty pounded the brakes.

Zellwood thumped to the floorboard.

"Jesus."

"Who the fuck is that?"

A man lay in the path, between the concrete columns.

The headlights seem to arouse him. He sat, arms limp at his sides. He rolled over, trying to stand, one arm definitely out of service. He ended up face in the dirt, ass in the air, pointing at the car. His pants were bloody on the left side.

Dupree said, "Un-un."

Marty said, "Look and see."

Dupree leaned over the back seat. "Ah shit."

"The one back there's not shot in the ass, is he?" Marty looked back at Dupree.

"Nope."

Harmonize on: "There's two of them."

[53]

EIGHT FIFTY IN the morning—a Sebring convertible in Eddie's drive. A man in plaid jacket and loud pants was putting out a sign.

The sign said the house was available for long-term lease, fully furnished, executive home and some other realtor shit.

Dupree said, "I smell rain."

Marty said, "I smelled rain last night when Stanley called."

"Well, wasn't like we were able, at the time, to react to young Stanley's phone call, was it?"

"No."

The way it went:

They load the other guy, the Arab or South American black guy, whatever he was. Marty pushes the old Mercedes towards civilization.

Stanley calls, tells Marty about a lump on

his head. About a woman called Anna who didn't seem to have a Caribbean accent or be a maid either one. About Eddie veering over to clip the cop.

About helping Eddie load the goodies into the Cadillac at gunpoint and Eddie finding Stanley's scooter, rolling it out into the road and running over it.

Stanley had decided Eddie liked running stuff over.

Then life really goes to shit.

Not too very long after Marty and Dupree get Zellwood inside the E-room, somebody sees the other guy—Zellwood called him *Bones*—in the car. Next thing, enough cops to write a decent pad are at the hospital.

The street cops aren't smart enough to separate Marty and Dupree right away but put them in what looked like the Baker bin. Padded walls, no seat to jump off and smash your head into the grimy concrete floor should the urge overcome you.

They get separated after a bit. A few hours later, a cop comes in Marty's cell, tells him the one guy's conscious and wants to see them.

Marty figures Zellwood had a lucid moment, called in brass who figured Zellwood plowed a wide acre. Marty further figures he and Dupree are going to jail.

He's only completely wrong.

Dupree beats him to Zellwood's private room, looks like he feels like Marty does: sideways pinstripes in the near future.

Zellwood's in plaster and traction. Jaw wired shut. Head bandaged extensively.

A youngish spectacled guy—flannel slacks, starched shirt and a decidedly normal tie—whispers in Zellwood's ear.

Zellwood opens his only available functioning eye, looks from one to the other. A grimace passes for a smile.

After the b sound, "Boys," is a monotone buzz from barely parted lips.

Heavy drugs. Good drugs.

"You did awright."

Marty and Dupree trade glances.

Zellwood shakes his head as if to clear it of the beeping sounds from the machinery hooked to him. "Little Eddie fooled us, huh?" The *huh* was bubbles between clenched teeth. "You *know* he's not meeting you, head start like this. Whatever the plan may've been."

Marty moves around like his feet hurt. Makes a face to match. "Listen, you wanna send us to jail, do it. But don't make us listen to this shit."

Zellwood blinks his good eye, focuses on Marty. "Jail?" Hesitation. Cool individual—he says, "Who's in here?"

Marty says: "A cop." Meaning the spook-in-training.

Zellwood says: "Tell him to leave."

Marty: "You tell him."

Zellwood does. The guy leaves.

Zellwood has to ask if the guy's gone.

He says, "My gracious, no, boys, I'm not sending you to jail. This is my retirement fund. Half, anyway. Here's the deal: you two go on and get it. I'll find you." A coughing sound bubbles out. "Half and half. I have to look for y'all? I take it all. Do what you like." The grimace played a smile again. "I'll find you. Wherever you go."

That was it. Got off easy. Marty says, *fuck you*, they leave, walk out into the dawn's early light.

"You even wanna stop, cuz?"

Marty thought about it, pulled to the curb. "Yeah."

The realtor looked up and got out a canned smile. It wasn't one of the expensive ones—he could read his clientele.

"Morning, gents. What can I do for you?"

"The folks living here move?" Marty put on a concerned face.

"Yes. Suddenly, unfortunately. The elderly gentleman who lived here passed a couple of days ago. His housekeeper called me yesterday." The guy did an acceptable job on sorrow-shared, head down, eyes averted.

"Annie Mae?"

The plaid sport-coat came back, got friendlier. "You knew Mr. Clarendon?"

Marty shrugged it off. "Business, mostly, but, yeah, my partner and I knew him pretty good. Had a few beers with him under the bougainvillea out back. We were working on his granddaughter's car." Marty thumbed at the Mercedes on the curb. "It's fixed." Remorseful face. "And Mr. C's dead." Pause to wish it weren't so. "Damn."

Dupree added his own condolences solemnly. He looked down. "You see the maid? The grandbaby?" Dupree looked as concerned as a funeral director.

"Oh, yes. The young lady. She left . . . " a look at a fancy watch, " . . . not ten minutes ago. Little thing in that big motor home, all her computer stuff."

"She say where she was going?" Marty didn't expect much at this point.

"No. But she asked the quickest way to the interstate highway. I told her to go straight down here and there it is. She says which way's west and I said . . . hey."

Dupree and Marty were hurtling across the St. Augustine grass.

No looks back. Too busy chasing the only piece of sunshine breaking through the rain.

Marty kept grinning but wouldn't tell Dupree why.

[54]

CARS THIS WAY; trucks, trailers and motor homes that way.

A rest area on the interstate. No more exciting or restful than any other. No more or less complex. Just the next one westbound.

A few RV's were sprinkled in the long spaces among ten to eighteen wheelers. A huge one with a stretched-out, abstract golden goose on its sides nestled between a Freightliner and a full-grown Mac.

The final leg of a bathroom run had the girl born as Gwendolyn Frazier moving over concrete to the beige beast. She could prove she was Gwen Frazier. Or Sarah McRay. Or Jennifer Reese.

Or Edy Margot.

Edy looked tired. Up all night, hitching and hiking back to town.

Gwen Frazier might have been affected by the night's events. Edy Margot wasn't.

Nothing but the forever road, the never-ending party for Edy.

Gwen was serious, responsible. Had to be.

After mom died when Gwen was eight, she had a sorry drunk called Daddy to raise. Daddy's priority in life, unequivocally: a twenty-pack minimum of Old Milwaukee every day. There was no money, no nothing and Gwen got school clothes from the gimme-bin at various churches around town.

Fate took pity, rescued Gwen when she was fourteen—a chain of events connected only by the thin fabric of the dismal situation.

Gwen wore a resale-store garment to school, a blouse with a small yellow stain on it. First period, a classmate claims the shirt, even related the chili incident that resulted in the stain. Back chatter went on until third period when Gwen loaded her backpack and walked the three miles home.

The neighbor, a Syrian widow, Mrs. Rafeedi, saw her come in early, crying. Mrs. Rafeedi, Gwen's only ally on the planet, had been the one who had coached her through poverty, fed her when the only thing in the fridge was Old Milwaukee, told her about periods and other pubic things.

Mrs. Rafeedi cried some too. Then she took Gwen to Walmart, bought her thirty-eight dollars' worth of new clothes. Then

Mrs. Rafeedi gave Gwen a ten-dollar bill and took her to a thrift store in the nicest part of town.

Being fiscally responsible, Gwen selected a heavy coat that would get her through the winter and a pair of sensible brown shoes with good soles.

Last fifty cents, she bought a Frank Zappa album to play on her dad's old fold-down stereo. She had never heard of Frank Zappa, but it was the coolest looking album in the sad pile.

The incident at school, the freedom of the shopping spree, the ugly brown shoes bumped against each other some, but, a few days later, the old man off swilling, she put Frank on, dropped the needle on him.

Brown Shoes Don't Make It came up and the world changed.

Not many days later Gwen Frazier packed a small bag with her few cool clothes, put the Zappa album under a bare arm and walked into a new life. She left the sensible shoes behind—brown shoes don't make it.

She caught a ride outside McAllen with some migrants headed to Florida to pick strawberries.

On the way to Plant City, Gwen found out how lucrative losing one's virginity could be. Over the next two years, she must have sold her virginity two dozen times. Got good at it. A nice mix of fear, pain, then pleasure. Wind it up, head arched back, little girl grunts deep in her throat, like her childhood was being torn away by the guy on top of her.

Living on the street, crashing wherever for a bit. Met some USF students at Skipper's in Tampa at an Iron and Wine show—the new Dead Heads—all of them sitting in front of the stage cross-legged, singing along to this neo-folk stuff, knowing every word.

Intrigued—the communal, hippie lifestyle, a big house funded by a trust fund, and having a place where she didn't have to worry about having to wake up and give blowjobs in the middle of the night like you did on the street—she moved in.

There was a good bit of fucking, but it was voluntary and almost silly. Mostly, it was computers. The group considered themselves cyber-revolutionaries, looking to liberate man from his earthly bonds by redistributing the world's wealth one checking account at a time.

Seemed to Edy, they were way better at shoplifting than revolting or redistributing. And that's what finally dissolved the cell. A couple of guys go down for like fourth, fifth offense shoplifting. The cops squeeze them, they pony out the cyber-revolutionary concept, it gets interpreted as cyberterrorism. 9/11, blah-blah-blah, the cops visit, get a few computers, a good bit of pot, a few hits of acid and some other unidentified pharmaceuticals. Edy watched from the drugstore across the street. The game was over, but not before Edy had found she had a knack for hacking.

But, on the street, hacking doesn't pay: back to the hustle game.

Stuck her hand in Eddie Margot's pocket at the Tampa State Fair. Eddie grabbed her slim wrist, never said a word, led her out to the parking lot, up to a new Cadillac. He spun her around and slapped her face—palm then knuckles—pushed her in the back seat and climbed in on top of her, fucked her roughly.

Then he said he admired her nerve, did she want a job?

The next year, Eddie goes to jail. Gwen—who is now Edy, bearding as Eddie's granddaughter—and Anna do okay scamming around. Lived pretty good on low-risk, nearly-legal games. Mostly the Big-Red-Hand game. Anna was good. The obeah woman, eyes rolled back, a touch of froth at the corners of her mouth. Did a damn spooky channeling voice to match.

The oldest shit known to man: air streams, trick candles, two pound monofilament. The best was the smell-of-the-deceased riff Anna ran. *Bring me an article of this person, something that has not had his or her aura laundered away.* That was visit one. Visit number two, the article. Then Anna did her thing: a single sniff, Anna could identify a perfume or cologne with amazing accuracy.

Go buy the scent. Edy pumps it in the room while Anna does her voice-of-the-dead voice. The pigeon almost faints.

They had fun. Then asshole Eddie gets out. He's got a big scheme, one to get him back into the high-cotton game where he belonged. They'd all be rich. Filthy.

He moves them to the new city, which wasn't bad. The university there was decent and Edy got some good legit courses in her pocket—the more access, the more understanding you have of programing and coding. And Eddie got her some decent shit, not the NASA-grade Mac stuff the Tampa rich boys had, but some good strong machines. It's for the game, he says.

End of game? Eddie left Edy two ingots. Not bad—more than she'd expected. Even hot, she'd get maybe two, three hundred grand each.

Bullshit, Anna left it. Eddie would have left her squat.

Edy found keys in a jean's pocket, unlocked the door of the motor home. She climbed in, took the captain's seat, re-familiarized herself with the controls. Ignited the beast. Adjust side mirrors. Adjust rearview, although you couldn't see much out the rear window.

But she could see two faces: Marty Pell, Shad Dupree. Smiling in the mirror at her. Dupree said, *Hey, girl*, to the rearview. She killed the engine, spun the seat to face Marty and Dupree on the back bench seat.

The two ingots were stacked on the floor. Dupree's crossed feet rested on them, one shoe missing a heel.

Edy didn't speak. Nobody spoke. Edy and Marty watched each other. Marty's smile got her. She gave it back.

"Would you find it hard to believe I'm glad you found me?"

Marty held the grin, put a shrug with it. "I'd find it harder to believe you didn't know how to get to the interstate. Or which way was west."

Edy nodded gracefully, points of hair almost meeting at her chin. "Thank you."

Marty leaned forward, elbows on knees, face turned up, eyes on Edy. "What's your name? In real life?"

"Gwen."

Marty thought about it, nodded. "That's alright." More nod. "I like it." Gwen fit better but why mention it?

"Before you two swoon, maybe we oughta talk some business."

Marty's face stayed on Gwen's, but he talked to Dupree. "Where you at, cuz? Right now?"

Dupree didn't answer and Marty looked over.

Dupree, eyes on the ceiling and off in thought, draped an arm over the back of the seat, swapped his ankle position, put the other shoe on the gold. He looked at Gwen for a beat then looked away, out a window.

"You know, bread, we first thought about this, I suggested we each take one. Here it is." Dupree bounced the heel on the ingots. "And, I was smart, I'd take mine, go up the road, live good for a few years somewhere."

When Dupree stalled for a straight-man's line, Marty said, "But if you were smarter . . . "

"I'd realize I could go to Central America, somewhere like that, for a couple of years—maybe five, maybe ten—live large as hell. But then I'm broke like a motherfucker, and I'm a few years older, and—my résumé's more fucked up than it is now."

Gwen watched Marty watching her, though she spoke to Dupree. "So, where does that go? You taking your piece or not?" Eyes on Marty.

Marty grinning, swiveled his head to Dupree.

Dupree looked pained, insulted. "Nah, girl. That means we're all kinda stuck in this arrangement. For a while anyway."

Gwen seemed to relax. "So, what are *we* doing?"

"Whatchu think we're doin, girl? All these computer machines, this rollin motel-room, whatchu know about the man, this grub-stake." Again the heel bump to the ingots. "We're gonna go lookin for Eddie Margot."

ABOUT THE AUTHOR

Suspected pop-noirist Bob Truluck resides in Orlando, Florida where he lives life to the fullest with his wife and ardent supporter, Leslie. Truluck has been nominated for some good stuff and has actually garnered a couple of fairly nice looking awards. His influences would include Raymond Chandler, Elmore Leonard, Charles Willeford, Nathan Heard and James Crumley, but not necessarily in that order. Bob has no favorite color or lucky number and will eat most anything but rutabaga. Truluck and his works can be scrutinized virtually at www.bobtruluck.com.